Who Knows You by Heart

Who Knows You by Heart

A Novel

C. J. FARLEY

WILLIAM MORROW
An Imprint of HarperCollinsPublishers

Without limiting the exclusive rights of any author, contributor or the publisher of this publication, any unauthorized use of this publication to train generative artificial intelligence (AI) technologies is expressly prohibited. HarperCollins also exercise their rights under Article 4(3) of the Digital Single Market Directive 2019/790 and expressly reserve this publication from the text and data mining exception.

This is a work of fiction. Names, characters, places, and incidents are products of the author's imagination or are used fictitiously and are not to be construed as real. Any resemblance to actual events, locales, organizations, or persons, living or dead, is entirely coincidental.

WHO KNOWS YOU BY HEART. Copyright © 2025 by CJ Farley. All rights reserved. Printed in the United States of America. No part of this book may be used or reproduced in any manner whatsoever without written permission except in the case of brief quotations embodied in critical articles and reviews. For information, address HarperCollins Publishers, 195 Broadway, New York, NY 10007. In Europe, HarperCollins Publishers, Macken House, 39/40 Mayor Street Upper, Dublin 1, D01 C9W8, Ireland.

HarperCollins books may be purchased for educational, business, or sales promotional use. For information, please email the Special Markets Department at SPsales@harpercollins.com.

hc.com

FIRST EDITION

Designed by Nancy Singer

Library of Congress Cataloging-in-Publication Data

Names: Farley, Christopher John, author.
Title: Who knows you by heart : a novel / C. J. Farley.
Description: First edition. | New York, NY : William Morrow, 2025.
Identifiers: LCCN 2024060888 | ISBN 9780063418639 (hardcover) | ISBN 9780063418660 (ebook)
Subjects: LCGFT: Novels.
Classification: LCC PS3556.A7165 W48 2025 | DDC 813/.54—dc23/eng/20250108
LC record available at https://lccn.loc.gov/2024060888

ISBN 978-0-06-341863-9

25 26 27 28 29 LBC 5 4 3 2 1

For Mom with love after love

Who Knows You by Heart

Chapter One

BLANK SPACE

There's more to life than what you do for a living. At least that's what your dad used to say before he died fifteen years ago, in the office, at his cubicle, of a massive subdural hematoma. He had been pulling another late night, and your mom found him the next morning, collapsed onto his ergonomic keyboard, when she went to his job to bring him a pick-me-up Caramel Frappuccino, just like he liked when he was putting in overtime. Ever since his passing, you've associated Frappuccinos, mochaccinos, macchiatos, espressos, lattes, flat whites, or anything coffee adjacent with death. The smell of cappuccinos makes you sob out loud. Every time you pass a Starbucks, you get to wondering about the afterlife. You turned thirty last month and you hated your job, and after your job started hating you right back you decided it was time for a change.

You still didn't think what went down at work was your fault, although with the benefit of hindsight you might have done things differently. But with the benefit of hindsight you would have bought Mee Corp stock early and often. Fuck hindsight. You had been working in IT at a nonprofit, Anthropocene Associates, that was trying to raise awareness about global warming, and it was supposed to be a transitory postcollege thing, but transitory transformed into five years, and you hadn't saved the world yet and you certainly hadn't saved any money. Raising awareness, you finally admitted to yourself, was something you were doing to get other people to solve problems you needed to tackle yourself. You decided it was time to grow the fuck up.

Leaving a job is like leaving a lover. When the little things start to drive you crazy, you know the big things will never be right again. You began to hate the crackle and hum of the fluorescent lights in the break room, the cardboard croissants at the morning meeting, the eternally ink-deprived printer. To distract yourself from the drudgery, you edited and wrote the in-house company newsletter, but the mundanity of it all began to eat at you like termites nibbling into a load-bearing beam. You hated that Patrick the executive director ran Ironman Triathlons in different parts of the world every season and that Sheila in communications attended Renaissance fairs on the weekend. But you didn't really hate your colleagues or their side gigs; you personally had no problems with carb-deprived middle-aged men like Patrick trying to recapture their glory days by swimming twenty miles down the Volga, and if Sheila wanted to celebrate an era in which everybody got dysentery on the regular, that was her right. You just hated that your fellow employees chose to make their true passions secondary, and you hated it because it was a reminder that you were doing the exact same shit.

Cynicism isn't a feeling, it's the absence of one. You wanted to feel passion, and, more than that, you wanted to feel that passion existed. But you couldn't fake it anymore. So you decided to get someone else to do the talking about the office for you and you created a chatbot version of the newsletter. You modeled it after a friend from work who was gone. You figured it would be like bringing them back. What you came up with wasn't exactly a large language model—you needed many more flops of computing power to do an LLM right, not to mention the backing of a company with a lot deeper pockets. Instead, you worked around scaling issues by tapping into datasets that were close at hand to get training material, like documents and videos stored on the company server and the conversation archive from the employee messaging app. Then you turned up the heat, focusing on creativity/randomness instead of accuracy/correctness. Everyone loved what you created—until it all went screwy.

Your friend Kenise reached out to you at 3:00 a.m. the night your little chatbot beta went live. You operated on different levels now, so you had to accept that you never saw her in person, but you were happy to hear from her via text. You and Kenise both went to Columbia together. You met at the Caribbean Students Association mixer during the first week of freshman year. She was born in Kingston and your grandparents had roots there, and she loved Jamaican black cake and Jamaican men with the same emotional intensity you felt about both. You and Kenise were connected in a biological way, like schooling fish swimming in synchronicity around a coral reef. Being a woman in tech is like being a Black guy in golf—even when you're better than everyone they view you as the exception and not the default. You were always a great software engineer. Both of you would study together. Kenise wouldn't have gotten an A-minus in Applied Machine Learning if you hadn't spent two weeks drilling her on obscure regression algorithms and conditional probability. Kenise was the studious one, the sensible one, but you had that Roman candle craziness you both needed sometimes to score the really great grade in a class or have a really good time at a party. That's why people in the computer science department gave you the nickname "the Big O." The moniker confused you at first, but then Kenise explained that it was short not only for your first name but for "Big O Notation," which, of course, is a tool coders use to describe the efficiency of a program. In other words, your classmates were paying tribute to your problem-solving skills, albeit in the most techie way possible. You and Kenise always supported and looked out for each other; when the Audre Lordeless world tried to tear you both down, you complimented and complemented each other. After you graduated, you spent many months traveling and bouncing around from gig to gig, and it was Kenise who helped hook you up with a stable position at Anthropocene.

????

Open the attachment I sent

                                      Kenise—why am I looking at a mugshot of Douglas from compliance and regulatory?

DUI from five years ago

Your chatbot sent it to everyone in org

                                                      Shitmotherfucker

You tell this chatbot my secrets? Like what we did at Club Duat?

What happens in Morningside Heights stays in Morningside Heights

So whatthefuck

                                           Algorithm trained on dataset of publicly available info

Not potty trained evidently. Your chatbot 💩 the 🛏️

                                  Personal info must have been mixed in training data. Could also be hallucinating

AIs do love to hallucinate. They make up names, statistics, stories

I don't know if storytelling makes them more human or just more fallible

People have an infinite capacity for self-hallucination

How soon can you turn off

                                    Office is closed and VPN down. Monday soonest

You better check with Patrick before that

                                              Fuck. Just tell me Kenise

    Kenise didn't need to tell you, she forwarded a link that showed you. A chatbot is a pretty small and unintelligent chunk of code, so to turbocharge yours you had fine-tuned an open source LLM with all that data you had found sitting around on the company servers. Big mistake, because the datasets turned out to be a shit show, as you were now finding out. Employees had been routinely storing super-intimate photos, videos, and email attachments on their company-issued phones and laptops, and all of that had gotten backed up on the company servers. The result was a mess—your chatbot had uploaded a series of clips into the newsletter of Executive Director Patrick having sex with Gloria from legal, who had a side gig running a charity that purchased prosthetics for three-legged pets. Apparently, Patrick celebrated every Ironman Triathlon that he finished with intercourse on the completed course and in the most picturesque locations he could find. Gloria, perpetually in search of the next labradoodle in need of a bionic limb, was his go-to partner. There was a clip of Patrick going down on Gloria on Sugarloaf Mountain in Rio, another with the pair conjugating on the bank of the Yangtze River in Shanghai, and one more with them doing it doggy style near the Wai-O-Tapu sulfur springs in New Zealand, complete with a three-legged terrier, newly rescued by Gloria, looking on. Something about the sex tape left you disgusted and envious at the same time. You had never felt that kind of love or lust, much less the need to memorialize it on your phone. But you did know that you were going to get screwed for broadcasting their round-the-world fucks.

So you quit your job before it quit you and updated and uploaded your résumé to all the usual employment sites. You always hated those mass emails people send out to everyone in the office when they resign—they felt both extroverted and pitiful, like a flaccid dick pic. So instead you sent Patrick a text on Monday morning informing him you were stepping down and that they could keep everything you had left at your cubicle, including a half-empty tin of breath mints, a dog-eared paperback of Mary Oliver's collected poems, a wilting potted hydrangea that you hoped one of your now former colleagues would give a proper home, and a striped pashmina wrap you always kept draped over your chair because, although Anthropocene Associates was dedicated to fighting global warming, the offices were ironically always fucking freezing. You didn't feel triumph or relief over leaving your job, just a sense, like the chill in the air before a summer rain, that it was time to go. That existential coffee was coming for you, just like it came for your dad, and you wanted to lead a life that mattered before that life was over.

The day after you quit, a few friends from the office stopped by to say goodbye and drink pinot grigio, but pretty soon the wine ran out and so did the friends. At least one of them brought you back your pashmina wrap. Nothing happened for weeks after that and you were getting worried, and to conserve your dwindling funds you were eating off-brand ramen noodles for breakfast, lunch, and dinner. You began to worry that employers had found out about the fuckup with the algorithmic newsletter—or that maybe thirty years old was too old to start over in tech—when out of nowhere you landed an in-person meeting with the most corporate corporation that ever incorporated: Eustachian Inc. Even Kenise, who was always your hype girl when it came to professional development, couldn't hide in her texts that she was surprised you had scored an interview with one of the biggest tech companies on the planet.

It's harder to get into Eustachian than it is to get into an Ivy

> I know that Kenise. I don't want to fuck this up

You're the best programmer I've ever met

You've got this

> I hear the interview process is like the Spanish Inquisition times the bar exam.

Just do you

> Why do people say that? Just do you? The whole reason I'm changing jobs is I want to be someone else. Someone who makes a lot more money

It's not about changing who you are. It's
about getting paid what you're worth.

                                                        What if I'm not worth that much

Don't ever talk that way

You are a priceless child of Jah

Which is why whatever you do

Don't take the first offer. Ask for 10 percent
more

                                                        I haven't even gotten any offer

I'm renewing my Eustachian subscription
right now

I believe in you. Onward to Zion you go

                                            Like I'm not under enough pressure 😔

    The position you had applied for was vague. Here's how the job description started: "Are you a great storyteller *and* a great listener? Can you thrive as a programmer in an ambiguous atmosphere? Have you read the *Dao De Jing*, the Bhagavad Gita, and *The Fountainhead*?" The Ayn Rand nod was some bullshit squared, but the important thing was that the salary range, even at the low end, was three times what you had been making. You had been hoping for a marginal upgrade, maybe something with benefits and dental and, best-case scenario, a working printer. This, if it worked out, could be so much more.

A job possibility in Big Tech was a betrayal of all your ideals, but it was also financially fucking phenomenal. Like most people who weren't getting paid by Big Tech, you had this ephemeral notion that Big Tech was not the engine of modern life but somehow destroying it. That social media and search engines and artificial intelligence were somehow stealing human jobs, breaking the social contract, and turning the milk of human kindness into some curdled pretender liquid squeezed from oat or soy or a hazelnut, with no connection to love or lactation. But now that you had a shot at landing a Big Tech job, you were willing to reconsider all your biases against the industry. You were sick of off-brand ramen and you were tired of being broke. You were ready to trade your worn-out green values for a more lucrative shade of emerald. You felt you needed to do this before the inevitable arrival of that final, fatal Frappuccino.

When you were a freshman at Columbia you took a class called Poetics and the Meaning of Life, and you read these lines from Rilke: "Death, especially the most completely felt and experienced death, has never remained an obstacle to life for a surviving individual, because its innermost essence is not contrary to us ... but it is more knowing about life than we are in our most vital moments. I always think that such a great weight, with its tremendous pressure, somehow has the task of forcing us into a deeper, more intimate layer of life so that we may grow out of it all the more vibrant and fertile." You changed your major from English to engineering within minutes of reading that passage. Your father's death, just three years before you went to college, still haunted you, and you needed to use it to grow, like a flower sprouting from the dirt of a grave. STEM was a challenge, a goal, and switching from the humanities to the sciences would demonstrate that some change would have come about in your life from his passing. You had always been better at (and more interested in) math and science than liberal arts and *The Canterbury Tales*, and the Rilke epiphany pushed you toward your true path. It seems a contradiction, but there is something life-affirming about a funeral. Seeing the photos of your dad in his youth, at his wedding, at work, and with you and Mom, and hearing the truth-telling eulogy from your mother about his warring impulses, how he was single-minded but mercurial, family-oriented but a workaholic, was cathartic. Far from being a sad experience, the service inspired you, albeit with a three-year delay, to try to use his fully examined death to lead a truly examined life.

You sit down on the futon in the center of your studio apartment in the West Village in Manhattan. To get yourself in the right frame of mind for the interview, you put on your headphones to listen to some Noelle Swizzler. That wasn't her name, but that's what you called her in your head. You had run into her once at a restaurant on Waverly Place that was so expensive you ended up only getting an appetizer and the check. Well, you hadn't exactly *run into her* run into her, but a waitress had breathlessly confessed to you that *the* Noelle Swizzler had made a real reservation under that fake name just the week before, and ever since that close encounter you felt like that pseudonym was a secret connection between you and the superstar you never met (and maybe the waitress, whose name you never got). You're more into neo soul, hip-hop, and Afrobeats and artists like SZA, Kendrick Lamar, and Tems, but you find yourself listening to Swizzler's music more and more lately, not because you like it necessarily but because you want to decode the secret to her success. Swizzler seems to have it all: artistry, glamour, business smarts. You would settle for two out of the three, even one out of the three.

You lie in bed afterward unable to sleep. You weren't a money person. You didn't want a fancy car or fancy clothes or fancy anything. You understand that money, like race or beauty, is just a social construct, a tale that people tell themselves, just another fiction, like a ghost story, a bedtime story, or a Tinder profile. You had been seeing a psychotherapist before you quit a few months back. The therapist had dark, judgmental eyes that hovered above the rest of her face like an umlaut. After about a year of sessions with Dr. Umlaut, the only lessons you came away with were 1) you needed health insurance with a lower deductible, and 2) you needed more affirmation in your life. You want someone to tell you that you are worth more than you have been valued so far. There was this scene in that TV show *Mad Men* where junior ad executive Peggy complains to her boss Don that he never tells her thank you, and he barks back at her, "That's what the money's for!" You never really fucked much with *Mad Men* because you couldn't stand the sexist (if historically accurate) way the female characters were treated, but that scene resonated with you. Money was a sign of appreciation and respect, and you wanted more of all three. Not because you were greedy but because you deserved it. Yes, Kenise was right, and you were a priceless child of Jah and all that. But your current weekly wages were far less than priceless.

Tomorrow you were going to find out how much you were really worth.

Chapter Two

ELECTRIC TOUCH

You wake up to one thought: You are going to follow Kenise's advice and you are not going to accept their first offer. This, you decide, is not a counting-your-chickens-before-they're-hatched kind of idea. This is a positive-vibration thing. Breathe in, breathe out. This is yoga for the soul that you're doing now. You are manifesting a good outcome to the day by assuming that at the end of it you will be fielding offers, not dealing with rejection. The only question is how big your win will be. As you get out of bed you notice spotting on your panties—your Mee Corp FloFinder tracking app was off, and your period's arrived early. Breathe in, breathe out. You decide that this is a positive thing and the blood is a human sacrifice to the power you are manifesting. You are a goddamn fertility goddess, and you will make the whole tech industry go with your flow. You insert a tampon, get dressed, and prepare to seize the day.

The apartment you live in on Waverly Place used to be your mom's place. After your dad passed, she had used the death benefit from his life insurance to move out of the widow-unfriendly suburbs and buy the place. You lived there only about a year before heading off to Columbia, but you moved back in when you started working for Anthropocene Associates, because nonprofit salaries are an oxymoron. Part of your mom still seems to be there because the things she treasured are still there. There's a magic to everyday objects. One of your favorite poetry collections is Pablo Neruda's *Ode to Common Things*, where he pays tribute to stuff like socks and soap and saltshakers. One of your favorite songs is "My Favorite Things" from *The Sound of Music*, which is all about brown paper packages tied with string and snowflakes on eyelashes. And you like hip-hop that's about real stuff, like sneakers and turntables, and about how much everyone misses hip-hop that was about real stuff like sneakers and turntables. Heroes in movies and fantasy books and video games are always going on heroic quests for magical shit like the Holy Grail or the sword in the stone. The best stuff is the stuff that's already all around you, the lived-in things, like favorite chairs, neck pillows, and your go-to black dress. You don't want a life full of new things that glitter and glow. You just want to make enough income to not lose the familiar things you already love. You needed to make a lot more money if you were going to keep living in this apartment, and landing a job at Eustachian was the only way you could see to make it happen. You decide you need some comfort food to steel yourself for this interview so you eat half a slice of Jamaican black cake for breakfast, brush your teeth, and then open the fridge and finish the other half because fuckit you deserve it.

 You head to the subway and transfer to a New Jersey Transit train. The location of your interview is Arkhaam, NJ, the headquarters of Eustachian, the global leader in audio entertainment products. It's an intensely secretive company. When you arrive, you have to sign an NDA about signing another, more expansive NDA, and they even give you a retinal scan without explaining why. You are getting anxious, and you sometimes say things you regret when you get anxious. You make a joke to the epauletted guard in the lobby about the commute from Manhattan and how the E-ZPass toll booths should be paying you for going from New York to New Jersey, and the woman doesn't laugh, she just stares straight ahead like one of the sentries with the furry Seussian hats outside of Buckingham Palace. "I was born and raised in East Orange," the woman growls. You make a mental note: No more jokes about Jersey while in Jersey. Eustachian strikes you as a pretty tight-lipped place. All the stealth and mystery at Eustachian should turn you off, but instead they stoke your interest. You feel like you're entering a strange new world in a hidden corner of Silicon Valley. In New Jersey, no less.

The company is located in a repurposed cathedral that had been the cornerstone of a thriving cultural center before white flight became a thing, Black unemployment boomed, and large masses of people of all races decided that God was dead. People look at buildings like this and say things like, "They can't build them like this anymore." It makes you question the forward march of progress when you hear things like that. You also can't escape the irony that this mighty tech company is housed in an antique structure in part because "they can't build them like this anymore." Rising up from the back of the cathedral is an architectural acknowledgment of the modern age: a glass-and-steel column some thirty stories high that houses the bulk of Eustachian's operations. The vintage glamour of the cathedral was, in many ways, just an anachronistic facade, and the real workspace was this tower of power, sleek and contemporary. The column thrust itself into the Arkhaam sky with what could be seen as enthusiasm or impudence—it was either an upraised hand from a teacher's pet or a middle finger from an incel. Then again, like most things men build, maybe it was just a penis. The tower—you can't unsee its phallocentrism once you notice it—is tippy-topped with a spire that makes it the tallest building in Milton County, NJ—though, as you would hear Eustachian employees joke, it was still only the 1,079th biggest dick in Big Tech.

But the premodern cathedral part certainly made its own impression, with its twisted Gaudí-ish towers, flying buttresses, neo-Gothic archways, and stone gargoyles hunched evilly and medievally over every entrance. There are ogival stained-glass windows lording majestically on every wall of the facility, but instead of depicting religious figures, there are images in red, blue, and yellow panes of the divinities of technology, like Thomas Edison, Nikola Tesla, and Steve Jobs. You can't help but notice that there are no women venerated on the stained-glass windows. Astronaut Mae Jemison didn't make the cut, and neither did programming mastermind Ada Lovelace, computer maverick Grace Hopper, search engine trailblazer Elizabeth Feinler, computational linguistics genius Margaret Masterman, LED pioneer Vivian Wing-Wah Yam, robotics entrepreneur Ayanna Howard, or any of the sheroes from *Hidden Figures*. Even in a cathedral dedicated to modern technology, women can't be priests. There are no images of men of color on the windows either—no tributes to video game entrepreneur Jerry Lawson, or traffic light inventor Garrett Morgan, or botanist George Washington Carver, or Bi Sheng, the Chinese commoner who came up with the idea of movable type four centuries before that Bible-thumping slowpoke Gutenberg. It probably wasn't a coincidence that all these people of color were passed over for veneration on the walls of the Cathedral of Technology. The Founder of Eustachian had been born in apartheid-era South Africa. He moved to New Jersey as a child, and after his start-up really geared up, he established the headquarters permanently in Arkhaam. It was a great public relations move and a canny business decision, because labor and real estate in the city were cheap. And the fact that the entire city hailed the Founder as a savior didn't hurt. He had been a bullied handicapped nerd with a funny accent back in Arkhaam High, but he had returned to the area as a high-tech hometown hero. All his scars had become stigmata.

You arrive precisely fifteen minutes early for your nine a.m. interview and are ushered into a glass room on a floor full of glass rooms. A sign on the wall reads "Eustachian: We Get What's Between Your Ears." Another glass wall is emblazoned with the Eustachian logo, a giant green ear with a blue eye staring out of the ear canal. You feel as if you are on nonconsensual display, like a lobster in a tank at a seafood restaurant or a spectator caught on a kiss cam who just wants to watch the game in peace.

As you wait, you pull out your phone and pass the time shitposting and doomscrolling. There's a bunch of stories about the fact that Mee Corp, one of the largest companies on the planet, is rumored to be exploring a purchase of Eustachian, a blue whale trying to swallow a sperm whale. It was Wall Street whale-on-whale violence. If the deal went through, the buyout would give Eustachian a massive infusion of cash and the resources to swamp all its competitors. Training AIs, like training elephants, requires a lot of resources, so bigger companies have a scale advantage. Smaller companies were likely to get stomped on by the hungry, undisciplined pachyderms they were trying to disrupt. You take a selfie and post it with the caption "Is a picture still worth 1,000 words when you're in the waiting room of a major audio technology company?" The observation is silly, but you want to memorialize your interview at Eustachian, and nothing feels real unless you photograph it and post it. A second after you post, you wonder if you just violated the NDA you signed five minutes ago. You put away your phone.

You are suddenly and intensely conscious of how you are dressed. You don't know what the sartorial rules are in the tech world when it comes to interviews, and you didn't ask anyone because you were kind of embarrassed that you had quit your old job before you had locked in a new one. Nobody these days wears suits, except for funerals, weddings, and television sportscasting, but you wonder if you should have worn something more formal to make a good first impression. You're wearing a tweed button pocket sheath dress that used to be your mom's, but you're now second-guessing yourself. Maybe the outfit is too girly or too girlbossy, or maybe you should have shaved your legs, which you suddenly realize are as furry as a Muppet.

"Octavia Crenshaw?"

A thirtysomethingish Black man walks in the glass room holding a closed laptop. You were expecting someone older and techier and whiter. There's a glint of gold, and you see he's wearing four clunky gold rings and you hate that. One of them looks like a college ring, another is maybe a frat ring, and you don't know what the other two are for, but they ain't wedding rings. You hate jewelry on men, sorry but you just do. Four rings? You once had a bad date who took you to see a rereleased 70mm version of *The Lord of the Rings: The Two Towers* and neglected to tell you that it was the second movie in a trilogy, and so you couldn't tell what the hell was going on except it involved a lot of rings, which you've hated ever since. You couldn't give a fuck about a hobbit or jewelry. Too many rings is a definite turnoff.

The Black guy sits down and smiles. It's a slightly goofy smile, with teeth and a horsey flash of gums. This guy is a doorless refrigerator—no chill. This is the kind of guy who plays *Fortnite* on a Friday night, and stays to the bitter end of Marvel movies to watch the post-credit scenes, and debates why there are no zero-g scenes in *Star Wars*. He's a Black Nerd, and the smile is evidence.

"I'm Walcott," Black Nerd says. "I'm so glad to see you here."

You relax a little bit. The way he said that he sees you sounded like he meant it not just literally or figuratively—he meant it Afrocentrically. When another Black person acknowledges your shared Blackness, it's a good sign they're not in the Sunken Place.

"Are you not getting a lot of Black applicants?" you ask.

"Well, I don't know if it's legal for me to say or not, but we're trying."

"I guess the company needs to try harder."

"Listen, if this is about the whole *Jungle Book* controversy..."

You sit up. "*Jungle Book* controversy?"

He looks away. "Uh... Never mind."

You remind yourself to google "*Jungle Book*" and "Eustachian" and "controversy." "I actually was referring to your DEI numbers..." Like any good applicant, you had googled the company before your interview, and the DEI shit turned up on the first page.

Walcott sighs. "The numbers aren't good with any of the Big Tech companies, and the courts have made it tougher to—"

"That's not an excuse." You throw this out with a little more heat than you intended.

Walcott is now on his guard. You can tell he feels like his racial bona fides are being challenged. His back is up and his Black is up. "I didn't say it was an excuse. And I'm not saying this place is perfect. Every workplace is full of microaggressions. I don't even call them micro in this industry, because they don't feel small when they are happening to you, and micro adds up to macro pretty quick. I call them technoaggressions. And I'm the last person who's going to defend the hiring records of Big Tech."

You make a mental note of that coinage—"technoaggressions." You are kind of feeling the technoaggression all around you right now. You know that as a Black woman with thick-ass hips and natural hair you don't fit in here, and that out-of-placeness is spurring you to overcompensate and act out. Your natural default mode is bitchiness, but you silently castigate yourself for letting it show during a job interview. You usually try to hide your bitchiness until third dates and definitely until after job offers. But you can't help yourself most of the time, because being a bitch is a necessary psychological coping mechanism in a world full of microaggressions and macroaggressions and mansplaining. You'd rather be sorry that you went too far than regret that you rolled over and took it. What you're about to say isn't going to help you land this job, but you ran out of fucks at age thirteen when your tits came in and you started clapping back to leering venture capitalist bros on the F train. Plus you're officially anxious, and you say things you regret when you're anxious. You hear yourself declaring, "So if you can't defend Big Tech, why are you an interviewer for Big Tech?"

Walcott's eyes narrow. "Because I want to change things."

"That's like a wildebeest thinking he can change things after the lion has swallowed him. Once you're inside, it's over."

"Why are you *here* then?"

"I'm *here* to make money."

He looked like he had tasted something unpleasant but only realized how nasty it was after it was so far down his throat his swallow reflex had finished the job. "Isn't that . . . shallow?"

"This whole company is about to be sold. Isn't that about money?"

Walcott shrugs. "That's just financial media speculation . . ."

Your initial passion may have been performative—you wanted to show some spark—but your indignation is becoming realer every moment. "All I'm saying is this is a money-oriented company in a money-oriented world, and I want in. And I don't think that's anything I need to apologize for."

"I'm not saying there's anything wrong with making money. I just think it should be a side hustle and not your main motivation."

You shouldn't have done this, but you wagged your finger at him. "I'm guessing your family always had it good. I bet your dad had a crystal stair."

Walcott couldn't hide the flash of anger that passed across his face, lightning on a cloudless night. "There's no time for this," he says under his breath, more to himself than to you. Then he recovers, and the energy in the room shifts. The shared Blackness tone in his voice is gone, and suddenly he's all business, as if he were processing your forms at the DMV. "Let's reset. Why do you think your skill set would be a good fit for this company?"

You clear your throat. "I worked in IT at my last job. That prepared me for this."

"How so?"

"I have an engineering degree and I'm a coder. Eustachian is a digital entertainment company, and so my skill set is a great fit. But the job description was vague. If you could fill me in on details about potentially what my duties might be, I could tell you more about why I'm . . ."

Walcott powers up his laptop to a chorus of electronic angels and types something.

"Did I say something noteworthy?" you ask.

"Apologies," Walcott replies. "Eustachian has a highly sophisticated rubric of things they look for in a hire, and so I have to take notes so I can accurately tally a candidate's final score. It's really for your benefit, because it removes the subjectivity. It's very data driven."

"What are some of the qualities that you're scoring?"

"The Founder created the questionnaire. If you get hired here, you may get to meet him—sometimes he surfaces at big events, like the All-Hands meetings. Last I heard he was on an Antarctic expedition with Greta Thunberg and Snoop Dogg. He's a fascinating guy—when he was at MIT he didn't major in anything scientific, he studied theology. Before he dropped out sophomore year, of course. He's super-brilliant but he tries to be relatable—did you know he's into *Star Wars*?" Then Walcott added, sotto voce, "But do *not* mention the prequel trilogy around him." Then, in a normal voice, "The Founder is less involved in the day-to-day here than he used to be, but he reads all the interview notes. You ever heard of übersectionality?"

"The social science thing?"

"It's a theory that seeks to unite all the liberal arts fields—from economics to sociology to psychology—under one umbrella, kind of like the grand unified theory in physics. Übersectionality can be used to forecast social trends for masses of people, but it's useless for predicting the actions of individuals. So the Founder developed a variant, Microsectionality. It's a proprietary mathematical modeling algorithm for business use that can predict how prospective employees will fare in a company. It's 57.7 percent accurate."

"So it's only 7.7 percent better than a coin flip?"

"Fortunes are won and lost on margins like that."

"How come I've never heard of 'Microsectionality'? Like *ever* ever?"

"Because everyone that's ever heard of it has signed an NDA. Anyways, all I need is for you to answer a few personal questions."

"How personal?" You shift in your seat uncomfortably.

Walcott presses on. "What's your biggest fear?"

An image pops into your mind of a venti cappuccino. "Why would I tell anybody that?"

Walcott types something on his laptop.

You're fucked. All you had to do was pretend you were someone else, someone a little less bitchy, for a couple hours, and you couldn't even do that. Now this nerdy Black brother was dropping the Afrocentric bonding and putting you through some sort of bullshit business psychosocial profiling test like every other applicant. No doubt this Microsectionality exam is hella racially biased. "Was that the right answer?" you ask. Your voice sounds sheepish in your ears, like a little Black lamb bleating in a flock of white sheep.

Walcott looks up from his keyboard. "I guess we'll find out soon enough."

• • •

Technoaggression #1: You go to the restroom between interviews. A young white woman begins talking to you in a familiar fashion. You wonder if this is part of the job interview. When she hands you a sheaf of papers, you realize she has mistaken you for someone else and you tell her that. "Oh my god," the white woman says, putting her hand to her mouth. "You look just like this temp we had named Chloe—I thought she was back! She's tall like you." The woman walks away. You are not tall, you are medium height—and you are not a temp. You are certain Chloe is Black.

• • •

You endure a full day of questions. At first it's like a television game show, but by the end it feels like the House Un-American Activities Committee. After Walcott, several other Eustachian employees come in to grill you about your life and career interests. Each one arrives armed with a laptop, dutifully taking notes and filling in a rubric that will summarize your worth to the company. And each one, at some point, poses a question that is head-scratchingly existential. What do you think happens after we die? Does free will exist? What makes any action right or wrong? How do you know that other people perceive colors the same way you do? Can you tell us one thing you changed your mind about? What is time? If the past is what we've lived through and the future is what's ahead of us, then how long is now?

You've always believed that standardized tests are a joke. They never measure anything other than your ability to prepare for standardized tests. In high school, you took the SAT three times and suffered through two years of prep courses until you got a perfect score and secured your admission into Columbia. Now that you know about this Microsectionality bullshit, you decide to game the system. People think data is objective, but it's for damn sure not sentient. Data is always subservient to power. "Data driven" is something that people with power say to justify decisions they would have made without the data. But you're an engineer, and you know how to skew results. It was time for you to be the Big O again and crack this problem.

Since the test was designed by a man, you figure he's not really looking for the best candidates, he's looking for the candidates who are the most like him—other men. You think about that Noelle Swizzler song "If Girls Were the Man" about how if she were a dude she'd be celebrated for all the things her critics rip her for. You try to channel that spirit. You are a fox turning the tables on the hunters. The human interviewers might not like a woman acting like a man, but the algorithm might just eat it up. You decide to answer all your interview questions like a man. You are arrogant. You interrupt. You speak boastfully of your individual role in projects you worked on that were actually team efforts. When you are asked to discuss your greatest failure, you sit in silence for a full thirty seconds until the interviewer moves on. You riff about the back nine at Augusta National, the brilliance of the first two *Godfather* films, your love for *Grand Theft Auto*. You monologue. You mansplain. You manspread on the conference chair. You can feel the Y chromosomes coming alive in all your lady cells. CRISPR technology ain't got shit on you.

After eight hours of this you have sweated through your tweed button pocket sheath dress and you are desperately hoping that 1) your perspiration stains aren't visible through the tweed, and 2) your deodorant hasn't failed. Over the course of the day, you've slurped your way through so many decaffeinated Coke Zeros that they have to be adding up to positive integers at this point. At 5:15 p.m., Walcott comes back to escort you to the lobby of the building, where you sign another NDA.

"You guys love your NDAs," you say as you sign.

Walcott doesn't smile. "Eustachian is all about safeguarding data. We're not just the global leader in audio entertainment—we support our customers."

"I saw the sign. 'We Get What's Between Your Ears.' Did AI write that copy?"

"That's the company motto. NDAs are a part of fulfilling that promise and protecting personal information that belongs to the company and our customers."

You hand him back the signed NDA. "Listen, about our interview..." you begin.

Walcott raises an eyebrow. "What about it?"

"Well, I said some shit I shouldn't have said. At least in the way I said it."

He shakes his head. "That's one of the worst nonapology apologies I've ever heard."

"It wasn't an apology. It was more of an explanation."

"You're incredible," Walcott says. "Well, you can stop nonapologizing or whatever it is you're doing. I'm not supposed to tell you this until a little later, but you've got the job."

"You know this already?"

"It's just math—you scored higher than any other interviewee on the Microsectionality algorithm. We like to move fast—one of the company's mottoes is 'Tomorrow Is Today.'"

You suppress the urge to do a celebratory dance you recently saw on NikNak. You have never before had the urge to do a celebratory dance you saw on NikNak, much less had to suppress that urge, so you know that you're feeling alarmingly gleeful. So you don't dance at all, in part to preserve what little professionalism you have left, and partly because you're wearing two-inch heels and your ankles are used to Nike low-tops. You know that you have successfully gamed the system, but you are still surprised. "Can I ask you a question?"

Walcott nods.

"Why in hell would a Big Tech company like Eustachian want to hire me?"

"You're really selling yourself, aren't you?"

"I'm just being real."

"Maybe the algorithm has a crush on you. It likes your life story and wants to follow it up close—I don't know. Maybe the algorithm thinks you have a 'particular set of skills,' like Liam Neeson in *Taken*. Didn't you create a chatbot at your last job?"

Your face feels hot. You hate when people know more about you than you want them to know. You've got things you'd rather not tell just anybody. Shit, you've got things you haven't even told yourself. "How did you hear that? I certainly didn't list that on LinkedIn."

"Your chatbot was a shit show, wasn't it?"

You are worried now. Has he been waiting this whole time just to let you know that he knows you're a screwup? You decide the only course of action is to admit everything. "Yes, it was a shit show. And on weekends, it was a shit matinee."

Walcott's next words aren't accusatory or angry, they are comforting and calming. "Do you remember John Lewis?"

"The civil rights pioneer and congressman?"

"That's the one. Like he said, there's good trouble."

"My chatbot newsletter was not good trouble—it was a total fuckup. I unleashed an AI that spilled everyone's secrets at work."

"That was bad trouble, but maybe good trouble can come out of it. Our algorithm says that you're perfect for this new position, and I trust the algorithm."

"About that—can you tell me exactly what the position is?"

"Not yet, but soon." Walcott's expression turns serious. "I love my job, I'm not ashamed to say that, and I definitely don't want to get fired. But you're wrong about thinking the best reason to join a company like this is just for the money. I like money as much as the next Capitalist with a capital C, but Eustachian is something more. That's why we're in Arkhaam, New Jersey, and not San Francisco or Seattle or Brooklyn. You can do something here—*we* can do something. Black people have been shut out of tech for too long. People of color helped invent STEM—we were doing advanced mathematics in sub-Saharan Africa thousands of years before Pythagoras was born. And, by the way, Pythagoras visited Egypt and that may be where he learned to do real math. But I'm digressing. Tech is like this far green country, just waiting to be settled, and Black people have a chance to plant their flag..." Walcott shakes his head. "Sorry, I'm ranting."

You smile. "You are kind of ranting."

"I almost forgot!" Walcott hands you a slip of paper. "The most important part."

The offer—the moment of truth that Kenise texted you would come and that you manifested into being. You fight the urge to unfold the folded Post-it note that Walcott has just slipped you to unveil how much you are worth. Kenise told you not to take the first offer, and that's exactly the advice you're going to follow. Whatever they think you're worth, you are worth more. Money is just another story, and you are taking control of the narrative. You are Scheherazade, motherfuckers! You tear up the slip and let the shreds fall into a nearby recycling bin.

Walcott drums his fingers on top of the bin. His four golden rings click and clank in the silence. After a few beats, he says, "That was your compensation number."

"I want ten percent more."

"Yeah, I get that—I know how negotiations work. But you didn't look before you threw the slip away. How can we give you ten percent more of a number you didn't see?"

"You work for a tech company, so I assume you're good at math. You'll figure it out."

"You are mental, has anyone else told you that?"

"I'm a priceless child of Jah, and your algorithm picked me."

Walcott reaches toward you, and you instinctively jerk back.

"Relax," he says, and he seems to pull something out of the air near your ear. You see that he's now holding the folded-up Post-it note in his ringed fingers. The same note you just ripped up and threw away.

"Is that some sort of magic trick?" you ask.

"Abracadabra." He stuffs the note in his pocket. "So—ten percent more and we're good?"

"Ten percent more."

Walcott blinks, shrugs, and holds out his hand. "Welcome to Eustachian."

You shake his hand and try not to think about the rings.

Chapter Three

BLACK STAR

You are dreaming about the last lecture you ever heard your mom give. It was a small talk in front of a dozen New York University grad students. Her mind was already starting to slip, but she was still an icon in the philosophy department. Your dad had always been the one with the unpredictable career; he had stints as a journalist, an internet entrepreneur, a children's toy inventor, a realtor. He was always launching some new venture, watching it crash and burn, and then sorting through the wreckage to build something new. Your mom was the steady one—she had been one of the youngest instructors to ever get hired at NYU, and once she got there, she relentlessly rode the tenure track all the way to Grand Central Full Professor. As long as you could remember, she had the same NYU office at the same NYU address at 5 Washington Place in Greenwich Village, a historic six-story building that had been there since the days of Mark Twain, the Gilded Age, and the Benjamin Harrison administration.

You were a sophomore at Columbia, and your dad had passed four years before, when you took the subway downtown from Morningside

Heights to the Christopher Street station to meet your mom. You were going to grab lunch together after she finished her classes. It was a clear, warm day, and she had taken her students out of the stuffy classroom and to a grassy spot in Washington Square Park.

"What makes you really you?" your mom said, with the students gathered around her in a semicircle. "There's a thought experiment the British philosopher Derek Parfit writes about that can help us get to the heart of what really matters. Imagine if there was a transporter beam that could beam you to another planet. The way the transporter works is that it dismantles all the cells of your body and transmits them, at the speed of light, to their destination. Would you get into such a transporter? If your body was taken apart, for even a short time, you might not regard your reassembled form to really be you. So we might say that continuity of the body could be important when it comes to identity. But maybe you're okay with being beamed up. So now let's say that the way this transporter works is that it destroys your body and reassembles an exact copy at the point of destination with different atoms. This is where you might finally draw the line and say no way, you refuse to be beamed up or out or anywhere. But you're already in the transporter—because this story isn't science fiction. Our cells change over the course of our lives, and yet we consider ourselves to be the same person. Every time we go to sleep or go under anesthesia, we suffer a break in our consciousness, but when we wake up, we consider ourselves the same person. The mind is not the person because people's minds can change. The body is not the person because bodies change. Memories aren't who we are because people can share memories and be different people or lose memories and remain the same person..."

Your mom continued her lecture, warming to her subject, until a student raised her hand and began to speak before she was even called. "Professor, you gave this same lecture last week." The class began to rustle like autumn leaves. "Are you okay?"

Your mother froze for a second, sunlight on her face. You took a step forward, dropping your backpack off your shoulder, wondering if your mom needed your help but having no idea what you could do. Your mom's eyes looked like they were focused on something far away—not on some skyscraper in the distance, but on a point deep inside her. Then the sunlight faded and she dismissed the class. You and your mom had lunch—a great West Indian place on Houston Street—but you never talked about what happened. And she never invited you to another one of her lectures.

• • •

Even the swirling roar of your blender mixing your morning pomegranate power smoothie can't drown out the sound of the trucks. You look out the window of your kitchenette to confirm your suspicions. The trucks have the logo of Mee Corp on the side: the ink-dark eyes of Ines Mee, the daughter of the founder of the company. You've always found it ironic that the trucks have eyes, because they don't have any drivers. Mee Corp is constantly delivering things to people's houses: books, toiletries, furniture, groceries, whatever. The trucks arrive, the back doors roll up, and tank-treaded robots roll each delivery to the correct front door. The mascara-limned eyes on the trucks observe it all, unimpressed, unemotional, unblinking. They might as well be looking over a lake of ashes.

The trucks and the robots make a lot of noise, but there's nobody to complain to. You called Mee Corp customer service once to protest the racket, but the line kept transferring you to one automated operator after another. That's what the world has come to—humans having nobody to complain to but robots about the bad shit that other robots have done. You live in a cave resounding with echoes. The sound of the trucks is just something everyone has to live with, like gerrymandering and global warming. You would think the trucks would be electric, but the company probably likes calling attention to itself. Most mornings, when you wake up, there are more Mee Corp trucks on the road than there are cars. The company exploits a hole in the system by using public roads for private gain. Maybe that's what the eyes of its trucks were trying to say. The biggest crimes weren't in the shadows, they were in plain sight.

You down the smoothie, plop down on the toilet, and flick on your phone. You google "Jungle Book controversy," and nothing comes up except stuff about Rudyard Kipling and colonialism. Whatever the furor was all about, the company seems to have scrubbed it from the web. You sigh and start to watch nature videos instead. You've been following the social media account of an oceanographer who is trying to use artificial intelligence to communicate with sperm whales. The theory is, if AI can be used to translate Mandarin and German and whatever else, maybe it can help us talk to cetaceans as well. The way current translation neural networks work is basically by training them on pairs of translated sentences—that is, you need translated examples to start with, a sentence in each language talking about the same thing.

Now in theory, you could try to train a general translator AI that could decipher any language, even ones it had never heard before, just by ingesting lots of other tongues and then extrapolating a shit ton, but since pretty much all the translation data we have is for human languages, you doubt that it would generalize to undersea mammalian languages. But neural networks work better than they should, according to classical statistical analysis, so maybe cetacean translation has a shot. It's weird that we've been living on this planet with intelligent species like whales and dolphins and squid and octopuses for thousands of years, and we have no idea how to meaningfully communicate with them. It's like living in the same house with a Frenchman and never once saying "bonjour." If we can't even hold a chat with a squid, what makes us think we'll really be able to understand machine intelligence when it fully blossoms? Hell, humans can't even communicate with one another. *Homo sapiens* have been around for three hundred thousand years, and you still don't get what goes through most men's brains, or know for a fact that there's anything going on in there at all.

In the video, the researcher takes a small boat from the coast of Húsavík, Iceland, into the waters of Skjálfandi Bay. He's trying to plant recording devices on passing sperm whales so he can record their clicks and whistles and develop a big enough database for computers to absorb the information and figure out some patterns. The latest theory is that people have been going about speaking to animals the wrong way. It's not about understanding; it's about brute force. If you collect enough information and stuff it into a black box, the AIs will figure it out. That's one of the dirty secrets of AI—it takes a shitload of data to teach machines anything. To train a computer to communicate, you have to tap into a language dataset that's too big to fail, like social media posts or Wikipedia articles, and even those resources aren't big enough if you want to create a really convincing conversation. And the thing is, whales aren't being cooperative about letting researchers plug into their colloquies. Maybe they don't want their language cracked. Maybe humans are just too tiny for them to care. Maybe whales are pissed that *Free Willy 2* didn't live up to the original. After several attempts at tagging the sea animals around him, the researcher's boat is capsized by a whale fluke, and the Icelandic Coast Guard has to pluck the scientist out of the water and take him back to shore.

A text from Kenise pops up on your phone.

You're in the big leagues of Big Tech now

Treat everyday like your first and your last ✊

[Link to Peter Tosh song "Jah Guide."]

I wish we could celebrate. Go to Yan Wang Palace like we used to

You are going to love love love your new job

You don't believe in love. There are only two possibilities: Destiny or Dice. Either love is a random event, and therefore as meaningless as winning the lottery, or love is the result of biological programming, and in that case, human beings are just fleshy robots, lacking in agency, dumbly following the commands of nature, like an ant following a pheromone trail. Destiny or Dice. Either possibility makes for a depressing greeting card. "Happy Valentine's Day! Thanks to a cosmic coin flip, I love you!" or "Happy Mother's Day! We're all basically bugs!"

Loving a person, loving a job, loving anything—what did any of it mean if love isn't a real choice? You were cynical about love—didn't trust it, didn't pursue it, didn't care much about it. You weren't a prude or anything and had no problem with giving a guy a blow job if he had done enough to deserve the honor. But most guys made you feel dead inside, like you were a machine full of gears, grinding away the way you were built to grind, instead of feeling something that felt warm and right. That's why you became a coder. Writing programs that could control systems and machines gave you insight into the way life really worked. Even the most complex things could be reduced to a series of simple commands, from the operation of a video game to the flight of an airplane. Unfortunately, the men you met in your engineering and computer science classes didn't exactly stoke your romantic fires. Many of them weren't even men—they were boys, irritating and solipsistic, barely able to articulate their own needs, much less acknowledge and satisfy the desires of the opposite sex. Some of them weren't even frogs, waiting for princesses to kiss them into royalty—they were pollywogs, limblessly wriggling in the shallows, with a lot of growing up to do before they'd even be ready for the possibility of any magic. You know all that sounds a bit harsh, but hearing some of those pollywogs talk shit about you and female engineers had hollowed out your heart more than a little bit. But coding filled the void. Others could dream about love and romance. Emotion was under the dominion of the heartless happenstance of the universe. Coding was control at your fingertips.

• • •

Before you leave home, you have a brief virtual meeting with Polly from HR about getting your employee ID. Polly has a virtual background behind her of tropical waterfalls. They look just like Dunn's River Falls in Jamaica. You and your parents used to climb the falls together when they took you to the island on vacations. Thinking back on those happy family times makes you immeasurably sad, and so you try to stay focused on the present. You hate virtual backgrounds. They make conversations feel inauthentic, the same way cheesy fake backgrounds in car-driving scenes in movies prevent you from suspending disbelief. Every so often Polly would melt into the background like that meme of Homer Simpson disappearing into a hedge. But Polly is efficient and friendly. She praises you for your high incoming Microsectionality rating. You begin to wonder if Polly is also a virtual creation. You suppose, in the future, it will be harder to tell such things. The virtual background will become the foreground. People only seriously resist fake stuff before it becomes indistinguishable from the real deal. Once you reach certain levels of verisimilitude, outrage recedes. That's why I Can't Believe It's Not Butter! is a brand and You Tricked Me, Bitch! This Shit Ain't Butter! is not. And as a coder and engineer, you will be one of the people turning lies into a reality that's too satisfying to question.

As much as you complained about your last job, and the one before that, and the one before that, you're glad to get back to work. You feel like a single sock when you're not paired with a position. First job IDs are evidence of how much people love leaving the ranks of the unemployed. Just look at the smiles on those virgin IDs—ear to ear. Anyone who still has an ID that has the photo from the first day they were hired knows that the image captures an almost naive optimism that slowly fades, almost beyond memory, as the workweeks grind on into infinity. That first ID is like the "Most Likely to Succeed" photo in a high school yearbook—full of joy and promise and instant nostalgia. Like that fleeting glow you have at the start of a new diet, when you don't care that you've eaten only baby spinach for seven days straight because you've already lost .2 lbs, .4 lbs if you remove your socks, panties, and bra and balance on the scale on one leg in just the right way. You love that glow.

Second ID photos, taken after you lose the first one at a hotel bar, tell a different story. They have the joie de vivre of police booking photos, with worse lighting. There are rarely smiles in replacement ID photos, and once bright eyes devolve into bovinity. Second ID subjects have accepted mastication as their lot and milking as their fate. But that's a possible future; right now, you have the fresh face of a first ID. Experience has yet to crush your joy.

You arrive at work and are alone in the elevator. Your employee orientation meeting is supposed to be on the top floor, the twenty-sixth floor. You notice there's an extra button above that, but it's not marked 27, it's just unnumbered. You let one indecisive finger hover above the blank button. There's something about unexplored rooms that's always enticed you. You read *The Lion, the Witch and the Wardrobe* when you were a kid and loved the scene where the children find a hidden room in a large, antique house in which there's a closet filled with fur coats, and they squeeze through the coats and find themselves in the magical world of Narnia. You were six years old when you read it, and your first thought was: *These British twats just had a reverse birth into a giant vagina.* You never thought about your vagina in quite the same way ever again, and the idea of a secret space that could take you on a magical adventure has stayed with you ever since.

You press the elevator button that should be marked 27 and it doesn't light up. You press it again—still nothing. You keep pressing it, and then an alarm goes off. The lobby guard who didn't laugh at your Garden State joke on your interview day enters the elevator, pulls a key out, sticks it into the elevator control panel, and turns it. The alarm stops.

"The top floor is off-limits," the guard says.

"Why?" you ask. "What's up there?"

The guard scowls at you as the doors close.

• • •

There are five other new employees in your orientation group. A young woman in braids smiles at you. She has a dewy enthusiasm like she just threw her graduation cap into the air three seconds ago. Turns out, you were only a few weeks off—she graduated from East Arkhaam College last month. "I grew up in Arkhaam," Braids says, grinning. "I always dreamed of working here!"

"What was your major?" you ask.

Braids looks apologetic. "History," she half whispers. "I probably should have done something more STEM-y. But my focus was the history of technology, which is how I managed to land this job. My thesis was 'Rage Against the Machines: Social Reactions to Technological Shifts from the Luddite Movement to the Algorithmic Justice League.'"

"Luddites? Like the idiots who didn't believe in technology at all?"

Braids warms to her subject. "That's a common misconception—Luddites weren't ignorant, they were revolutionaries. They were the Robin Hoods of their day, taking jobs away from machines—like nineteenth-century automatic looms—and giving them back to the people. There's this Luddite poem that goes: 'You might as well be hung for death as breaking a machine...'"

You like this girl, but you do not want to hear Luddite poetry in this life or any future reincarnation, so you interrupt. "What department are you in?"

"Customer service," Braids replies, her thesis trance broken. "At Eustachian, they call it 'customer experience' to be fancy. That's where most of us go, you know." The way she says "us" makes clear that it's code for "Black," but she's being oblique since whitey is listening. "I'm taking night classes in coding, and I'm hoping to work my way onto the data science team."

When you tell her you're a software engineer, Braids is impressed. "A coder already! Go on, Ms. *Hidden Figures*! You're inspiring the rest of us!"

You spend the first hour of orientation signing NDAs and clicking submit. You know you should read them carefully, maybe show them to a lawyer, but the orientation group leader assures you it's all standard. You realize that's Satan's secret to getting people to sign away their souls. One contract is suspicious, but a thousand is routine. There are only so many Terms & Conditions you can read before you just start scrolling to the bottom and checking the box so you can get on with your life. Submit, submit, submit. During all this submission, you notice a now familiar sign on the wall reading "Eustachian: We Get What's Between Your Ears."

The class gathers in a small glass-walled room, and you are each issued Eustachian-branded laptops. You open yours up, and the Three Company Commandments appear on the screen.

One: You're Your Product
Two: Tomorrow Is Today
Three: Profits Are Prophecy

The orientation leader looks younger than you, or at least around the same age, but she says she's been with the company ten years. She's wearing simple but fabulous clothes and has chili-pepper-red hair and a hint of an accent. Where was that accent from? Australia? New Zealand? Old Zealand? You know nothing of the lands of kiwis and kangaroos other than you can hear an echo of down under down deep in her voice. She makes it work, this pinch of worldly charm blended with an abundance of effortless style. You're impressed by her sleeveless top that shows off her yoga-fied arms, the Fortune 500 elegance of her slightly flared pants, the comfortable chic of her slip-on shoes. As they catch the light, her stud earrings sparkle greenly—girlfriend is crisp as new money. You missed her name so you make one up in your head and decide to call her Wombat. You hope you don't get anxious and call her that name by mistake. That would be so you. Wombat says she's the company's "chief people officer," whatever that means. In that role, she oversees Eustachian's DEI program.

"Let's have a yarn, shall we?" Wombat says. "The Three Company Commandments were written by the Founder himself. What's amazing is he had the vision for them when he was in middle school. He suffered from diabetic retinopathy from a young age, and because of his failing eyesight he was never picked for teams in gym class. So he spent the time plotting out the company he was going to build. One day, sitting in the bleachers playing with a battery-operated lightsaber while the other kids played kickball, the Three Company Commandments came to him. Can any of you tell me what the first one means to you? Speak up—there're no wrong answers."

A young woman with brown bangs raises her hand. "I know, I know!" she calls out. The eager new employee has an unblinking stare, like a snake's. You decide, in your mind, her name is Parseltongue. "In his book *Hearing Is Believing*, the Founder wrote that the First Commandment was a reminder that the things you sell should be manifestations of your truest identity."

Wombat is impressed. "Good on ya! I'm so glad you read his book!"

"I've read all the Founder's books," Parseltongue says brightly. "*Eardrum Empire, Inaudible Man, Do Bad Algorithms Go to Electric Hell?*..."

Wombat tries to move on. "Very impressive..."

Parseltongue isn't done. "The audio versions, of course, are the best." She starts to talk about the fact that a big-time actor—you think of him as Mr. Hollywood—does the narration.

Wombat cuts her off. "Let's get back to the Founder's commandments. Does anyone have any thoughts about the second..."

You know the answer to this, but before you can say anything, Parseltongue is already back to monologuing. "'Tomorrow Is Today' is a declaration that in the tech world you've always got to move fast to get things to market and not worry about breaking things."

"Right again," Wombat replies. "Anyone have thoughts about the Third Commandment... other than Parseltongue?" Wombat doesn't actually say Parseltongue, of course, but you imagine she does. You always imagine people are calling people by the same nicknames that you are in your head.

This time you speak up. "I think the Third Company Commandment means that if something sells, you should do more of it. That maybe the market is always right?"

"Correct," Wombat says. "Okay, next I'd like us to—"

"But does that make sense?" you interrupt.

"Does what make sense?"

"The Third Commandment. I mean, just because something sells doesn't mean you should keep making it. There are some products that you should stop selling, even if people are buying them. Like asbestos, or cigarettes—or lawn darts."

Wombat's eyes narrowed. "Remember what I said about there being no wrong answers? Maybe I was wrong about that!" She smiles in a way that she probably thinks is disarming but that is actually completely arming. "Here's what is so great about the company you now work for. The social media revolution has failed. All the tools that were created to bring people together have split us apart. Digital communication has divided us into separate tribes, placed us into separate bubbles, with separate streams of information, so much so that we can't understand each other, much less communicate with each other. To quote the Founder, 'It's an epistemological disaster on an epic scale.'"

Parseltongue raises her hand, but Wombat, who is getting warmed up, motions for her to put it back down.

"Digital platforms for communication abbreviate and infantilize information. They provide more heat than light and leave us unable to grapple with the big issues of the day, which require more information, not less, to understand them. Climate change, wealth inequality, racial discord, the erosion of democratic values—these are macro-subjects that can't be addressed in micro-posts! But the amazing thing about the platform that the Founder has created is that it gives you more information, not less. People will sit and listen to an audiobook or a podcast or an audio lecture for hours on end. Books aren't outdated tech; they are the building blocks of high tech. Text is tech. Judaism, Christianity, Islam, are each rooted in a single text, so much so that their adherents are known as People of the Book. Virtually all major religions are text-based. Books are at the heart of who we are, but social media has taken us away from that. The Founder, and this audio company, are returning us to our human roots, to the oral traditions of Homer and Charles

Dickens and Jay-Z. As the Founder famously said at an All-Hands meeting ten years ago: 'The revolution isn't on the screen or the streets but between your ears.'"

Parseltongue can't hold back. "The Founder wrote in his book *The Cursor Never Blinks* that 'the ears, not the eyes, are the window to the soul. And it is through them the future will come rushing through.'"

Wombat laughs. "You're an incredible reader. If all of you learn to be good listeners too, you'll be a success at this company."

• • •

Technoaggression #17: You are in the elevator to your apartment. "Hold it!" a voice calls out, and you stick out your arm and risk losing a hand to stop the doors from closing. A white woman, swallowed in entitled silence, steps into the elevator without even a thank you. You recognize her from work, but she acts like she doesn't even see you. You float your finger over the elevator buttons, waiting for her to say her floor number, but she just stares straight ahead. So you ride the elevator up. When you get to your floor and get out, the woman doesn't exit the elevator with you. As the doors close behind you, you see her finally pressing the button for her floor. You can't see which floor she's going to—that was surely the woman's intention—but you make a guess. You run up three flights of stairs, and you do it fast so you can beat the elevator to its destination. When the elevator doors open you are standing there, gangsta leaning against the wall, when the bitch exits. She clutches her purse as you stare her punk-ass down.

• • •

When you get inside your apartment, you take a shower to wash off your first day of work. You found everything incredibly interesting, but if you're being honest, sometimes the workplace atmosphere at Eustachian felt more like a cult than a culture. Maybe that's the way all tech companies operate. God was dead, patriotism was corny, and COVID had broken the bonds of friends and communities everywhere. People work better and harder when they believe in something, so, in the tech industry at least, the workplace was the new church, and bonuses and corporate perks had replaced the sacraments. Tech was changing everything, and you felt guiltily proud that you were now part of making change happen and not waiting for it to happen to you. It had always been agency-sapping to see news stories speculating about what the tech industry was going to do and where it was going to go next, like it was something out of human control, like a tornado or a dragon. Now you were riding the dragon. You were one of the *Homo sapiens* making fire, and not one of the Neanderthals huddling in a dark cave hoping a saber-toothed tiger wouldn't drag them off into the night. Okay, maybe that was shitty and elitist to think of techless civilians as Neanderthals, but you have to admit being part of the cultural wave feels good.

That Walcott guy seemed to believe in the company and that there was some way Big Tech could improve the fortunes of Black people. You didn't know if you believed that, but you had to admit you wouldn't mind believing in something. But you're not doing this for belief. You're not even doing this for yourself. Your ledger is soaked in red, and you've got to turn it black. Your mom left you with a debt you have to pay, and now that you have this job, you are one step closer to doing that. So what if you have to fake a little enthusiasm so your fellow employees think you're down with the program? You know what you believe in, and it's not in Big Tech or the Easter Bunny. You're in Big Tech to get paid. Bitch better have my money, you feel me? As you're toweling off, you see an email pop up on your phone. Speak of the devil.

From: Walcott Neville
To: Octavia Crenshaw
June 3

You finally plugged in! You're probably still processing your first day at work. Beginnings can be hard, but they're better than endings. I'll reach out and try to find a time on your calendar in the next week or two to get the download on how your onboarding has been going so far. My first few months here were really hard because there were a million things to learn about how things got done and none of it was written down and none of it was intuitive. My advice is to wipe your mental hard drive of the old ways you used to do things and leave room in your head for the new. If you have any questions about anything, feel free to reach out to me directly, and I'll try to help or find someone who can. I have a feeling we'll be working on a project together soon, but until then I hope you mesh well with your initial assignment. Remember, there's more to making money than making money!

—Walcott

    You notice that he sent you the email from his private account, not his work email, and it came to your private account, not your work one. Did that mean this note was more personal than professional? Was it a digital flirt? Your head was too overloaded with data from your workday to parse or process this any further. You are tired, but you want to get back to him before you go to sleep, so you dash off a return note thanking him for checking in and recounting in James Joycean stream of consciousness everything that happened to you on your first day at work, and by the time you're done your account is just about as detailed as Bloomsday, and you probably sound like either an avant-garde writer from Dublin or a crazy bitch. You hit send.

    Black Nerds were not your love language. You were attracted to guys who were dangerous but intelligent. Guys who drove motorcycles but wore helmets. Guys who free-climbed El Capitan in Yosemite and were tenure track at Stanford. Guys who drank Jamaican rum to excess and were militantly vegan. Audre Lorde–quoting, dreadlock-wearing, six-foot-tall or taller motherfuckers who give foot rubs, are always down for going down on you, and have credit scores of 700 or higher. Those are the kind of guys you were into. Your first boyfriend, Ezra, from your eighth grade Latin class, had a self-inflicted tattoo on his forearm that read "Alea iacta est." He said that because of his body art, he could never be buried in a Jewish cemetery, since the Torah prohibited the marking of one's skin. He told you Leviticus 19:28 declared, "You shall not make gashes in your flesh for the dead, or incise any marks on yourselves. I am the Eternal." Quoting the Torah was a huge turn-on for you because it felt deep and mysterious and eloquent. Plus Jewish boys had chest hair and that was hot. The taboo-breaking nature of Ezra's tattoo turned you on even more. So the night before his bar mitzvah, you let him slide into second base because hearing him rehearse the Hebrew portions of his d'var Torah made you horny as hell. Later, in college, you briefly dated a cantor at a Reform synagogue who told you the stuff about tattooed people not being allowed to be buried in Jewish cemeteries was a bullshit myth. "The Nazis tattooed Holocaust victims," he explained. "Are we really going to bar someone who's suffered through Buchenwald from the family plot?" Whatever he said after that was muffled by the contractions of your thighs. You weren't here for a history lesson; you figured you were doing your part to combat anti-Semitism by trying to come on this cantor's face. In any case, your tattooed grade school fling remained sexy in memory. Last you heard, Ezra was a civil rights lawyer in New Haven. He still had a wild side—you came across a photo of him on Instagram perched on the lip of a volcano in Maui. You needed more tattooed guys in your life and fewer ring-bearing nerds. You plopped face down on your futon.

You had your Big Tech dream job. Now you just had to learn how to do it before everyone realized you were a goddamn imposter.

Chapter Four

CHAMPAGNE PROBLEMS

A few months after her funeral, you found your mom's diary when you were cleaning your apartment. You had been clearing some space on a shelf for an urn with your parents' ashes when you spotted the diary hidden behind a trio of books about the intersection of epistemology and machine learning: *Of Two Minds: The Future of Hegelian Thought in the Age of AI*, *The Algorithms You Meet in Heaven: A Dialogue on Neural Networks and the Afterlife*, and *Minding the Machines: Foucault and the Digital Panopticon*.

The diary was a booklet bound in red leather with an embossed image of a doctor bird on the cover. Flipping through it, you discovered it wasn't a diary in the standard sense—your mother seemed too guarded and unsentimental for that—it was a journal that a marriage counselor had recommended that she write. The first entry suggested that Dad had been asked to write one too. The last entry was dated about a year after his death, so Mom had probably forgotten where she had even hidden the journal. Maybe she wanted it to be found; maybe she would have preferred it was forever lost. You felt a little creepy reading something your mom may or may not have wanted to keep private, but not reading it would have been like letting her die all over again. You kept reading.

In my darkest marital moments—and I'm not proud of this—I hate my husband. He pisses me off because he didn't turn out to be as successful as I always thought he'd be. A lot of the things that I thought made him special—his quirkiness, his creativity, his compassion—turned out that in the corporate world they're character flaws. I've got tenure at a major university; he's an SEO engineer for a start-up news website. The fact that he earns so little makes me have to work harder, and the frenzied pace of my academic career feels unsustainable and unhealthy like the way fracking helps produce oil and gas but also pollutes the groundwater and triggers the occasional earthquake. I don't want to be associate dean for undergraduate affairs because I'm already teaching a full course load, but I have to do it because we need the money. I don't want to travel the East Coast lecturing on post-Cartesian theories of personal identity, but the honorariums and stipends add up to real income and help bridge the gap when my husband is between jobs. So why do I stay with him? My daughter, first of all, I'm not going to lie about that. But also something else. Maybe it's the way he asks me about how my day went and shows genuine interest. Maybe it's the way when I'm sick, he'll take off from work too—if he's employed—and cook pepper pot soup with callaloo, okra, and allspice just like I like it. Maybe it's a million little things, like the dots on a Seurat painting. Up close they're just splotches, multicolored mistakes, but when you take in the big picture you've got A Sunday Afternoon on the Island of La Grande Jatte. *I don't love Thurgood because he succeeded. I love him because he tries. And he'll keep trying. I have to keep the big pointillist picture in mind.*

You had never imagined your parents having problems. They never argued in front of you and never discussed any money problems in your presence. You suddenly felt guilty that you had intruded on your mom and dad's private emotional space by reading this journal and perhaps even sullied your memories of them together. But that feeling faded pretty quickly. You started hunting around the apartment to see if you could find Dad's journal next.

• • •

You listen to Noelle Swizzler on a podcast as you run on a treadmill at the company gym.

Interviewer: What inspires you?
Swizzler: I don't write about the road or about hotels. I write about feelings—how people make me feel and how I wish they would feel about me. Fame is an alien planet to most people, but everyone has the same emotions.
Interviewer: Do you feel that your early fame has cut you off from experiences that might have fed into your songwriting? Any regrets that you became so successful so young?
Swizzler: Dolly Parton once told me that you should never regret anything because you make choices in life in the moment, not in hindsight. Nobody knows the past, present, and future at the same time. So I never look back, I look at where I am. Now is the most amazing place.

• • •

You've been at the company eight days and you still haven't figured out all the software. You're a software engineer, so this is extra-embarrassing.

There's an app to submit business expenses, another to put in for vacations, and another to register to use the cafeteria. That's all standard. But then there's an app to log ideas for new proposals, another to submit proposals that have been approved for evaluation, and still another app to actually move the project into the development phase. Each of these apps required separate two-hour-long training sessions. You could have created your own app in the time it took to train yourself to use these. And at the end of your second week, a company-wide memo went around that the idea-logging app and the development app were being replaced, and that new three-hour training sessions would be scheduled to get everyone up to speed on the new processes. There's also an email in your inbox about a new training session on "Safeguarding User Data: The Key to Corporate Reputation Building." As an engineer, you're used to training sessions and programming and things that require plenty of keystrokes. But you hate wasting time and you'll never get used to that.

You get to wondering why so much of the tech is so clunky at what is, after all, a *Big Tech company*. Then you realize the problem is all about being proprietary. Big Tech companies hate using the software of other Big Tech companies because 1) it undercuts the client company's image of being visionary and independent, and 2) it gives the company making the software leverage and bragging rights. So Eustachian was always developing its own shit to use in-house and on its own owned platforms even when there was better stuff out there that did the same thing. As a result, the in-house apps were second-rate knockoffs, like the designer purses for sale on the sidewalks in midtown Manhattan. The other explanation for the sucky software is that Big Tech companies, once they get big, aren't great at innovating, they're good at dominating. Creating cutting-edge stuff gets them to the top; monopolizing and buying out the competition keep them there.

You notice that while you were contemplating the clunky apps, your Microsectionality rating dipped a few points. You try not to think about it.

You open up the video that accompanies the "Safeguarding User Data" training session. Your coding background makes data security and authentication protocols etc. all SOP for you, but this bullshit course is something every employee has to suffer through. The clip features the DEI Players, a multiethnic troupe of actors who play out scenes that are meant to teach you about data safety, diversity, sexual harassment, and other aspects of corporate culture. In one video, a guy in a porkpie hat surreptitiously tapes a virtual conference call and manages to record an employee typing in his password—and Porkpie uses that password to hack into the company's records. You wonder if this training session is really safeguarding user data or just giving hackers ideas. The training session couldn't end soon enough for you.

You are seated on the ninth floor with many of the other coders and software engineers, and you're constantly getting calendar invites from people who are desked only a few feet away from you. Nobody at the company wants to just quickly hop on the phone to discuss a topic, or send an email to clear up an issue, or even walk down a hallway to connect face-to-face and make sure everyone is on the same page. Instead they schedule virtual meetings, usually an hour long, to hash out something that could have been handled IRL in five minutes. The nonconsensual meetings would often just appear on your electronic calendar, without warning or explanation, like uninvited wedding guests, and sometimes at the last second. You'd suddenly find your laptop pinging you that you have a meeting in half an hour that you didn't know you had, and you'd spend the first few minutes of the meeting, if not the whole thing, trying to figure out what the meeting was about, who was on the call, and why it couldn't have just been handled via text. One time a meeting started up while you were on the toilet with your laptop balanced on your knees, and you had to quickly make sure your camera was turned off; another time you almost clicked into an unexpected morning meeting before you realized you were still wearing a bright yellow skin-detoxifying mud mask from that night.

You get that every company has meetings, but Eustachian was addicted to them in the way that junkies get hooked on the methadone that's supposed to get them off drugs. There was recently a meeting about planning a meeting to address the glut of meetings. That was just too much turtles all the way down for you. So the meetings kept emerging, unwanted, unstoppable, like broods of cicadas. Nobody wanted to make a mistake that could get them cast out of the land of milk and money, so they were always checking with each other, groupthinking, and making sure there was an electronic record that whatever bullshit decision they made had been authorized by a quorum.

Within a few weeks, you've learned to defensively fill up your calendar with fake meetings so your colleagues can't pull you into their useless two-hour assemblies from hell. Another problem solved—they didn't call you the Big O for nothing. You give the fake meetings fake names like "Expense Reports from Monopolated Light & Power Company" and "Yoyodyne Industries Training Session" and "Lunch with Sasha Fierce." You don't know if people even notice the names of your fake meetings, maybe all they register are the blocks of time blocked out, but it still amuses you to see your calendar filled up with fictional happenings. Fantasy is a great defense against reality.

Your laptop pings. Someone has invited you to some other meeting. You are annoyed. You believe that calendar etiquette demands that someone call or text you first before simply inserting themselves into your calendar. There's something invasive and #MeToo-ish about an unwanted calendar advance. Your time is at least as precious as your body. People need enthusiastic consent before they can kiss, so why do they think it's okay to grope and grab on to someone's time before seeing if it's okay?

You are about to reject the invite, but you decide you need a little more information first. You look the dude up in the company directory. The guy who sent the invite has blue hair and glasses, so you call him Blue in your mind. It seems like Blue couldn't be bothered to upload a current headshot onto the company database. In the photo, he seems like he's twelve years old. If this is really what he looks like now, he's either a prodigy or a case of arrested development.

"Good to e-meet you," you email the guy. "What's the meeting for?"

"Your first assignment," Blue emails back.

"Which is?"

Blue doesn't respond, so you google him. Born in Seoul, raised in

Alexandria, VA, graduated from Berkeley with a BA in political philosophy (interesting) and from Caltech with an MS in computer science (predictable). He has a healthy track record of news stories about his work. But the guy doesn't have any social media accounts you can see. You never know whether to be impressed or horrified with people who aren't on social media, because it feels like a holier-than-thou indictment of all the people who are on social media. Everyone understands that social media is for attention whores. But you don't have to slut shame everyone else by refusing to patronize the digital brothel. You snap a selfie of yourself at your desk and you don't even know why you took the picture; it happens reflexively like popping another potato chip into your mouth. You decide that Blue is the world's biggest asshole. But you RSVP yes to the meeting because it seems like you kinda have to if he has info on your new assignment. You've been here for almost two weeks now and all you've been doing is training. You don't even have a boss yet. Eustachian has a practice of peer-to-peer hiring, so Walcott is a colleague, you're not his direct report. You need a manager and a department. You are mentorless and sponsorless.

You've heard whispers at Eustachian that Blacks and women and especially Black women sometimes go weeks without direction until the only direction left is the exit. It's Big Tech's way of saying thanks for helping our inclusion numbers, we tried, now here's the door. If you wash out of this place, you don't want anyone to say "I told you so," because the truth is nobody has told you anything. Not yet, anyway. You feel like you did that one time when you were driving to visit Kenise at her family's place in Jamaica and your GPS cut out in the Blue Mountains. Kenise had gone there to get some R&R after her big operation. You had no idea where to go, and you had to keep driving for an hour in the wrong direction until your Waze reconnected. You needed some direction right now. Saying no to Blue's request would be like Tom Cruise choosing not to accept a new mission in *Mission: Impossible*. The answer has to be yes or there's no movie. Immediately after you RSVP, Blue sends you an email with an attachment: It's an NDA. You don't even read it before checking a box and sending it back.

• • •

Blue sets the meeting to take place at his desk on the eleventh floor. He's doing a deskside meet because all the conference rooms were booked for that time slot. They always are. The conference rooms at Eustachian are all named after famous New Jerseyans. Bruce Springsteen, Frank Sinatra, Philip Roth, George R. R. Martin, Thomas Edison, and Meryl Streep all have rooms. You didn't even know Meryl was from New Jersey— you could have sworn she was from Connecticut or Vermont or someplace with ski lifts. She had so thoroughly de-Garden Stated herself, it's easier to imagine her speaking like a Danish aristocrat than a Jersey girl. Whitney Houston and Lauryn Hill don't have rooms yet, which is crazy. And for some reason the lactation space on the twelfth floor is named after Jon Bon Jovi. Nobody seems to know why.

The conference rooms are always filled because nobody has an office at Eustachian, and there aren't even cubicles. Everyone just sits at democratizing desks, from the newest intern to the c-suite team (or they would be the c-suite team if there was actually a c-suite instead of just more desks). Even the Founder sits at a desk (with a 7,500-piece Lego model of the Millennium Falcon hung on wires above it), although he's rarely seen behind that desk or in the offices at all. If you need to meet someone or have to make a personal call, you have to book a conference room, and to get one you have to reserve it at least a week in advance, like a table at a hot restaurant in SoHo. But anticipating when you might need a little privacy is hard to do, so people end up having to conduct a lot of their personal business in public. You've overheard colleagues talking to their divorce lawyers, their Tinder hookups, their gastroenterologists. You suspect this isn't a bug, it's a feature. The company, like the church, wants you to bare your whole soul. So if you need to call your pharmacy to check on your birth control pill prescription, or to break up with that passive-aggressive dude you were seeing only because you hate sleeping alone, you may have to do it on company grounds.

You decide to spend your lunch break looking into whatever's on the twenty-seventh floor. A new approach is what's needed to find out what's really up there, you decide. You take the elevator to the twenty-sixth floor and get out. You walk around the entire floor but don't see a stairwell to the level above. Every floor plan in the building is roughly similar, but there's a big wooden filing cabinet where you thought the stairs would probably be. When you get really close to the cabinet you think you hear the faint sound of music. Old-timey church music, pre-hip-hop gospel that makes you think of Aretha and Mahalia and old Black women in primary-colored wide-brimmed hats. You once saw a performance of Alvin Ailey's *Revelations*, and the music filtering through the walls behind the filing cabinet makes you think of that. You look around, but everyone is working away, and nobody else seems to hear the music but you. You open up a drawer in the filing cabinet, and it's stuffed with company-branded T-shirts, tote bags, and coats. You pull out one of the jackets. It's warm, with faux fur lining and "Eustachian Inc." emblazoned over the front left breast and the creepy blue eye inside the green ear company logo across the back. There's a scrap of paper in an inside pocket that you unfold. It reads "DEI = DIE."

"Having a Captain Cook?"

You turn around, and Wombat is behind you, her red hair blazing.

"Um... what?"

"What are you looking for?"

"A snack," you lie, stuffing the scrap of paper into your pocket.

Wombat smiles. "You're in for a treat."

• • •

You end up joining Wombat for lunch at the Grapevine, Eustachian's main cafeteria. The place is one of the wonders of the world—or at least the world of tech. There's a pandemonium of mushroom-cloud-hatted chefs, and the menu changes every day. There are food offerings from around the world: navratan korma from India, bibimbap from South

Korea, saffron-infused plov from Azerbaijan, and the list goes on. The tables have grills built right in, like at Japanese steak houses, and the food preparers will come up to where you're sitting and cook shrimp, chicken, and chunks of Kobe beef right in front of you. The hot dishes are hot, the cold ones are cold, everything smells great, and everything is free. There are visiting chefs from restaurants across Arkhaam who get to do three-month all-expenses-paid residencies at the Grapevine, boosting awareness for their establishments, helping to support the local economy—and making sure the food at Eustachian is varied and top-tier. You've had dates take you out for superexpensive meals that weren't half as good as the food at this workplace cafeteria.

Your stomach is growling at all the great dishes. "They must do this so we never leave."

Wombat winks as she piles egg rolls onto her plate. "Is it working?"

You both take your trays and grab seats, and you get a good look at Wombat. She is one of those women who, through sheer force of will and a mastery of makeup, stopped aging at thirty-five years old. Or maybe forty. Or maybe thirty. It was impossible to tell how old this woman was. There was a timelessness about her, like vintage Chanel.

"Have you signed up for FLIT?"

You quickly swallow a bite of a Swedish meatball. "What's that?"

"Female Leaders in Technology. It's an affinity group I cochair. It's sisters at work trading stories and trying to stay sane. I read in this book *Invisible Women* that female business owners get less than half the VC investment that men get even though we generate more than twice the revenue. Even when we succeed they don't cover us like they do Jobs and Musk and Gates and Altman and Zuckerberg. How many times have you ever heard a female business leader called a genius? We have to help each other because nobody else is."

You're still trying to piece together this woman's story. She's a high-ranking executive here and she's talking to you like you're equals, but you're totally not. She's a senior manager and could fire you if she wanted. Plus her eyebrows are flawless. Although that's not something you typically give two shits about, this woman's brow game is something to which attention must be paid. You're still trying to figure out how old she is. You notice that she cleverly avoids references that could carbon-date her. The songs she mentions are all on the charts right now. When the question of college comes up, she doesn't mention anything about when she graduated or even which school she attended. She talks a lot about "the juggle" and "work-life balance," but she doesn't drop any hint about whether she's married or has any kids, or if she's planning to reproduce by cellular mitosis. She's an expert at saying a lot without saying anything. It's a masterful conversational technique because it pulls you into talking just to match her word count. You're not as good at saying nothing—few people are—so you end up saying way more than you intended.

She is nibbling on a curry chicken patty. "The food brings them in, but what really keeps people here are the RSUs."

"I know I should know this, but what's an RSU?"

She puts down her patty. "Are you serious?"

"I'm just playing," you lie. "I saw that I got a bunch of them, and I know how they work. I just don't know how they *work* work. 'Cause nobody explained it."

Wombat laughs—with surprise, not because she thinks what you said was funny. "I'm sorry, I'm laughing because we spent a lot of money on our onboarding process and clearly we have a long way to go. RSUs are restricted stock units. New employees get a grant of them when they're hired, and high-performing staffers get a new bunch every year. Every November they vest, meaning you can cash them in. You own a piece of Eustachian, girl. And if you last to the end of the year, and the stock performs, you're going to have loads of money. A lot of people earn more through their RSUs than they do in salary."

You try to hide your excitement, but you know your face isn't doing a very good job of it. You could use this RSU money. Not to buy things for yourself, but to help you sort out the financial mess your mom left you.

You don't say any of that, of course. "Oh my god, that's incredible," you say. "I guess they did tell me at least some of that in onboarding, but I didn't quite understand."

Wombat smiles. There must be a million kinds of smiles. You cataloged thousands of them as part of an image recognition project for a course back in college—W4731: Deep Learning for Computer Vision—and you were amazed by their variety and specificity. You had to run through an endless stream of upcurled lips, dutifully labeling each one for a dataset. There are big smiles, tight smiles, half smiles. Grins, leers, and smirks. There are smiles that are really frowns, and those are maybe the saddest things you can do with your face. And there are smiles that are acts of bravery, and they can bring tears to your eyes to witness them. Then there are mocking smiles where the smiler is smiling at you, not with you, and cruel smiles meant to lip-lash the viewer into submission. There are smiles that don't involve the eyes (and when the eyes are alienated you know those smiles are fake as shit) and smiles that barely curve the mouth beyond a straight line (evidence of emotion too deeply felt to conceal). Then there are smiles like the one Wombat is smiling—wide, inviting, both rows of teeth flashing like paparazzi cameras, crimson-lipped, deeply-dimpled, crinkles bracketing her eyes like greater than and less than symbols in a math equation. Smiles like hers oxymoronically wrinkle the face even as they rejuvenate it. Wombat's smile is a smile that says you and she have both arrived, and you should take a seat, feast on the bounty you now share. Hers is a smile that makes you smile back.

Wombat, the smile dancing in her voice, offers you a plate of cookies. "Wrap your laughing gear around these!"

• • •

You go to the third floor to get some peace of mind. You sometimes come to this level because this is the data compilation floor and data compilers keep their restrooms immaculately clean. It's also a very quiet floor, with very little small talk, and most of the employees are bent over their laptops data compiling. Most of what's done by this department was pretty rote: filing NDAs, reviewing Terms of Service agreements, and processing the info that came in through the Eustachian app's Hearing Is Believing program, which compiled user data to help generate and personalize product and service recommendations. Some of the customer experience staff occupy a few of the desks here as well. They were probably all going to be replaced by AI in the next few years or months. Any job you think could probably be done by a robot eventually will. The truly creative coding, the kind of stuff you specialized in, took place on the higher floors with the more senior employees.

But the best thing about the floor is that, tucked away in a corner, there's a cozy little recording studio. They probably put it here, in part, because the area is so naturally quiet. Or maybe it's a vestigial room from some earlier floor plan, like the way humans have appendixes or snakes still have pelvic bones. You stumbled onto the area when you were exploring the building. Apparently, visiting podcasters use the room, although you've never actually witnessed any actual podcasting taking place in it. It's a small space with a glass partition bifurcating the control room and the recording booth. The soundproofing is thick and damn near impenetrable, which is great for incubating creativity. Once you close the thick studio door, the outer world falls away, and all you can hear is whatever genius sound is being created inside. It's like walking into Beethoven's head. The studio is the perfect place to get some alone time in the middle of a crowded day.

This time, when you enter the studio, there's someone in the recording booth.

Braids.

She can't hear you behind the thick double glass of the partition, and she can't see you because her eyes are scrunched tight, like overstuffed suitcases. You can't hear her either, but you can see what she's doing. She appears to be screaming—a primal scream, with her whole chest and gut, her neck straining and her fists clenched. You flick on the intercom, and her scream fills the control booth, awful, incendiary, feeding back into itself.

"Braids?" you say into the mic.

The scream cuts off, and Braids looks at you through the glass. Her eyes are dark and full of secrets like the windows of a haunted house. You see your reflection in the partition blending into her image.

Braids blinks. "I thought I was alone."

"Are you okay? Can I help? You're not alone here..."

She wipes away a tear. "I...I...I'm sorry. I was just thinking..."

"About what, babygirl?"

"...about the Luddites."

"About the *Luddites*?" you reply. *Are you shitting me?* you think. You hand her a Kleenex from a nearby dispenser.

Braids blows her nose. "Have you heard the story? I mean, the whole story? The asshole British government, siding with industrialists against workers, launched this horrible wave of political and social repression..."

You put a hand on her shoulder. "Babygirl, you need to..."

"...employing spies to infiltrate the Luddite movement, sponsoring armed gangs, and ordering soldiers to kill everyone who was buying into the Luddite point of view..."

"Braids..."

But Braids brushes your hand off her shoulder, rushes out of the booth, and exits the studio before you can say anything more.

Damn, that was weird. You wish you could have helped her more, but on the flip side, at least she didn't recite any more Luddite poetry.

• • •

Technoaggression #42: Two white women are standing next to the fridge in the break room discussing a trip to Santorini. One of them—Parseltongue from your onboarding group—turns to you and white-womansplains that Santorini is an island off the coast of Greece like of course you wouldn't know. You pull out your phone and show them photos of you in Santorini from a trip you took there three years ago. There you are with the blue domes and white walls of the island behind you. There you are taking a tour of the ancient, ruined columns and buildings. There you are walking the black sand beaches as the sun sets on the vin santo–colored Aegean Sea.

"We didn't mean it like that," Parseltongue says.

"How did 'we' mean it?" you ask.

"'We' didn't say 'it' at all," says the woman who didn't say it at all. "There's not a 'we.'"

"There's no reason to start accusing people of racism," Parseltongue says.

You cross your arms. "I didn't accuse anyone. You assumed I was accusing you, just like someone might reasonably assume you assuming that I had never been to Santorini is racist."

Parseltongue slithers away.

The other woman turns to you. "You realize I barely know that bitch, right? She's not even in my department."

• • •

Braids sends you a text after work apologizing for being such a hot mess and thanking you for your kind words when you tried to comfort her. "I'm sorry," she says. "I was feeling bad, but it wasn't really about the Luddites. I'm going through stuff at work. When I'm ready to talk about it, I'll talk about it." She also forwards you an encouraging email she got from Walcott.

From: Walcott Neville
To: Braids
June 28

There are some memories you can't delete. Back when my dad became the first person in my family to go to college, he had to sleep in a hallway between two white students' rooms because nobody would rent to him. He didn't let intolerance stop him. He went on to get a BS in computer science and go into the industry. His successful struggle to get his education has always inspired me. I graduated from a public high school in Rockport, a tiny town in upstate New York. I went on to graduate from Howard University and MIT. Now I'm an executive editor for Eustachian, the biggest audio entertainment company on the planet. Yes, we all know our world is collapsing. Police brutality continues to ravage our communities. It's harder to get a job, even harder to keep one. But there's hope—the Black Lives Matter movement demonstrated that demonstrations matter. People took to the streets to demand their rights and to topple statues and monuments that represent racism and intolerance. Don't be frightened by the future. The whole world is rebooting and your time is now. Let the bad stuff go, like a program running in the background. Find your space, just like my dad did. Use that space to make yourself, future generations, and this company better. Be yourself 2.0.

You wonder how Walcott found out about Braids, but in any case you're impressed that he's walking it like he's talking it and trying to support other Black employees. Without any available mentors and sponsors for employees of color in the whitewashed world of tech, it was nice to at least have peer support. Maybe he was more than just another Black Nerd after all. But what's going on with Braids? She seemed so tough and cheerful—what had gotten her so upset?

Chapter Five

NO SURPRISES

How's the new job Octavia?

There's a lot to process.

Isn't it interesting how more and more people use computer metaphors to describe what's going on in their heads? People talk about processing or not having the bandwidth. Whenever I was overwhelmed at work I used to go to Cafe Beatrice just to make room on my mental hard drives.

I remember you saying that Kenise

Computers are thinking more like humans
and humans are thinking more like them. The
singularity is a two-way street

> Maybe humans and AI will end up using machine
> metaphors as the default. And human brains will
> be analogies for obsolescence and limitation.

If that happens, I'll know your job in Big Tech
is going great!

> I'll make it happen. They didn't
> call me Big O for nothing

You know I hate when you call yourself that

• • •

You would have liked to have eaten lunch alone under a tree in the park across the street from the Cathedral of Technology. You would have loved to have gotten some alone time and cleared your head of all the swirl at work. Instead, you were roped into a lunchtime meeting of FLIT. Wombat had come to your desk so you couldn't get out of it. The only other person who showed up for the meeting was Parseltongue. At least she was coming of her own volition.

Wombat, you, and Parseltongue pick up drinks from Hannibal's, this smoothie place on the edge of the Eustachian parking lot, and stroll around outside. The day is hot and breezeless, and the Eustachian tower throbs in the sun. Lots of employees are eating *en plein air*, and that term floats into your mind because the color and light of the afternoon remind you of a show of French impressionists you saw once at the Met. It was fascinating that a small group of people could change the way the world views itself and that there is this ever-changing duet between science and culture. You learned in the exhibition that technology gave painters ready-made paint in tubes that allowed them to work outside more easily, and research into color contrasts spurred artists to experiment with fresh palettes, like plopping down a sunset-orange boat in a cobalt-blue lake. Images were rendered in dots and hazy brushstrokes that emulated the way the then-emerging field of optics said people actually saw the world. Wombat motions for you to hurry along, and you stop daydreaming about museums. You pass kids kicking soccer balls and seniors playing chess. The women employees you see cross the street or turn around when they spot your FLIT trio coming. They had clearly seen the invitation pop up unsolicited and unwelcomed on their calendars and wanted to enjoy the nice day without the sister-to-sister banter.

As you walk down the sidewalk, homeless people intermittently come up to you and ask for change. You fish out a few quarters. Arkhaam's streets were teeming with unhoused individuals and families, and some of them wouldn't leave you alone unless you paid them to do so. You knew giving them money wasn't going to help much, and you felt kind of shitty and bourgeois paying people to stay away from you. Parseltongue just keeps her head down when approached for change. Wombat has her own approach: She has a roll of five-dollar bills in her purse, which she doles out one at a time.

"That adds up," you say.

A wistful look passes over Wombat's face. "When I was a little girl, my dad used to always quote this one passage from Matthew: 'Then he will say to those on his left, "Depart from me, you who are cursed, into the eternal fire prepared for the devil and his angels. For I was hungry and you gave me nothing to eat, I was thirsty and you gave me nothing to drink, I was a stranger and you did not invite me in, I needed clothes and you did not clothe me, I was sick and in prison and you did not look after me." They also will answer, "Lord, when did we see you hungry or thirsty or a stranger or needing clothes or sick or in prison, and did not help you?" He will reply, "Truly I tell you, whatever you did not do for one of the least of these, you did not do for me."'"

You did not expect Wombat to quote Scripture at you at work, and at such length. It's a bit oversharing-y, like someone pulling down their pants to show you how their Brazilian wax turned out. "That's very biblical," you say.

"That was a long time ago." Wombat smiles, running a hand through her flame-red hair. "I haven't gone to Sunday service since I was a child." She winks. "Now the only commandments I follow are from the Founder. I hear he's got an audience with the pope next week! Or maybe it was the ayatollah."

You and Wombat and Parseltongue stop and take seats on the grass under the very tree where you had wanted to spend your lunch break alone. A group of laughing uniformed Catholic schoolgirls are perched on a bench nearby sipping bubble tea out of clear plastic cups.

"I'll break the ice," Wombat says. "I'd love for us to each share something about our experiences as women at this company. One of our biggest problems as women in the workplace is that we go through things alone. We're not alone, and when we share, we succeed." When both you and Parseltongue stay silent, Wombat presses on. "I'll go first then. I'm not from this country, as you may have noticed from the little trace of an Aussie accent I still have. I grew up in Oodnadatta, which is a very small, very remote, very oddly named town in the Outback. My mother married a clergyman who was on a mission in the area, and so when I was still a small girl, we moved to New Jersey, the last place I ever expected to be. So you see, I have had the full immigrant experience, and it really informs me as an executive and as a woman."

"How so?" you ask. "I mean, how have you had 'the full immigrant experience'?"

"I know what other immigrants are going through. The language barriers and all that."

"But they speak English in Australia, right? Like English English?"

"Not if you ask the British." Wombat laughs. "Now tell me about you."

Parseltongue sips her smoothie and looks away. You guess that you will have to fill the silence. "What's *The Jungle Book*?" you ask.

Wombat turns to you. "What about it?"

"I keep hearing about it. What was that controversy about? It sounds like it was something pretty bad and #MeToo-y."

"I wasn't working on that project, so I can't say much about it," Wombat replies. "But what I will say is that people sometimes make mistakes."

You hate when people say "what I will say." It suggests that there's plenty that they're unwilling to say and that's the good shit you want to hear. But you shrug this off and say, "It seems like the people who are making the mistakes are usually monstrous men."

"So are you saying they should just be canceled?"

"Depends on what they did. You have to strike a balance, create a formula—a Bechdel test for monstrous men. How big of a genius is the person? And how bad did he screw up? It's like Chris Rock said about the difference between R. Kelly and Michael Jackson. They both messed up, but we can go the rest of our lives without hearing R. Kelly's 'Bump N' Grind' and we'll be just fine. Michael is a little different—he's too big to fail. And besides, he's dead, so he's not gonna profit from his alleged crimes. So I can dance to 'I Want You Back' with no guilt."

"Trust me, the people associated with the *Jungle Book* incident have been dealt with appropriately. That's about all I can say about it. And monsters aren't always men."

"You never hear about Noelle Swizzler pistol-whipping her enemies. A lot of her enemies began as her friends, but she handles betrayal with class. The monsters are dudes like Picasso, Philip Roth, and Omari. There's a reason 'geniuses' rhymes with 'penises.'"

"They don't rhyme, but I take your point. What about Alice Munro?"

"Alice Munro, the Nobel Prize–winning short story writer?" you ask.

"No, Alice Munro, the captain of the Adelaide Strikers cricket team."

You play along when you realize she's making a joke. "I don't follow cricket."

"Of course the writer."

"But she's Canadian," you reply.

"You say that like 'Canadian' is a synonym for 'harmless'—it's not. Munro's second husband abused her daughter from her first marriage, and when Munro found out about it, she did nothing. The daughter even wrote an article about it."

"I love that Alice Munro story 'The Lottery,'" Parseltongue says between smoothie sips.

"That's Shirley Jackson," Wombat replies.

Parseltongue takes another thoughtful sip. "'Everything That Rises Must Converge'?"

Wombat exhales. "That's Flannery O'Connor, who also wrote 'A Good Man Is Hard to Find.'"

"I thought that was Georgia O'Keeffe," Parseltongue says.

"You're as useful as an ashtray on a motorbike," Wombat says testily.

You shake your head. "Munro does sound like a monster. But that still comes down to the man, doesn't it? Her husband was the one doing the abusing."

"My point is this: I just don't like it when people try to act like women are gentler creatures than men. The lack of a killer instinct is an evolutionary deficiency, not an advantage. Great men are monsters because monstrosity is often what greatness demands. If a woman wants to succeed, she has to be prepared to do terrible things. We can't shy away from being called 'witches' or 'bitches' or 'ball-breakers' or even 'monsters.' You're going to have to step on a lot of faces on the way to the top, but once you get there, those faces will be smiling up at you."

You wonder if you have what it takes to succeed in business. You don't want to step on anyone else's feelings or toes, much less their faces. You've heard there's a theory out there that rich people are all psycopaths and sociopaths, because apparently being a -path of some sort is the only path to success. Can you be a homeopath and do good in corporate life? You think you'd be good at mixing home remedies from cane sugar, dandelions, and crushed honeybees. But knocking rivals off the corporate ladder, maybe not. You once got subbed out of a basketball game in middle school because you stopped to help out a girl on the other team who had tripped, and you got to talking about STEM classes, and honestly you didn't know your team was down by one point with fifteen seconds on the clock until the coach put your butt on the bench and told you to consider another sport, like maybe chess.

The FLIT meeting is wrapping up, and you all get up from the grass to get out of the sun and head back to the office. A group of a dozen preschool ballerinas, recently released from a class, run giggling around you as you prepare to depart. The tiny dancers, in tutus and sneakers, pirouette and sauté as they skip through the park, a blur of brown and pink and green. Their mothers—and a dad—trudge behind the girls, earthbound and parental. Just then, Braids comes up to you and Parseltongue and Wombat. "How are you doing?"

Wombat fishes into her purse and brings out a quarter. "I'm all out of fivers, mate."

Braids puts her hand to her mouth in surprise. "Um . . . I work at Eustachian."

Wombat puts away the change. She smiles, but not with her eyes, which are glittery but guarded, like sapphires in a display case. "And so you do," she says. "And you're late."

• • •

You hear sobbing coming from the Jon Bon Jovi Lactation Room. You crack open the door and you see Braids.

"We have to stop meeting like this," Braids says, dabbing her eyes with her blouse. "You can come in, I'm not breastfeeding or anything."

"What are you doing in here?" you ask, closing the door behind you.

Braids smiles through her tears. "This is one of the only private spaces in the office."

"What's the matter? And why were you late for the FLIT meeting?"

Braids starts to speak, but you hold up a finger before she can say a word.

"And for the love of Christ, not a single goddamn word about the Luddites!"

Braids looks at you, chokes out a laugh—and then she loses it. "My Microsectionality rating is shit!" Braids sobs. "They put me on the PIP!"

She collapses in your arms.

The PIP—Performance Improvement Plan—was something that managers implemented when an employee wasn't living up to company goals. You had seen a video about it during your onboarding and overheard talk about it at the Grapevine. Originally, the PIP had been designed to help struggling employees, especially women and people of color, by giving them clearly delineated benchmarks for success. It can be tough on an employee from a diverse background when a boss tells them they're not performing but then fails to articulate what they have to do in order to improve. The PIP process was purportedly created so women and people of color would know exactly what they need to do to succeed—and bosses couldn't just terrorize their DEI hires by not giving them clear guidance on how to thrive at their positions.

The way the PIP process worked was that an employee was given a PIP plan that set goals and dates by which those benchmarks had to be met. The goals could be things like selling a certain amount of advertising or producing a certain number of audio products. The employee was then given a choice: accomplish those goals and retain their job, or take a small buyout and leave the company. But accepting the PIP came with a risk: If the manager determined that the goals weren't met, the employee could be released without severance. On the other hand, if the employee took the buyout instead, they would typically lose their RSUs before they vested. Being put on the PIP was like walking a tightrope in a hurricane. It was possible to make it to the other side, but there were lots of ways to fall, and there was no net.

"The PIP used to be a way to help people like us," Braids says. "Now they use it against us. Half the Black girls in customer experience are on the PIP. I just got to this company, and they got my ass on the PIP. Managers use it to bully us—and sometimes they extend it for months to keep us on a short leash, like we're children they're walking to preschool. And once you're on the PIP you're under so much pressure, you're almost sure to fuck up. That's the way they do us around here. They want to make us fail so they can prove that they were always right about us."

Braids says she's going to fight for her job and go on the PIP for thirty days. Like you, she needs that RSU money. Plus she was the only person from her graduating class at East Arkhaam College to get a job at Eustachian this year, and she didn't want to let down her professors, friends, and family. She wipes away her tears and fixes her makeup, ready to go back out.

"They say they want Black people, but they really don't," Braids says. "They hire us, but they don't promote us. They promote us, but they don't pay us. They pay us, but they don't value us. They give us jobs, but they deny us careers. They want us in a revolving door, so we're in and out quickly and they can point to their numbers and act like they're doing something."

You want to help Braids, but you have no idea how. You once dated an older guy who couldn't get it up and sat at the edge of the bed crying. You thought about giving him a hand job, but instead you decided to go into the kitchen and make smoothies for the both of you. The smoothie didn't help then and it probably won't help this situation either. Corporate life makes you feel as impotent as that old guy did—you don't have the power to hire or fire or promote. All you can do, which is what you do do, is take Braids's hand in yours. "I'm so sorry you're going through this."

"I'm the only person in my family making real money. Good-paying jobs are hard to find in Arkhaam. You know, my family had a house on this street, they used to go to a church in this very spot before the Founder bought everything up and made it what it is now. This was a thriving Black neighborhood—they used to call it New Carthage. Doctors, lawyers, clergymen—all Black—used to live on this block. There were churches, banks, and schools. There were a couple places that refused to sell out at any price, like Hannibal's Smoothie Shack, but they were the stubborn outliers. Now New Carthage is pretty much all gone, not even a plaque. And they won't even let us rise in the ranks in the company they built over the bones of what we had."

You don't know what to say. "Maybe you should join FLIT."

"You mean FLITE? As in white flight? That's what all of us call it. That group isn't for people like us. I only showed up today because the PIP thing made me desperate. Look where that got me—Wombat thought I was a street person. The only way to join them is to fight them."

Her words echo in your head. "People like us," she said. You had ten years of experience in IT. You knew how to do your job. You couldn't ever see yourself being put on the PIP. Were you and Braids really an *us*? You haven't even been assigned a manager or a department yet. Is this the way they do sisters at this company? Just leave them hanging and wait for them to fail?

There was this video you saw once about the spider layer of the atmosphere. Scientists called it the "aeolian zone" after the Greek god of wind, Aeolus, although it also made you think of Anansi, the spider-deity of Jamaican legend. The zone in question was a band of stable air some fifteen thousand feet up teeming with tiny, windblown creatures like mites, beetles, moths—and baby spiders carried by silk balloons they spun themselves. All these bugs and insects were riding high and moving fast and completely subject to the whims of the weather. They had sacrificed agency for the high life. You saw some other videos that said the whole spider-layer thing was bullshit and there were flying arachnids and beasties at various altitudes, but you couldn't shake the metaphor. You were aloft and your skin was crawling. Had your career reached new heights? Or were you just another spider blowing in the wind?

You decide to take the stairs back to your desk on the ninth floor. You hear footsteps echoing above you. Way above you. You wonder if someone is going to the twenty-seventh floor. You start to walk quickly up the stairs. The sound of the footsteps is heavier now, so it seems like you are getting close. You stretch out over the rail and look up to see what you can see. It's dark in the upper reaches of the stairwell, but there is definitely someone up there. The sound seems to be coming from the twenty-third or twenty-fourth floor—and rising. You start to run now; you are closing in on whoever it is ahead of you. They seem to be half carrying, half dragging something. You can hear something scraping against the stairs, along with the increasingly loud sound of the footsteps. You look down and notice scuff marks on the steps. You stretch over the rail again and look up to see how close you are to catching up. You can hear heavy breathing from the person ahead of you, but you still can't get a clear look at them. They are definitely carrying something. It's casting a shadow down to where you are—it looks like it could be a large cross. You've reached the twenty-fifth floor now, and you hear the sound of a key in a lock, the rattling of a chain, and the sound of a heavy door opening and closing. By the time you reach the twenty-sixth floor whoever was there and whatever they were carrying are gone. There's just a blank wall. You now notice there's a keyhole in it. Clearly it leads somewhere. But wherever it goes, you just missed it.

Chapter Six

POLYETHYLENE (PARTS 1 & 2)

You're watching a nature video about killer whales. You always figured they were good hunters—"killer" is right in their name—but you never knew they were so crafty. They often hunt in pods, working in concert to track down their prey. Their favorite targets are Weddell seals, which live in and around Antarctica. Weddell seals aren't dumb, but they're not as smart as killer whales. You see this one clip of a Weddell seal chilling, literally chilling, on a large chunk of frozen sea ice. As the seal suns itself, a pod of killer whales pops up from beneath the waves to size up the situation. If the seal spots them, he doesn't show it. In any case, he probably thinks he's completely safe, given that he has about one hundred yards of frozen ice all around him. There's no way a predator could break through that and get him, right? Wrong. The killer whales whistle and click at one another and call some more orcas to join them. They're strategizing, like football players in a huddle or executives in a boardroom, and they come up with a killer plan. They all swim beneath the ice floe together, beating their tails as one to produce a subsurface wave. It's incredible to see animals demonstrate this level of teamwork. The collective wave breaks up the ice their prospective prey had been resting on. The seal suddenly realizes the danger he's in, but it's too late. The seal tries to wriggle away, and it's both comic and tragic, but there's nowhere to go. The large chunk of ice around him is now broken up into ice cubes. There's no protection, no place to hide. He's basically floating unprotected in the icy water, like Jack at the end of *Titanic*, only there's no Rose to offer any sympathy (not that Rose was much help since that floating door was totally big enough for both of them). The killer whales quickly live up to the first word in their name, and the ice-blue water turns red. You are drawn to, not repelled by, the spectacle of animal murder. Animals seem so innocent, so pure, but they are capable of cold-blooded homicide. You've seen lions rip each other's balls off. You've watched chimpanzees eat the brains of bonobos, which is pretty much cannibalism. Even plant eaters are killers. You've seen zebras stomp baby baboons to death just because zebras are assholes.

Is murder what it means to be alive? Is competition hardwired into us? Or is the ultimate in evolution to somehow transcend all this baboon-stomping, ball-ripping gore? Someday you have to study the secret lives of plants. Maybe you can learn some gentler life lessons from photosynthesis or pollination or something. You are about to click on a nature video when you get a text from your lawyer. You don't read it because you don't want to deal with it right now. You can guess it's about your mom's apartment and it's about money. Not today, Satan. You were getting the hang of your new job, and new money was coming in—whatever the lawyer wanted, it looked like things were on track to handle themselves. You would deal with him when you had the time and when your Big Tech money started adding up, but for now you would bury whatever he wanted away somewhere deep in your brain and pretend it wasn't happening. First things first.

Chapter Seven

HOW TO DISAPPEAR COMPLETELY

You often think back to that moment on the BET Awards when the rapper Omari took the stage to take the mic away from Noelle Swizzler when she was about to receive a big award for Video of the Year. Noelle had just started to say thank you to her friend Aimee when it all went down. You know you shouldn't be wasting brain bandwidth on this kind of trivia, but there was maybe a learning moment there. You had been watching the awards show with Kenise in your apartment. Actually, she wasn't *there* there, you were texting each other in real time as the show went on. Kenise partly sided with Omari because she agreed with him that it was a crime that Geesellé, a righteous Black female singer, hadn't won the award, and she thought Omari was standing up for artistic excellence in general and Black women in particular. And what was that white girl Swizzler doing at a Black awards show anyway, much less winning an award? It was all very triggering. Some of your other Black girlfriends said they liked to see Black men fight for Black women, so they were Team Omari all the way. For them, it reaffirmed what should be the basic social contract between the genders, that males should protect the females. Any woman who said she didn't like men fighting for her was just lying to herself, they argued. Helen of Troy probably fucking loved the fact that they sent a thousand ships to fetch her fine ass back to Sparta. But something about the whole Omari-Swizzler thing struck you as stinking of toxic masculinity like a rugby team locker room, and you and Kenise agreed on that point. White women weren't necessarily your allies, but you were wary of purportedly chivalrous men pulling you into their fantasies of protectiveness and retribution by disrespecting other women. So you were Team Swizzler even though at the time you liked Geesellé's music and Omari's music way more and you weren't really checking for Swizzler's acoustic folk shit. Sure enough, Swizzler turned out to be way more down than Omari, siding with progressives and feminists during the presidential election while Omari showed up at the White House surrounded by white people and wearing the dreaded purple hat that was the symbol of the Sunken Place if there ever was one. Omari ended up writing a song about Swizzler called "Blue Check Bitch," which he tried to get her to duet on and she very smartly decided not to, because the song was about how he made her famous, which he totally didn't do. The weird thing is that Swizzler never really wrote a song specifically and overtly about him, although writing songs about the men who pass through her life is kind of her thing. You heard her talk about it in an interview.

Swizzler: I don't know if what happened was a tragedy or a comedy or both. That's why I don't like talking about it. But if you listen to my music, it's all there. There may not be a specific song, but all the details are in my lyrics. That's why I write music, that's why people make art. We have a million different feelings about a billion different things, and songwriting forces you to figure out how you singularly feel about something and fit it all into eight bars. Whenever I'm feeling lost or confused, I write a song about it to figure out what I'm really thinking.

• • •

You run into Wombat in the elevator at Eustachian.

After a few beats of silence you break. "I have a friend who's been put on the PIP."

Wombat blinked. "And?"

"I just know she's having a rough time with it. It seems like a lot of the people they put on the PIP are Black."

Wombat shook her head. "The PIP was created to help women and people of color. I know this because I helped develop the PIP program at this company. There's nothing more frustrating than when a manager gives a direct report a bad review without clear guidance on what they need to do to improve their performance."

"So is there anything we can do to help her?"

The elevator dings and Wombat steps off.

"These things generally end one of two ways," she says. "One, she goes on the PIP and learns how to be a better employee, and she'll be apples. Or two, she lawyers up and wastes a lot of money trying to save a job she's already lost. Let's just hope Braids makes the right choice."

Your mouth opens in surprise—how did Wombat know whom you were talking about?

Wombat raises one perfect, omniscient eyebrow.

The doors close but the elevator doesn't move. You realize you haven't pressed the button for your floor. You wonder what Wombat's deal is—is she there to help other women or just herself?

• • •

You meet Blue at his desk on the eleventh floor. In real life his hair is even bluer than in the photo. It's a bold blue, a cartoon blue, a Gatorade blue. His hair is also thick and lush, and his eyes are dark. Blue is a babe. In fact, you think he looks like a K-pop star, and you wonder if thinking that about a Korean guy is somehow racist. Anyway, this guy could definitely get it.

You're not a woman who is always thinking about sex. You know that men are different in that regard—a man sees a woman, and the first thing he does is imagine what her tits look like under that top or beneath her hijab or her space suit, whatever she's wearing. Your impressions of men are usually framed in transactional, not sexual, terms. Is this man going to change my tire? Can this guy get me fries with that? Is this dude going to murder me? Men see sex everywhere, read sex as text and subtext in every situation. That's why men and women talk past each other. Men are thinking that a cigar is not just a cigar, and women are wondering why the men are smoking that fucking stinky cigar. But Blue has you thinking about sex the minute you see him. His thick, stylish glasses can't conceal his dark, soulful eyes. He's got tattoos on his forearms, his neck, and across his clavicle area, which is tanned and toned. The tattoos are only partially visible—all you can see on his exposed flesh are curly, pointy tails, so the images could be of snakes or seahorses or dragons. Whatever the beasts are, real or mythological, they are slithering or swimming or swooping down toward his lower body. You think about touching those tattoos. These are NSFW thoughts; these are not feelings you usually have. You set them aside like a simmering dish you're pulling off the stove. You try to stay professional.

"Hello?" you say.

Blue is locked into whatever he's doing on his laptop.

You try again. "Hey, hey, I'm here."

Blue still doesn't look up.

You wave a hand in front of his face, and he instantly turns to you.

"Hey," Blue says, clicking and activating something on the temple of his glasses. "Built-in hearing aids—it's Mee Corp tech," he explains. Now you feel like a fucking jerk for waving a hand in front of his face. You feel like you just pulled into a handicapped space and didn't notice it until it was too late and everyone saw you do it. You make a mental note to yourself to not turn into an asshole. "So you're the new hire, right?" Blue continues. You notice that Blue is seated in some sort of electric scooter and is missing his right leg, from just above the knee. You wonder if the missing limb and the hearing impairment are related. You also can't help but notice that when Blue is looking right at you he's even hotter. Some men undress you with their eyes. This guy seems to be mentally slipping you into different outfits, like that inevitable scene in a rom-com where the plucky heroine goes clothes shopping or tries on different wedding gowns. The way his gaze flicks ever so subtly across your body, like REM sleep with eyes wide open, makes it seem like he's reimagining you in varying poses, maybe some of them from the Kama Sutra. How can a guy say so much with his eyes? And why didn't any of this hotness come through in his emails? You try to stop thinking about all this and focus on what he's saying.

Blue explains that you're going to be part of his network security team—but with a twist.

"What's the twist?" you ask.

Without answering, Blue has you sign another NDA. You've signed so many at this point that you barely even read it. You're on autopilot, like a movie star autographing posters on the red carpet. Blue glances at the signed NDA and files it away. He explains that he's been working at Eustachian for three years, which in tech years is more like twenty-one years, because in tech nobody stays at the same job or the same company long. Good coders are in demand—at least until the latest tech bubble bursts—and so you go where the money is or where the action is happening or ideally both. Like whales following swarms of krill.

Before coming here, Blue was at Mee Corp for two years, and he says that it wasn't a fun place to work. There were perks—like his high-tech hearing-aid glasses which he upgrades every year—but start-ups that become leviathans are horrible places for creative people. The founders of the start-ups act like they're gods whose dictates must be obeyed. It's like working inside the Statue of Liberty if the Statue of Liberty were your boss. It's hard to argue with the thing you're inside of. Start-ups that become leviathans are cults of personality whose quirks become dogma and places where fresh ideas are crushed in favor of the played-out directives of whoever founded the place, he says. Employees are constantly reminded they are laboring inside the torch that the founder of the company lit. "Eustachian hasn't gone that route yet, but when it does, I'm gone." Blue snaps his fingers. "I'm a coder with a code."

"So what's the twist?" you ask again, a little impatiently.

"I'm getting to it," Blue replies.

Blue walks you through what he wants you to focus on. His pod is called Team Ryeo. All the departments at Eustachian are called "pods," and each pod is given a pod name that may or may not be related to its function. The Founder got the idea from the mnemonic idea of the "memory palace." When people lose their memories, one of the last things to go is their memory of the layout of their home. For evolutionary reasons, where you live is imprinted deep in every human being's brain, deeper than what you studied in college or the name of your spouse. If you ever want to remember something, one way to do it is associate the thing you're trying to recall with a room in your house. This internal "memory palace" helps with recollection. So the Founder decided to name every department after some famous fictional place. That way, he reasoned, the name could burrow its way into the collective consciousness of employees while remaining opaque from the understanding of outsiders. You didn't quite follow the reasoning on this, but you are still an outsider trying to find your place inside, so maybe that was the point. The assignment at Team Ryeo was this: You had to figure out ways to prevent threat actors and others from stealing Eustachian's user data.

"I know that you appreciate the company's motto is 'We Get What's Between Your Ears,'" Blue says. "Customer support is a core company value. A data breach would send the stock into free fall."

Blue says that the rumor that Mee Corp is sniffing around Eustachian had spurred a new round of threat actors trying to break into the system. "Some of the intrusions are rival companies, some are investors looking for insider tips, some could be attackers sponsored by Mee Corp trying to tank our stock to make us easier to buy," he says. Blue explains the attacks take many different forms. "It's like a Hydra, you cut off one head, two more grow back." There are Structured Query Language injections, where attackers inject malicious SQL code into input fields, giving them access to sensitive information and allowing them to delete data and disrupt operations, he says. Then there are zero-day exploits, which are weaknesses in Eustachian's security software that haven't been patched because the company doesn't even know they're there yet.

"You're covering stuff I already know..." you begin.

"I just have to make sure we're speaking the same language," Blue continues. "Ironically, some of the worst intrusions take place outside the system. Like man-in-the-middle attacks, where bad actors monitor communications between our people in public places, like if they've plugged their laptop in at LaGuardia or are on the wi-fi at Starbucks. We also have to watch out for watering hole attacks—that's when hackers target our employees at websites they frequently visit. We often get those reports late—it's embarrassing for employees to have to tell managers their laptop picked up a virus on HeavyNaturals.net."

"Great, I get it," you say. "So what kind of data are we protecting?"

"That's proprietary," he snaps. "But trust me, it's worth defending."

"So why did you choose me for this job? I'm not a cybersecurity expert."

"Eustachian has a tradition of cycling some new hires through a couple positions before they settle in—it gives them the lay of the land. Plus, threat actors are always changing their techniques. Network threats are like pandemics—the same vaccine doesn't work every year, so we have to keep changing the formula. We need fresh eyes on this, original thinkers."

"Thanks, I guess."

"You come from a brilliant family." Blue closes his laptop and whirs around in his scooter chair to face you. "You know, I studied your mom back in college."

"That's not at all a weird thing to say about a person's mother."

"I read her book—*Broken Vases: Philosophy at the End of History*."

"My mom read chapters from that to me as bedtime stories. Put me right to sleep."

Blue laughed before he saw you were serious. "Well, then you know what I'm about to say. I'm paraphrasing wildly, but she had this elegant thought exercise..."

"The Fog of Forgetfulness."

"That's it! That you could create a just society if the Founding Fathers and Mentoring Mothers of that society wrote a kind of Magna Carta slash Constitution while in a kind of amnesiac state, not knowing their personal history, their socioeconomic background, or what their status would be in the society they were writing into being."

You always thought the Fog of Forgetfulness was a rip-off of philosopher John Rawls's Veil of Ignorance, but you don't say that out loud. Your mom used to argue that her concept went way beyond Rawls in part because ignorance should never be seen as a virtue, but letting some traumas slip from the conscious mind, at least temporarily, could be a blessing. "I know my mom's book," you say to Blue.

"I'll get to the point. The algorithms we create are like the decision makers in the Fog of Forgetfulness—they have no skin in the game. That's why we can trust them with our secrets."

"Maybe—if algorithms were making the decisions. You would never say the Brooklyn Bridge has no skin in the game so that's why we can trust it when we drive from Dumbo to Manhattan. It's the people who have made decisions about the bridge—the architect, civil engineers, law enforcement, safety inspectors, politicians, corporations—who we have to worry about. Their attitudes are part of the blueprint. The real question is: Who's making the calls?"

Blue doesn't answer. You don't say this out loud, but you always thought the Fog of Forgetfulness was bullshit, even when you were a kid. It didn't make any psychological sense. You couldn't imagine yourself—your true self—without your individual characteristics. Your race, sex, personal history—those weren't just clothes you slipped in and out of; they were what made you into you and not someone else. Computers didn't have those things, and that didn't make them more objective, it made them objects. Objects that could be used and abused by people with agency.

But you don't want to argue with Blue, and you certainly don't want to talk about your mother who is oxymoronically a famous philosopher. You want to try to accept that this is your new job, and if it was okay with your new blue-haired manager and his anonymous but super-important data, it was okay with you. But you blurt out stuff when you get anxious.

"This database isn't full of *Eyes Wide Shut* Illuminati-type shit, is it?" you blurt out.

Blue laughs. "As far as I know, you don't have to worry about that!"

"So this all seems like standard network security stuff. What's the twist?"

Blue smiles. "The twist is we're not trying to stop break-ins, we're trying to do them."

"What?"

You leave the meeting in a haze. When you get back to your desk, your Microsectionality rating is trending up.

• • •

Technoaggressions #119 & #120: You are at a meeting in a conference room. You have arrived early and nobody is there. The next person to come in is a white man, and he takes a seat on the opposite end of the conference room from you. You both sit there in silence staring into your respective laptops. The next person to arrive is another white man. The two white men introduce themselves to each other and strike up a conversation. Neither man introduces himself to you. You are the person who booked the room.

• • •

The streets are filled with Mee Corp trucks. You imagine the things they are delivering. Boxes of granola. Air mattresses. Matisse posters. V-neck cardigans. Handheld bug-zapper rackets. Bottles of adobo seasoning. Driveway salt. Packages tied up with string. Socks as soft and warm as rabbits. Neruda could write another poem. The trucks will stop beside apartment buildings, hotels, and cul-de-sacs. Robots will roll up sidewalks and driveways and plop the deliveries in front of gates and doorways. Mee Corp is such a massive company it's hard to imagine its scale. All those trucks, all those robots, all those insouciant customers. You are glad you don't work for Mee Corp. You still see yourself as a nonprofit person who is temporarily profiting from Big Tech. You're a temp at heart. And at least you don't work for Mee Corp. That would be too big, too much to handle. Everything is for sale, everything has a price.

The twist was that Team Ryeo was a red team. You had heard rumors about red teams, but you didn't know that they were a thing. The name, Blue explained, had roots back in the Cold War, when CIA agents would impersonate KGB spies to test American defenses and weaknesses. The technique was adopted by tech firms decades later, and certain employees were dubbed "red teams," role-playing as hackers and various threat agents to see if they could infiltrate the company's firewalls and safeguards. Nobody in the rank-and-file at Eustachian, other than you and Blue, knew what you were up to—secrecy was the point. The best way to beat your enemies is to learn how to think like them. So the company wanted you to safeguard its data by figuring out new ways to steal it.

You don't know how to feel about your assignment with Blue. You are skittish about having no idea what's in the databases that you've been entrusted to protect. Sure, banks, hospitals, and political campaigns scrape some problematic shit, but that doesn't make it right. Something about this situation just feels wrong, like when a stranger offers you cash to carry a locked briefcase for them when you're about to board a flight to the United Arab Emirates.

Every tech company has data it needs to protect, but Eustachian was uniquely aggressive about blocking its own employees from peeking into its vaults—and that was suspicious. Sometimes alarms themselves are alarming, whether they go off or not. You try to aggressively rationalize away what you just heard from Blue. You wish rationalizations could burn calories—you'd be a lot more fit. Anyways, you kinda have to do it. You need to keep this job. It's your mom's bank's fault in the end. Everything already costs so much, and settling this situation with your mom's bank is costing you even more.

The rumble of passing Mee Corp trucks is in your ears. There's all this stuff to buy, but the only way to buy it is to sell yourself. Many of the jobs that matter don't pay enough money to live the life that most people want. Schoolteachers, college professors, restaurant chefs, first responders. Kids say they want to have these jobs at career day in grade school, but then they get older and they learn the reality of what things cost, and they go into finance or tech or the law. They work in fields that manufacture invisible things like derivatives or digital streams or baroque legal transactions. You can't make a living making stuff that actually adds to life in a real way, like writing books or poetry or teaching kids to write books or poetry. You certainly couldn't make a living trying to save the world from global warming. You tried that, and global warming won. You wonder if you should call Dr. Umlaut, your old therapist, and make an appointment. The old existential issues are creeping up your sides again, like ivy on a wall.

When you get inside your apartment, your first paycheck from Eustachian has arrived. You opted for direct deposit, but the first check, by company tradition, is always sent via snail mail. When you open it, you know why. A screen couldn't quite convey the numbers you are seeing. The base pay is what you expected, but the starting bonus is more than a cherry on top, it's like a whole cherry tree. That was the secret to these tech companies: The extras were extraordinary, and they hooked you in, hoping for more. Maybe money can't buy happiness, but it can lease it for a while. Suddenly your moral rationalizations seem a whole lot more rational. New money always feels like it could go as far as forever. The road to utopia leads through myopia. You snap a selfie of yourself smiling like an idiot and photoshop gold coins over your eyes. You nearly do one of those celebratory NikNak dances you've been resisting doing. Fuckit—you put Noelle Swizzler's "Song 4 You" on and you turn it up loud, and you begin dancing around your studio apartment like a madwoman and you post the whole ninety-second video. Halfway through the song the music cuts out and suddenly you're hearing "Samsara Sheriff" by that British–West Indian art-rock band Mama Legba, and the lyrics running through your mind begin to rattle and shake and you are kinda feeling the song a little bit, but you turn back to "Song 4 You" anyway. You are beginning to love early Swizzler, when she was still a folk singer and before she was cool. There was something pure about her music and bracing about her ambition, and her hair was crazy curly and her clothes were straight outta Nashville. You are knocking shit over as you dance—a signed paperback of Chimamanda Ngozi Adichie's *We Should All Be Feminists*, a vinyl copy of Rosalía's *Motomami*, a framed photo of you and your mom when you were eight and your mom was actually smiling. You keep dancing your just-got-paid dance.

You are not the kind of person who cares about money or designer brands or zip codes or second homes in the Hamptons. But you are the kind of person who cares about getting away from the insolvency that's been infecting your body and spirit like long COVID. The money you're making from this job is going to put you on your way to solving some of your biggest problems. Maybe not your existential fear of death that's triggered by coffee and coffee-adjacent beverages, but some of the personal financial shit. Like your mom's bank's stupid nuisance lawsuit about your apartment. After putting it out of sight, out of mind for days, you finally scroll through all the increasingly frantic texts from your lawyer. The fact is you owe your mom's bank a shit ton of money. Your mom died in debt, and you were legally on the hook for paying it off. You are not someone who runs away from problems; in fact you see yourself as a problem solver—the Big O. You're an engineer, and you just have this baseline belief that if you think hard enough there's a solution to everything—at least in math and science. In personal finances, sometimes shit just don't add up. You don't want to blame your mom for the mess, especially since she's passed on, but it's hard not to feel a magma-hot resentment for the fact she left you alone to clean up this mess. You wish she had left some clue in that secret diary about why she borrowed all that cash, but the only writing she left behind was about philosophy and family, not finances. Because there was such a huge amount of money to pay back, and because you literally had no idea how you were going to come up with all that cash, you found yourself doing what you never do and just buried the whole thing deep in your brain, like the corpse of a Mafia hit off the New Jersey Turnpike. Maybe you and your mom were alike in that way: You both had parts of your brain that were compartmentalized. But the therapy stuff was for another day—for now you needed money and lots of it. Sure, if you're honest with yourself, you're not okay with protecting the company's secret data without even knowing what those secrets are, but nothing powers a rationalization more than money. You remember something your mom once said, before she lost everything. She said the Fog of Forgetfulness wasn't about dissipation, it was about revelation. She said that once you lose everything, you find out what you really have.

• • •

You found your dad's journal. He had jotted some notes in a blue leather booklet—complete with embossed doctor bird on the cover—that he must have gotten at the same time Mom got her red leather version. He had written only a few pages of thoughts before apparently abandoning the whole enterprise, but you felt tremendously fortunate to recover this direct connection to your dad. You flipped open the journal. He was writing about a period of time where he had lost his job. You don't ever remember your dad not working.

I headed home, still in a funk. I was jobless and hopeless and didn't know where I was going next. It was like my soul was back in the bad old days before GPS, when people had to actually pull their station wagons over to the side of the road and unfold multicolored maps to figure out directions. I had quit my job in a huff after they refused to give me my long-overdue raise, but then I realized huffs are a really terrible mode of transportation. Being without a job is like being without a purpose. I'm not one of those people who defines themselves by their paycheck. But I do think we're hardwired to be hunter-gatherers, and when we're not hunting or gathering, something ancient and deep and saber-toothed within us begins beating against the cave walls of our souls, pounding out the message that something has gone tremendously wrong. All that studying I put in from grade school to UVA through internships and climbing the corporate ladder—for what? To find myself further behind than when I started, because at least at the beginning I had youth and promise on my side.

Maybe more than all of this, I felt like I had let down Sojourner. We married for richer or poorer—the vows didn't say anything about just scraping by. What if they wrote that in? Do you take this man not for richer, or for poorer, but for absolutely average with rock bottom right below you and success so close your fingernails are scraping against it? Would people still get hitched then? Mediocrity is worse than doing poorly. Mediocrity is limbo, neither here nor there, a no decision. When you're in the middle, you lack the moral clarity of feeling oppressed, and you're missing the moral superiority of being on top of the heap. Even feeling sorry for yourself feels somehow unearned.

When Sojourner married me, I had felt more honored than anything. She was a hotshot from Harvard with a hot job at NYU, and she could have had any guy, but she chose me. It was a vote of confidence, and as the years passed, it became clear that I had failed to live up to her expectations. That hurt worse than anything. She had bet on me and she had lost. I felt like a championship horse, once heralded as a possible Triple Crown winner, now headed for the glue factory. I tried to figure out which disaster I should tell her about first. The toilet? The basement? My self-inflicted unemployment? Definitely the toilet, then work my way up to the bigger impossible-to-solve tragedies.

It hurt to read about your dad hurting. But it was comforting to see he had gone through some of the same things you had—the slow, torturous hunt to find a job after having lost one. You couldn't believe that Mom had ever really been disappointed in your dad, despite what she wrote and no matter what he wrote. You wish you could have comforted him when he was alive, but you were only fifteen when he died. You were barely old enough to grasp your own emotions, much less understand what your parents were going through. And you feel like you're even less of a grown-up now than you were then.

• • •

You are falling behind on your mandatory training sessions. You click on the latest video from the DEI Players, who have been renamed the Inclusion, Civil Rights, and Title IX Players. In the video, we see the guy in the porkpie hat talking to a blond woman with dreads next to a watercooler.

"I have two great candidates—a white man and a Black woman," the blonde says. "They have similar résumés, so I'm going to hire the Black woman because she's good for diversity."

The scene freezes and Porkpie turns to the camera.

"One of the first things you need to know about 'diversity' is you can't use that word anymore," Porkpie says. "The d-word is a legal trigger that could spur a lawsuit."

The blonde plays along. "Wait—I can't call a candidate diverse? What should I say instead?"

Porkpie looks at the camera. "Use euphemisms like 'marginalized' or 'historically underrepresented' or my favorite, 'impoverished.' Everyone knows what you really mean."

"But won't people just start suing us over those words too?"

"Then we'll just find new ones!" Porkpie says. "As long as we stay one step ahead semantically, we'll be all right. A good storyteller knows which words to use and which to leave out. Today's corporate environment isn't about being color blind, it's about being color mute."

The clip leaves you unsettled. How did people clearly acting in bad faith manage to redefine dealing with the consequences of bias as bias itself? Anti-racists somehow lost the messaging war, and now you're all living in the racial Upside Down, where less than 2 percent of Fortune 500 CEOs are Black and only about 10 percent are women, but trying to do something about turning those numbers around makes you the villain, or at the very least the defendant. In your mind, branding anti-racists as racists is like a tumor charging an oncologist with malpractice. You don't think playing semantical shell games with language is the way to deal with the New Jim Crow. Maybe launching your own company is the way. But you've got your hands full launching your career at the company you're at now.

• • •

In the morning you have a Zoom call with Blue to go over the workflow for the day. He looks tired, lifting his glasses several times to wipe sleep from his eyes. He says he pulled an all-nighter fending off a denial of service attack from some teenage hackers in Kazakhstan who had gotten some inside information on Eustachian's cyber defenses. Now, it was his job, and yours, to plug the leak by trying to replicate it. Some employee had passed on a password or lost a laptop, and if you and he tried to impersonate bad actors yourselves, maybe you could find out what went wrong. That was just one task in what promised to be a long week. "This job is crazy," Blue complains. "If it gets any crazier..." He snaps his fingers. At one point, Blue motors away in his chair to grab a can of Mountain Dew Code Red from the fridge. As you wait for him to return, in the corner of the screen, you spot a naked woman, heading from Blue's bedroom to the bathroom. You don't see her face, but her legs are amazing, long and lean like those of a dancer. Then you spy someone else—a man, also naked, also fit, also emerging from Blue's bedroom. Wait—is this some sort of throuple situationship? What the fuck? Whatever's going on, Blue clearly has an active social life. You wish you could say the same about your own.

Chapter Eight

INVISIBLE STRING

Equal Rights, first pressing vinyl. $500 or best offer.

Reasons and Persons, first American edition hardcover. $150 or best offer.

Black Magic High, vol. 1, paperback signed by author. $3,000 or best offer.

Chesterfield antique wingback armchair, tufted burgundy. $750 or best offer.

Super Ape, first pressing vinyl. $300 or best offer.

French vintage bedroom armoire with mirrors. $2,375 or best offer.

We Should All Be Feminists, paperback signed by author. $100 or best offer.

Rare antique Haines Bros. square grand piano, circa 1870–1880. $2,700 or best offer.

Tweed button pocket sheath dress. $100 or best offer.

Broken Vases, paperback with notes in margin by author. $50 or best offer.

Feminism Is for Everybody, hardcover signed by author. $75 or best offer.

Striped pashmina wrap, $200 or best offer.

Rastafarian hand-carved wood mask. $125 or best offer.

Wedding ring, genuine Jamaican gold. $5,000 or best offer.

You spent the weekend cataloging your mother's things in your apartment and writing listings for Mee Pawn, Mee Corp's online marketplace. Every item evoked a very specific memory of your mom, but everything had to go. You were making good money, but you had run the numbers and you were maybe not making enough money to pay off the mess you had inherited along with this apartment. To keep the apartment, at least until that RSU money came through, you were going to have to auction off almost everything that was inside the apartment.

You hated to let this stuff go, even if some of it was junk. You remember your mom and your dad reading the first book of K. J. Rule's *Black Magic High* to you when you were a child; by the time the second came out, you were able to read the new installment on your own. You loved the fact that the series created a whole world with its own rules, its own names, its own history. Most authors create characters and plots; true creators bring whole worlds into being. There's no better way to pay tribute to the Creator than to create. "In the beginning was the Word . . ." Famously, Rule never wrote a third volume; the author wrote under a pseudonym, so nobody's been able to track him down to find out if he planned to start again or if he had an ending for the saga so all his fans could get on with their lives. The whole thing was a mystery wrapped in a dust jacket. You didn't want to part with a signed copy of the first book, but it was probably going to generate some real money in an online auction, and you needed the cash.

Toward the end, Mom stopped caring about any of this stuff anyway. At least that's how you try to rationalize the sale to yourself. First your mom forgot the names of people, then of places, and finally ordinary things. She would sit in silence at the breakfast table, struggling to remember what to call the container filled with that white crystalline stuff so she could ask you to pass it so she could shake some of it on her eggs. She forgot the names of all the things around her, like the thing in the corner with black keys and white keys that you hit with your fingers, or the black disc you spin around to make music, or the wooden thing with the mirrors that you store clothes in, and who is that person looking back at me anyway?

You realize you are humming a track from *Equal Rights* to yourself—"I Am That I Am." The lyrics are about keeping your shit together when the world around you is falling apart. Your mom loved this song. And now you were going to let some stranger buy it away from you.

What are you doing?

What the *fuck* are you doing?

You put all the things you were listing online—the Tosh record, the tweed button pocket sheath dress, the goddamn wedding ring—back on the shelves, in the closets, and in the drawers, where you got them. You're not selling any of this shit. Selling off the things that remind you of your mother is like losing her all over again.

• • •

Big Tech companies have elevated job evaluations into a science. Unfortunately it's junk science. Many companies have 360-degree job evaluations, where not only does your manager evaluate your performance, your colleagues and direct reports (if you have any) also weigh in. But at Eustachian, the Founder added many more degrees to the process, coming up with what he called *real time spherical* job evaluations. The *spherical* part meant that anyone who came in contact with you—interns, outside vendors, strangers from other departments—were asked to give feedback on your work, or even just pass on rumors they may have heard around the office. In some cases, customers were recruited to watch videos documenting your accomplishments and failures and asked to rate what they saw, like an audience at a test screening of a summer blockbuster. The *real time* meant that the evaluations are always on, and your Microsectionality score is updated every day, every hour, every minute, like a stock market ticker or an Uber ride rating. The Founder got the idea for real time spherical job evaluations when he went to the Museum of Modern Art and saw Picasso's "Les Demoiselles d'Avignon." But it wasn't the painting's revolutionary depiction of multiple angles simultaneously that inspired him to create the new job evaluation process, it was the fifteen-minute wait he endured for a chicken liver mousse sandwich at one of the museum cafés—he just thought there had to be a better way of getting workers to get off their asses. His system was designed to strip away the hierarchy of performance evaluations and allow employees to be judged holistically. The word "holistic" is one that they liked to drop a lot around Eustachian—it made people feel smart, like when you used to regularly drop the word "epistemological" into term papers back in college, even if the class was about web design. The actual result of the company's holistic system was everyone spying on everyone else, everyone judging everyone else, with every man, woman, and nonbinary person fighting it out for themselves—holistically.

During your junior year at college, you did an internship as a user experience designer at a video game company in San Francisco. You weren't much into gaming, but the UX gig paid good money, and there were free snacks in the commissary. You learned that there were two kinds of games: player versus player, in which people competed against each other, and player versus environment, in which people competed against the game itself. You realized it was a good way of not just categorizing games but looking at life. Is your real opponent the player or the game? The work environment at Eustachian was a dangerous hybrid—you were struggling to fit into the corporate culture even as you were competing against your fellow employees. It was player versus player versus environment. You were trapped in the most difficult video game ever.

In the upper right hand of your laptop screen, your Microsectionality score was eternally on display, in red blinking numbers, from 1 to 100, with 100 being perfect (unachievable) and 1 being disastrous (and meaning an employee had better look for a new job). If you clicked on the score, you could call up more advanced metrics on your work performance, such as "creativity," "availability," "sociability," and more. Having a score blinking on your laptop that more or less told people if you were a shit worker or not was wildly embarrassing, but it couldn't be turned off. You also had to make sure the scores didn't suck you in. For your first few days, you found yourself constantly monitoring your "sociability" score, like it meant anything. You knew that, just like college rankings, the SAT, and Rotten Tomatoes, numbers like your Microsectionality score meant less than nothing, but they were hard to ignore. For example, you knew, consciously, that movie ratings were bogus and that trolls and incels lurked on entertainment ratings sites, bent on tanking films that featured people of color and/or feminist themes. But you still wouldn't go out of your apartment to watch a movie that had less than a 90 percent rating on the Tomatometer. Movies were too long and life was too short.

Your Microsectionality score has been hovering between 85 and 91 all day. When it hits 90 you click your laptop shut and decide to take the win. You drape your striped pashmina wrap over your chair and head for the exit. Walcott is taking new employees for coffee after work. You haven't seen him IRL in weeks and you want to catch up. You aren't going to order any coffee yourself because of the fact that you link java with death, but maybe if you went you could convince people to sit outside and order lemonade or boxes of pinot grigio or something. You pack up and head out to meet everyone at a café down the street. It's nearing dusk, the air is cool, and it's a great time for a walk. The shadow of the Eustachian tower is already lengthening, Viagra-ed by dusk, across the gray sidewalks and the green lawns of Arkhaam.

• • •

"Where is everyone?" you ask.

You and Walcott are waiting in front of the café on the sidewalk where everyone is supposed to meet. But Parseltongue had texted her regrets, and the other employees who are supposed to show are held up at yet another unnecessary virtual meeting.

Walcott looks around. "Looks like it's just you and me."

This is fine by you; since you're now one-on-one, maybe you can ask Walcott about that secret cache of data at work that you're supposed to be guarding. You can't tell him about the red team, of course, but maybe he can give you some clues to help you understand your job a bit better. Or maybe you can ask him about Braids and the PIP. You notice Walcott has nice eyes, warm and dark like coffee. Weird that you would link Walcott and coffee. This makes you think about your dad. And then the whole line of thought starts making you anxious and that's when you tend to blurt out things. "So why do you wear so many rings?" you ask Walcott.

Walcott rolls his eyes. "Where did that come from?"

"I don't know—I'm sorry! Sometimes things just come out of me."

Walcott glances at his watch. "There's never enough time. You want to call this off?"

"You mean like *off* off?" you ask. "We're already out, so we might as well grab a drink. But can we choose another place?"

"The coffee's good here. And they do that thing where they make designs with the foam."

You stare off into the deepening shadows on the street. "I have this thing about coffee."

"An allergy?"

"I associate coffee and coffee-like products with my father's death."

Walcott is quiet for a beat. "Okay! Do you want to go somewhere cheerful?"

• • •

Walcott takes you to the far side of town to a tiny club called Potter's Place. There is a large wand on the corner of the marquee outside.

"Is this a Harry Potter fan club?" you ask.

"Not even close," Walcott says. He opens the door and ushers you inside.

The club is small, packed, and smells like cigars. This is what it must feel like to be locked in a humidor, you think. Nobody here seems to have gotten the memo that smoking is no longer permitted in public spaces like this. Most of the seats are taken, but you and Walcott manage to find a small table near the back.

You start to line up a photo of the club to make the place seem real, and Walcott motions for you to put away your phone. "When you take a photo, you take yourself out of the moment."

You shake your head. "If you don't take a photo, how do you remember anything?"

"Once you electronically record something, it's telling your brain it doesn't have to hold on to it. Your senses dial down, and you miss things you might have otherwise noticed because you are staring through the lens instead of taking in everything around you. Smell, touch, taste, sound, even sight—it all gets shut down. All these posts on social feeds—those aren't memories people have, they're memories they've lost. And now some tech company has them—training data for their AIs. Just live the moment and it lives longer."

Walcott seems like he wants to go into full off-duty mode, so you put away your phone. This isn't going to be a good place to talk about secret data or the PIP or anything work-related. You order drinks and try to keep things light. "So why's this place named Potter's Place?"

Walcott leans close. "You really don't know? See, this is why I'm at Eustachian! We have to find better ways of telling our story. We've done so much as Black people, but nobody knows our true history. The namesake of this club is someone everyone should have heard of. It's sad that more people don't know him! Every week I'm finding out about some Black person who did something incredible that never got recognized. Like Jerry Lawson."

"I know Lawson—he's the Black guy who led the team that created the first interchangeable video game cartridge."

"Jerry paved the way for the entire multibillion-dollar video game industry. All the kids playing Xbox and PlayStation and Nintendo should have his face on their T-shirts. If Black kids knew about him, maybe they'd be inspired to go into video game development instead of just playing *Grand Theft Auto*. We have to create new ways to tell our story."

"So who is Potter?"

Walcott tells you that Richard Potter, who died back in the nineteenth century, was the first American magician to win worldwide fame—and he was African American. "He may have been of Caribbean descent too," Walcott says. "Nobody really knows." Potter was an incredible showman who pioneered many new magic tricks and techniques, and his success and celebrity paved the way for the magicians who would follow him, like Harry Houdini. "Richard Potter got me interested in magic," Walcott says. "I thought the Harry Potter books were about him!"

You slap your forehead. "Duh! The school for magic in *Black Magic High* . . ."

"Was inspired by Richard Potter. Exactly! Most people don't get the connection."

Walcott orders another round of drinks for both of you. He tells you that he's always been fascinated by the intersection of magic and technology, which is maybe why fantasy and sci-fi books are read by the same group of nerds. Magic and tech are both about creation, bringing something into the world that hadn't been there before. The word "abracadabra"—the traditional incantation of stage magicians—might have been derived from the ancient Aramaic phrase "avra kehdabra," which translates to "I create with the word." "That's why the Gospel of John starts off with 'In the beginning was the Word, and the Word was with God, and the Word was God,'" Walcott says. "That's what you and I are doing at Eustachian. Audio is everything, conversation is creation. The algorithms we're coding are using words to bring new life into being. Abracadabra!"

You suddenly have the sinking feeling you are about to be forced to sit through several hours of something tragically nerdy. "Wait—so this is a magic club? A *magic* magic club?"

The lights dim and your question is immediately answered. The first act is terrible. A guy with vintage Air Yeezys on his feet and a deck of cards in his hands does a series of tricks with the cards. He starts by asking an audience member to think of a card, and then he cuts the deck and produces the card the man was thinking of right at the top. Then Mr. Air Yeezy pulls out a cobalt-colored crystal ball that he says can forecast the future and invites people to come on stage one by one, predicting the card each one will pull from the deck even before they do it. The crystal ball is big and glowing and hot and you can feel its heat on your cheeks from twenty feet away. The guy's big finale is making an ace of spades fly around the room. It flutters right by your left ear. It's an okay trick, but you are pretty certain you saw a wire glint in the stage lights.

The next act is better. A female magician named Jen takes the stage. She cracks some funny jokes about the lack of women in the ranks of professional magicians. She was a Yale graduate who got into magic when she was ten years old, after her uncle gave her a big orange book titled *The Royal Road to Card Magic*. She could have gone into finance after college, but she moved to Vegas instead, and now she tours the country with her magic act. Her patter is strong—she knows how to tell her story and how to narrate her performance. She tells the crowd exactly what she's doing as she does it, so it's easy and fun to follow along. She could have been a stand-up comic if she wasn't a magician. Her tricks are simple in construction but amazing in effect. She invites audience members to record her on their phones so they can see that her trickery is beyond any sleight of hand you can catch on camera. But maybe the phone thing is part of the subterfuge—like Walcott just said, if people are recording, they are less likely to be paying real attention. Jen does a trick where she gets a pair of dollar bills from an audience member, folds them, blows on them, and turns them into a hundred-dollar bill. Then she does another bit where she rips up a paperback copy of *Fahrenheit 451*, sets the pages on fire, and then reassembles the charred remains into a complete and unharmed book. "That's my tribute to hardworking librarians everywhere," she says. "We've got to battle against the book banners, everyone!"

You and Walcott give Jen a standing ovation, and the rest of the crowd joins in.

"Her technique was amazing," Walcott gushes. "The way she narrated everything she was doing gave the audience a false sense that they understood what was happening, so the magic took them by surprise. You'll never learn your lesson if you think you know it all."

"That will be hard to top," you say. "Who's next?"

"Let me check," says Walcott, slipping away from the table.

Next thing you know, Walcott is striding onto the stage, wearing a black top hat and carrying a wand in his right hand. You slide down in your seat a little and hope nobody you know knows you know him. Being on a date with a magician—if this turns out to be a *date* date—is even more desperate than dating a deejay or a podcaster. You knew this guy was a Black Nerd at heart, and now it's all on full display. You wonder if you can slink off to the exit without him seeing you from the stage. Too late—the show is starting.

"Ladies and gentlemen, I am Wondrous Wally," Walcott announces. "I'm a magician by night, but my day job is working at Eustachian, just across town."

Some audience members start to boo, but playfully, and Wondrous

Wally holds up his hand. "Don't hold Eustachian against me! Magic is not some side hustle with me. It's a discipline I practice every day. Some of you may think that being a tech executive who is into magic is stupid or strange or oxymoronic. But you might also have heard what Arthur C. Clarke, the author of *2001: A Space Odyssey*, once said: 'Any sufficiently advanced technology is indistinguishable from magic.' Big Tech and Big Magic are in the same business."

Just then a bouquet appears in Wondrous Wally's left hand. He taps the flowers, and they float out to you. You reach out and take them from the air. You don't see any wires. You smell the flowers—hydrangeas, peonies, and dahlias—all freshly cut.

Wondrous Wally waves his wand again and shouts, "Abracadabra!"

• • •

After Wondrous Wally's act is over, you slip into the bathroom to freshen up, but there's only a single stall and somebody is in it. Check that, somebodies are in it, because from the sounds it's clear that two magic club attendees are banging their Hogwarts together. You want to leave the restroom, but now you have to take a piss. Also, it's kind of a turn-on, like those soft-core thrillers on Netflix that you have to delete from your browsing history after you watch them so all the friends who share your account don't find out about your secret streaming life. There are no actual words exchanged by the two somebodies in the stall, just moans and grunts and slurps, and the bumps and rustles of bodies being repositioned. You can't remember the last time you had sex like that where you lose a sense of where you are and dispense with the need to speak in sentences or words and just focus entirely on the pursuit of pleasure. You close your eyes, and it's like you're in the stall with the two somebodies, grinding, rubbing, letting the world and its words wash away. But after a few minutes it's enough already and you open your eyes. Who the hell has sex in a public bathroom? If you think about it, that's a pretty nasty situation. You get to wondering who is doing what to whom in there. You hear sneakers squeaking on the tiled bathroom floor and when you sneak a peek beneath the stall you think you spot some familiar footwear. Could it be Mr. Air Yeezy with his bad card tricks and crystal balls? Maybe he was in there with a gullible audience member. You can almost hear him saying to himself *If you can fool them you can fuck them.* You really need to take a leak. The sexytime sounds have stopped now, and the stall door is ajar. You look in and the somebodies have disappeared. You take a quick piss and decide it's time to get up out of this magic club.

• • •

You and Walcott walk back to the office after the show. When you get to the Eustachian parking lot, you stop by Hannibal's to get some smoothies right before it closes. Walcott is going to head home to his place in midtown Arkhaam; you are going to catch an after-hours company shuttle to Manhattan.

"I still don't understand how you did that bouquet trick," you say.

"There are rules to stage magic just like there are rules to programming," Walcott replies. "And there are secrets too. So I can't tell you exactly how I did it—unless you want to join the community of magicians."

"When I was at Anthropocene Associates, it always bugged me that people would bitch and moan about the jobs they did during the week but have these fascinating things they did on the weekend. I think people should find a way to love what they do—otherwise they're wasting their lives, right?"

"So you're wondering why I'm working in Big Tech instead of getting a gig in Vegas as a magician?"

"I guess kinda."

"It's like I said about Arthur C. Clarke. In the tech world, if we do our jobs right, what we do should seem like sorcery or sci-fiction to outsiders. Like the Founder said, 'Tomorrow Is Today.' There's nothing I like more than seeing a product hit the market that makes people think, 'How did they do that?' That's why I study magic. It's not separate from my work, it's part of what I do. I want to conjure the kind of magic I do on the stage in the work I do in the office."

You slurp the last of your pomegranate power smoothie as you stand outside the Eustachian offices, waiting for your shuttle. The stained-glass windows glitter in the moonlight.

"I hope you enjoyed the club," Walcott says.

"It was cool," you answer.

"See you later."

"Good night."

Walcott begins to walk away. Then he pauses and turns. "Oh—and I wear the rings to honor my alma mater, Howard University; my fraternity, Alpha Phi Alpha; my membership in Phi Beta Kappa; and my late father, who always dreamed I'd be part of all those things."

Then he playfully flips you off with one ringed finger and heads off into the night.

Chapter Nine

I LOOK IN PEOPLE'S WINDOWS

Your duties as a member of Team Ryeo, aka the red team, were to be the worst colleague in the world. You looked over shoulders to sneak peeks at people typing in passwords. When collaborating with a team generating prompts for an LLM, you'd add in text in white, typically unnoticed by human coders but detectable by the machine, causing it to follow your secret commands. You would half finish sentences that would trick the autocomplete function into completing a passage drawing on private information ("Mike Smith, MeeCoverage Life Insurance number . . .") and then file a report to Blue to rebuke the coder who had screwed up and left identifiable personal info in the training data. You went for drinks after work with interns and squeezed them for birth dates, mothers' maiden names, the names of first pets, hometown addresses, and other information you could use to purloin passwords and identities. You told yourself you were just doing your job, but you were very aware that everyone says that to themselves when they are doing jobs they shouldn't be doing. You were ashamed and thrilled and determined and inventive and very good at being terrible. You hated yourself for how good you were at being bad.

> If you thought a company was doing something wrong is it OK to hack them?

Ma'am this is a Wendy's

> I'm serious Kenise

This is out of the blue and I'm busy. I'm about to order from Yeomra—that Korean food cart

BTW No one at Anthropocene has figured out how to turn off your chatbot FYI

> Obviously

So are you a whistleblower now?

> Just checking into potentially shady shit

Be smart and careful Octavia. It's not about right or wrong with these tech bros. It's about who has better lawyers ✊

• • •

You had to find out more about the data you were supposed to be protecting.
    The data was tightly held. You would need a quantum computer to even think about cracking it. System security practices at Eustachian, in part thanks to Blue, were pretty airtight, so it was hard to come up with

an angle to access the data you wanted. And Blue himself practiced excellent anti-hacker personal hygiene, hashing all plaintext sections of his coding and converting them into ciphertext elements, and salting his work with random characters and symbols to prevent easy decryption. Of course, this only really works for (some) web code. Most code that gets shipped gets compiled into machine code, and by the time the compiler is done with it it's borderline incomprehensible to humans anyways, and that's before it gets fed through a program that obfuscates that machine code. Blue is good at what he does, but he's a little old school—and that makes him vulnerable.

On a Zoom call with Blue, you catch a break. You don't spot any more naked people parading around his apartment, but you do spy something potentially more interesting than a throuple sighting. You notice Blue's high-tech hearing-aid glasses are reflective. You take a screenshot while talking to him, and after the call, you magnify the image and reverse it.

The best cybersecurity people sometimes go analog because they know things written in pen and ink can't be hacked. So you figured getting a look around Blue's home office might be revealing—and you were right. One of Blue's passwords is written on a Post-it note next to his laptop, mirrored on his lenses as he peered at his screen.

Octavia, aka the Big O. You have earned your nickname once again.

The next time Blue comes into the office, you make an excuse to go up and talk to him. When he takes a bathroom break, you jump on his laptop and plug the password in: #SangMookLee27. Now you could finally infiltrate what you were supposed to be guarding. You couldn't go deep into the database, but you went far enough to get a sense of what was behind the walls.

And what you saw was fucked up.

• • •

Technoaggression #273: You are writing an email, and the in-house proprietary spell-check autocorrects "Lauryn" to "Lauren," "Du Bois" to "the boys," and "Afrofuturism" to "botulism." That has to be fucking deliberate, this kind of shit. The Autocorrect Autocracy is in full effect, forcing everyone into a common conception of the norm. It's like when you're at Banana Republic and the largest pair of linen pants the store has in stock won't even slip over your hips, hips which you had always considered to be normal human size. A woman with a pelvis tiny enough to fit into these pants would not be able to give birth without a C-section. Also, don't men like curves? Isn't that the theme of every hip-hop music video and Shakespearean love poem? (You have long been convinced that the Dark Lady of the sonnets was a Nubian sister. That line in Sonnet 130—"If hairs be wires, black wires grow on her head"—is a clear shout-out to Black girls who code.) In any case, the message from clothing retailers and autocorrectors is clear: Fuck the bard, conform, or your ass will be hanging out. Resist if you want, but compliance is inevitable.

• • •

Walcott hooks you up. He scores you a visit to the recording studio, and you have to admit you are super excited about it. You even wear your hair out today, instead of pulled back and practical like you usually do, because you want to evoke a little bit of Afrofabulous glamour. Studio sessions were the fun, Hollywoody part of what the company did. Eustachian was the largest employer of actors in the tristate area. Someone had to narrate all those audiobooks, host all those podcasts, and provide voice-overs to all those audio documentaries. Your job as a coder really didn't have anything directly to do with making studio recordings. But the company reasoned that it was a good idea for employees to have a view of the operation that was "holistic." And you were certainly not going to object, because today you were going to get to see three-time Oscar nominee Mr. Hollywood narrate a book.

"Telling stories is at the heart of what we do," Walcott says on the phone.

"I thought money was at the heart of what we do," you reply.

"We don't manufacture money, we make audio products. 'You're Your Product.' Just go into the studio and listen. It'll give you a whole new perspective on the company."

You want to tell Walcott about what you uncovered about Blue and the secret data, but you think better of it. It could all be nothing, and you don't want to bug Walcott if it's nothing. You decide you need to talk to Blue first. Right now, you'll just enjoy the studio session.

Mr. Hollywood was one of the biggest movie stars around. He made serious-minded action films, like that samurai space opera *Zero-Gravity Ronin*. And that detective thriller he starred in, *Scars in Scarsdale*, kept you guessing all the way to the end, although it definitely didn't need to be in 3D. These days, Mr. Hollywood was emphasizing the more serious aspects of his craft, because he wasn't getting any younger and he wanted to finally win an Oscar. His new movie was a time-travel adventure movie called *Battlefield: Forever*, in which he played a soldier who gets unstuck in time and has to fight battles in ancient Rome, World War II, and the thirty-second century in order to find his way back home. To help promote his new war film, the studio had the idea to have the actor record a new version of Sun Tzu's *The Art of War*. The thinking was that recording an audiobook classic would add to his gravitas with critics and Academy Award voters.

You find a seat in the control room along with the director of the session, an audio engineer, and a portly guy scrolling through messages on his phone. Mr. Hollywood breezes in thirty minutes late, which you are told isn't awful for an A-list star. He has a smaller entourage than you would have thought—just a stylist, a vocal coach, and manager. The audio engineer sets him up in the recording booth, giving him a tablet computer with the script of the book, three sticks of spearmint gum (his request), and a bottle of gin (again, his request).

Mr. Hollywood, it turns out, is more of a physical actor than a voice actor. The session reminds you of those stories about silent film stars who couldn't make the transition to talkies. On screen, Mr. Hollywood had a rugged, renegade persona that pulled you in and made you root for him, even if you were a little afraid of him. But if you close your eyes, his voice can't convey the command of his visual presence. His vocal timbre is tinny and thin and, if you're being honest, kind of wimpy. He walked the walk but couldn't talk the talk.

"'The general who loses a fight doesn't plan much,'" Mr. Hollywood reads. "'The general who wins a fight plans a lot. That's how you can tell who is going to win or lose a fight. Study who studies the most before a battle. Then you can identify the winner even before the fight begins.'" Mr. Hollywood stops. "What's this word here?" he asks, pointing to his tablet.

He clearly hadn't read the book himself before he started to narrate it out loud. Narrating a book wasn't like reading a movie script. There were a lot more words, and there was often nobody else to play off of. You had to find the rhythm of the piece all by yourself, and you had to find a cadence that would pull listeners in without boring them.

You used to think audiobooks were a cheat, that they were somehow less intellectually challenging than reading a physical text. But since joining Eustachian and listening to more of the company's products, you changed your views about listening. Hearing a book read out loud unlocked another level of meaning. There was music and emotion in the words that weren't there on the page but that a great narrator could pull out. It was like the difference between reading a piece of sheet music and hearing it played by a symphony. Mr. Hollywood was trying to bring out the melody of the words, but he couldn't read music. Maybe that's why he had been nominated for three Oscars but had never won. He was going to have to settle for a future of Golden Globes and People's Choice Awards.

The Art of War is a brief book, and Mr. Hollywood pushes through it, wrapping up his work before lunch. He signs a few autographs, poses for a few publicity shots, and leaves. He apparently had a talk show taping to get to. After Mr. Hollywood and his small entourage exit, the portly guy who's been listening in the studio with you puts away his phone.

"So what did you think?" he asks you.

"I think he's a movie star," you reply.

The man winks and flips a porkpie hat onto his head. "I got you."

Now you recognize Porkpie—he's one of the Inclusion, Civil Rights, and Title IX Players (who were recently renamed the Organizational Effectiveness, Leadership Development, and Equal Opportunity Compliance Ensemble). The signature hat tipped you off, but you also recognize his voice—he's a veteran Eustachian narrator. Everything is clicking now. You've seen him in some minor movies, playing characters like "Uber Driver No. 2" and "Frozen Corpse." He has a voice that is as smooth and sweet as melting chocolate. You get to talking to him. He was booked for an evening session to record a new novel by a writer who was semifamous for a long-running mystery series about a crime-solving New Orleans sous-chef. Porkpie had recorded every book in the franchise, so it was pretty steady work. The new installment was called *Mardi Gras Mysteries: Blood in the Jambalaya.* "Narration work keeps the lights on for me," Porkpie says. "I don't know what I'd do without it. Movie acting sure don't pay the bills, and stage acting costs me money!"

Porkpie is great at what he does. Sometimes saying someone is "great at what he does" can come off like a backhanded compliment, because you are low-key suggesting that although the execution is excellent, the thing being done is questionable. And that's exactly what you were implying here. The book Porkpie is reading is pretty much crap—the usual procedural crime shit, with a few Louisiana clichés thrown in to give the plot some bayou flavor. But Porkpie elevates the material in a way that makes you see the source code was maybe better than you first thought; it's like Miles Davis covering "Time After Time." He's playing the pauses between the notes, breathing nuance and meaning into lines that might have otherwise just stayed flat.

Listening to a story demands the kind of attention that scanning words on a page doesn't. When you read a physical book, you go at your own pace; you can reread lines you find confusing, you can close your eyes and rest your brain for a moment when you need to before plowing ahead. An audio experience, however, forces you to follow more closely. Sure, you can rewind an audiobook or listen to it at a slower or faster speed. But usually you just have to jump on the verbal train and hang on. If your mind starts to drift, you miss words or important parts of the plot, so you have to listen. You find you are at your most relaxed when you are at your most focused—like a ballerina dancing, a rapper freestyling, or a coder coding, when you are fully engaged with a task you let go of yourself. There's a freedom in focus, and maybe that's why listening to a good audio book is both grounding and transporting. That's somehow comforting—in a world of distractions, it's supremely satisfying to have an art form that demands and rewards your focus, and yet can somehow also be enjoyed while driving on the interstate or exercising on an elliptical.

As Porkpie narrates, you are transported back to freshman year in college, when you and Kenise and a bunch of friends went camping during spring break. As a Westchesterian turned Manhattanite, you weren't wild about the wild. Your idea of a cookout was getting shawarma from a food cart on Sixth Avenue. But the back-to-nature experience won you over—you could feel something, you didn't know what, just above your head and beneath your feet. At night, you and your friends sat around a fire and told stories, getting to know one another better. You can feel Porkpie building that fire as the book goes on, pulling you into the story he's spinning. When he's done, you don't want it to end.

Porkpie picks up the bottle of gin that Mr. Hollywood left in the control booth. "I think I need this more than him." He winks. "You want to help me drink it?"

• • •

You go to that retro diner down the street, the Punic Wars Café. There was a huge mural of Hannibal and his elephants crossing the Alps on one wall, and on another a quote from Gustave Flaubert's *Salammbo*: "How can I return to Carthage?" Porkpie says he usually has to go into Manhattan, down around Canal Street or Mott Street, to find a good bar or coffee shop, but this café in Arkhaam is a solid one, and it's one of the few holdover businesses that refused to sell to the invading tech barbarians. Porkpie orders a glass of ice for his gin and some French fries. You ask for a glass of fizzy water but are surprised to see Jamaican black cake on the menu so you order that too. The cake turns out to be neither Jamaican nor black but it is cake, so whatever.

Porkpie has this theory about how audiobooks can save the world. So many of the problems out there are because people can't understand other people's points of view, he says. Social media and wealth inequality and a host of other insidious inequities are making things worse, circumscribing social circles, funneling information in useless partisan drips. But books allow you to have a mind-meld with another human being—maybe they're a refugee from Syria, maybe they're a billionaire in Silicon Valley. Once you get outside yourself, it's easier to see things from another perspective. And when you listen to an audiobook and hear another person's voice in your head, it connects you to the world in a new and needed way. You love to hear Porkpie's passion—it's infectious. When you're an employee at a place where people are excited about their jobs, it's like nobody is really working. As Porkpie talks, you nod, sip your fizzy water, and pick at your un-Jamaican black-ish cake. He gets a slice of pomegranate cream pie.

Porkpie wolfs down his pie. "So what have you heard about this Mee Corp thing?"

"I'm new," you tell him. "They haven't told me much."

"I don't trust big companies," he says. "I've worked with Mee Corp Books, and I don't like how they handle their business. Eustachian is big enough—I don't want them getting any bigger. I don't mind them hiring stars like Mr. Hollywood once in a while. But if they hire matinee idols for every project, working actors won't get any work. And I need this gig."

"I don't think that superstars are your competition," you say. "This is just between me and you, but I know audio companies are doing a lot of experimentation with artificial intelligence."

Porkpie laughed. "Isn't everybody?"

"You're not worried?"

Another laugh. "Did you hear me today? Do you think a robot can do what I do?"

"You were brilliant," you say, sipping your fizzy water. "Like *brilliant* brilliant."

"Fuck AI," Porkpie says. "If they want to rely on robots, they're just gonna get more *Jungle Book* situations."

"I keep hearing about that *Jungle Book* thing. What's the deal with that?"

"I signed an NDA."

"Of course."

"I can say this—that situation didn't make robots or humans look good."

"Well, as a programmer, I do know one thing. Anything artificial intelligence can do it eventually will do better than humans. If AI can play chess, in the end it will beat a grandmaster. If it can drive, eventually it'll be pole position at the Indy 500. It's just math."

Porkpie takes off his hat, scratches his balding head, and puts the hat back on. "I don't think you quite understand what your company is selling."

"Audio products."

"No, you're selling connections. I listened to this audiobook once about Nelson Mandela. His ghostwriter edited all the tapes he recorded when Mandela wrote his memoirs and, with the blessing of the Mandela estate, turned it into a podcast. Mandela said this one thing in Xhosa that stayed with me: '*Umntu ngumntu ngabanye abantu.*'"

"Impressive—you even threw in the clicks! What does it mean?"

"It's this African philosophical concept of ubuntu. Basically it means a person is a person because of other people. We don't exist without society, without our bonds with other people. Remember the first days of COVID? Man, I'm a single parent raising two teenage daughters. We were all quarantined together, and we couldn't go out, and I couldn't work. The situation was shit—but there was this silver lining. We had family dinner every night; we binged-watched *Watchmen* as a family. The whole neighborhood organized so we could all stay healthy together.

There's this isolationist ideology out there that we don't need regulations, we don't need each other, every man for himself. Like animals in the wild. Social distancing was evidence of the opposite: People saw that we're all interconnected, even when we're apart, and that our actions have consequences for the whole community."

"What does that have to do with AI recording audiobooks?"

"I'm getting to it! Man, I'm just trying to tell my story!" He laughed. "See, people don't just listen to me because of my voice..."

"You have a great voice."

"I appreciate the compliment! But it's not just about that. It's about having another human being tell you a story. That's why cave people used to gather around a fire. It wasn't just for warmth—it was to share stories with each other. If a robot is reading to you, it's meaningless. It's like shouting into a dry well and hearing an echo. It's not ubuntu. That's why people still go to movie theaters when they could just watch TV alone at home. That's why people go to Noelle Swizzler concerts or NFL stadiums. We're giving away the house! You can't connect to your humanity with a robot. We need to be with other people in order to be ourselves."

● ● ●

On your way home after work, you get a call from Walcott.

"So what did you think?" he asks.

"I thought it was pretty amazing," you respond. "Seeing Mr. Hollywood was nice, but that Porkpie is a real artist. I do worry, though, if he's gonna have a job in the future."

"Why's that?"

"I'm afraid he's going to get replaced—by either a bigger star or a machine. He's a great guy, but I think even he'd agree that he's kind of a dinosaur."

"We're all dinosaurs. The only ones who aren't dinosaurs are the dinosaurs."

"What does that mean?"

"Dinosaurs are used as this symbol of failure, and it's totally wrong. The dinosaurs survived and thrived on Earth for 165 million years. They might have lasted another 165 million years if it wasn't for some totally random meteorite crashing into the planet. Humans have only been around for maybe three hundred thousand years, and we've already almost destroyed the world. Nature didn't select dinosaurs for extinction, they weren't bad at evolution; they just had bad luck."

"So what does that have to do with Porkpie?"

"I'm just saying you can be great at what you do and still fail at doing it. Success isn't a sign of worthiness or of anything, there are too many factors out of our control. Maybe we'll all get replaced by artificial intelligence. Maybe we'll all be bought out by Mee Corp. Maybe we're all dinosaurs. But that's nothing to be ashamed or anxious about. Success and failure are flip sides of the same illusion. Just do your work and step back. Dinosaurs had a pretty good run."

But when you get home, you can't sleep.

You hope what you discovered about Blue and his data isn't an extinction-level event.

Chapter Ten

GLITCH

There's a new online nature series about wolves. The show follows the lives of a whole pack of them living in Alaska. For some reason, researchers assign wolves letters and numbers and not real names. They say it's to differentiate them as wild creatures and not cuddly pets with names like Rover and Babybug and Mr. Scrumdiddlyumptious. Of course, letters and numbers didn't stop the public from idolizing U2, 007, Eleven, Seven of Nine, R2-D2, and C-3PO, but whatever. The nature show features this one wolf named L-10, who starts off life as a runt but manages to survive through a difficult winter with very little food. One thing that attracts you to these nature videos is how the unspoken message of all of them is the threat of climate change. All these animals live in precariously balanced ecosystems where if one thing goes wrong everything is thrown out of balance. And of course climate change is throwing everything out of balance. The caribou that the wolves depend on for food have changed their migratory paths thanks to global warming, and now the pack is forced to trek farther out of their usual territory in search of sustenance.

The other thing you find interesting is how much animal interactions resemble human society. The constant battles between males for mating rights and dominance. The ruthless fights for food and resources. The ambushes at the water holes. Animals communicate, some even make tools, many of them care for their young ones and other members of their group. The main difference between humans and animals is the moral structure we make up to govern ourselves. Once we start to ignore that, are we any better than wolves? You have to turn away from gory scenes of the pack tearing apart a reindeer. The snow around them is spattered with blood redder than Rudolph's nose. L-10 waits for her turn to feed.

• • •

What you need to say to Blue is too important to text from your personal number. You go to a bodega and buy a burner cell phone so you can make a call that can't be tracked.

Blue answers. "Who is this?"

"Octavia from work."

"Why are you calling from this number?"

"Why do we have a concerningly humongous, multipetabyte-size database of customer and employee data?"

Silence on the other end, then laughter. "Researchers have been teaching apes sign language for decades, but you know what the apes have never done with it? An ape has never used sign language to ask a question. Not a single one! Either they're not curious enough, or they lack the imagination to understand that other beings might know things that they don't. Either way it helps explain why humans are on the moon and apes are in zoos. That's why I wanted you on the red team—you ask questions."

You can feel your anger building. "So you're saying I'm just a little better than an ape?"

"I'm saying that you have what may be the essential element for higher-level cognition, whether it's human or silicon."

"Let's keep it a hundred percent real. You implied there was nothing in the database for us to worry about—that's a lie."

"I said that as far as I know—and that's true."

You don't just feel rage when he says this, you feel a specific radioactive isotope of that emotion: outrage. This is more than anger, it's a boiling sense that lines have been crossed and wrongs need righting. "I want details."

"Don't get so worked up! Maybe the data is for health care plans or EEOC requirements. There are many good reasons to collect personal data like this."

"I know the data is personal, but I need to know how personal."

"That's the funny thing—I have no idea."

Blue had written an algorithm that ingested vast amounts of information from across Eustachian's system—customer data and employee data—and stored it without identifying the users or even the data. "It's kind of a loophole," Blue explains. "We tell users we don't traffic in any data that would identify them specifically. But we do need information to help the app be as useful and responsive to our customers as possible. So we gather terabytes of information and place it into what I call a 'digital blind trust.' We don't know what the information is and we don't know who it comes from, but the algorithms we write are self-learning, so they're able to search inside of the digital blind trust and pick out what they need."

"So we don't know anything about the data we're storing about our own customers."

"We would never betray our customers like that. I told you—I'm a coder with a code. And if it got out that we were mishandling customer data, the stock price would crater."

"'Eustachian: We Get What's Between Your Ears.'"

"Exactly."

"The motto is starting to sound less like a guarantee and more like a threat."

"Your point?"

"So we trust algorithms with the data that we don't trust ourselves with?"

"It sounds crazy when you say it like that, but that's exactly right."

You talk a bit more and then you hang up. You feel like a spouse who found a cocktail napkin with a phone number on it but doesn't have quite enough evidence to be furious yet.

The bank of data you're supposed to protect is sounding less like a bank and more like a robbery. It's one thing if the company was just storing names, addresses, and Social Security numbers. You wouldn't be surprised by that—you shouldn't be surprised by that. But the storehouse of data is so large that it suggests there's much more that's been scraped. Sometimes volume is a tell. If you check your phone bill and see your boyfriend's placed one call to Belarus, maybe you don't worry about it. But if you discover hundreds of calls to Minsk, Belgrade, and Bucharest, maybe you have some questions about human trafficking. There's something wrong about a company collecting this much information from customers when the customers have no clue how much you have on them. Maybe the CDC needs some of your personal medical data to protect public health, but does Tesla really need to know if you're calcium deficient? But because you still don't have details on what Eustachian is collecting, you try to rationalize it away again. It's a good thing, at least, maybe, you hope, that the data you're protecting is unidentified and anonymous. You're not hurting anyone, at least not anyone specific. It's like they say at the end of movies—no actual data was hurt during the production of this film. There's still only a very small chance there's *Eyes Wide Shut* Illuminati-type shit hidden in the database. You look at the calendar on your phone. Only a few more months until November. Only a little more time before you can cash out your RSUs.

• • •

The All-Hands meeting is today, so you come into work a little bit early to make sure you're on time. Everyone is supposed to gather in the Frank Sinatra Theater on the seventh floor. Most of the staff works remotely, so a lot of people you've never seen IRL before have come in for the event. You want to make sure you have a good view of the circus.

The theater is already crowded when you arrive, but you manage to find a seat near the back. You notice someone has scrawled these words with a Sharpie onto the armrest on your left: "DEI = Dead European Idols." You're trying to figure out what that means and whether it's racist, and you are feeling some kind of way about it when Walcott slides into the seat next to you, obliviously covering up the Sharpie scrawl with his hand. Walcott smiles; you hadn't noticed what a nice smile he has, maybe because when you first met him you were focused on trying to land this job. Back when you were categorizing smiles for W4731: Deep Learning for Computer Vision, you never came across a smile quite like his—knowing but not know-it-all, sweet but not sticky, the kind of smile that lights up the room but seems spotlighted just on you. Damn—Walcott's actually a great-looking guy. He's adorably lanky, dresses well, and now that he's sitting so close to you, you notice that he smells good too. He's not wearing cologne or anything, but there's a pleasant, manly, just-scrubbed scent about him. It's a forest-y smell, but in a nice, comfortable, cabin-in-the-woods way, not a dank-rain-forest-in-the-Amazon-with-snakes-and-bugs way. And now that you know the story behind those damn clunky rings he wears, they don't annoy you quite as much. But if he were ever your man, the rings would have to go. The bling would definitely not be going into bed with you. No, no—this Black man would have to submit to a ringless fuck. Damn it, you are doing it again. You can always tell when you think a man is perfect for you when you start thinking of ways you would change him.

"Nice to see you here," you say to Walcott. "I feel like I only hear from you virtually."

Walcott checks his watch. "I'm pressed for time. I have to slip out for a doctor's appointment."

"Everything okay?"

"Just a checkup." He shrugs. "How are things going?"

You think about telling him about the database stuff and Blue, but you're in an auditorium full of people who work for an audio company, so the risk of being overheard is a little too much. You keep it light. "I really appreciate all the emails you've been sending with the work advice and everything."

Walcott turns toward you, one eyebrow raised, like he needs more of an explanation.

"It's nice to get supportive messages," you explain. "It's a human touch."

"Okay," Walcott says.

You switch subjects. "So what's the *Jungle Book* controversy?"

"You're still on that? Forget about it—it's nothing."

"The fact you'd say it's nothing kinda tells me it's something."

He smiles, but for the first time he's not really smiling. "Do you want to get me fired? Because I would do just about anything not to get fired, and I'm not ashamed to say that."

"Like I said, if it was nothing you'd tell me something."

Walcott touches your wrist lightly. An emotional jolt goes up your arm, which isn't something you've felt since middle school. "That's a cool tattoo," he says. "Is that Chinese?"

"Stop changing the subject." You need to keep this professional, or as professional as you can when talking about your body art. You give in. "It's a quote from the *Dao De Jing*."

"What does it mean? And how many tattoos do you have?"

"Stop changing the subject." You lean over and whisper, "Does the *Jungle Book* thing have something to do with the Founder?"

"It's time," Walcott says, turning in the direction of the stage.

The main event is beginning.

• • •

The All-Hands meeting started out slow, which only added to the slow-burn tension. Various directors of this and senior directors of that came out to make PowerPoint-powered presentations on various subjects. At Eustachian, executives were ranked on levels ranging from 1 (the lowest) to 7 (the most august). The early speakers were all L2s and L3s.

They were the amuse-bouches to the coming entrées. The general vibe of the meeting was about how well the company was doing and how rapidly it was increasing its market share. People were signing up for more subscriptions, people were listening to more titles, and people were listening for longer periods of time. The marketing team talked about some new ad spots they had planned for the Super Bowl and some new celebrities they had signed up for new social media campaigns. You started to drift off. The whole meeting had a this-could-have-been-an-email quality to it.

Then a parade of senior vice presidents took the stage. These were serious people—L4s and L5s. They were armed with charts and graphs and animated videos complete with musical soundtracks. They had commissioned research, compiled metrics, and sponsored focus groups. They had dial-tested hundreds of potential customers ages eighteen to forty-nine, carefully studying reaction meters ticking up and down as participants registered their responses to Eustachian products in real time. Using data-driven decisions, the L4s and L5s broke down the consumers the company needed to pursue into three categories: the Don Drapers (customers who listened to history and how-to books), the Wonder Womans (romance and self-help), and Active Shooters (podcasts and true crime). People of color, you noticed, didn't seem to be a category Eustachian separated out and prioritized. The L4s and L5s delivered data-driven orations about the future of the company and the next steps for the entire audio entertainment industry. They weren't there just to get employees to focus on the work at hand; they were looking to inspire everyone to think about the tasks that were just beyond our reach and how tomorrow we might run faster, stretch out our arms farther, to grasp that green light——

But all of this was only prologue. Eustachian hadn't called an All-Hands meeting in months. You all knew there had to be a good reason for bringing all the employees together. Questions and rumors ran through the audience faster than Jamaican Olympians. Were we being sold? Were we buying some other company? Was some sort of reorg in the works? Was a new product launch in the offing? The company was always working on secret ventures. There had been Project Laputa and Project Westeros and the Mordor Initiative. Employees tapped for such tasks signed NDAs (of course) and reported to work in conference rooms booked for months at a time with all the glass windows sealed off from prying eyes with sheets of tinfoil. Sometimes the assignments would result in a new product for the marketplace or a new app for the workplace. Sometimes the project would just disband, with none of the participants able to say what they had been working on or how it ended up. But either way, it was considered an honor to be selected for one of the stealth project teams. Nothing boosts your rep in a corporation more than making it widely known that you're working on something secret.

A buzz suddenly runs through the audience, quickly turning into a high-voltage electric current. The Founder! The Founder! The Founder is going to speak. That would explain the buildup and the presence of so many top executives. There is time for only one more speaker, and so it has to be the man himself. The opening acts are over, and now it's time for the headliner. Nobody has seen the Founder in months; you hadn't spotted him since you got a job here. There was a rumor that he was scheduled to visit the International Space Station; office gossip had it that he was planning a run for senate; others whispered about a possible Coachella cameo with St. Vincent. Everyone around you is dying to hear what he has to say. What new three-year plan did he have for the company this year? What commandments is he bringing down from the mountain?

But the Founder doesn't take the stage—instead, the final speaker is an L6. A disappointed groan rumbles through the crowd, but some women stand and clap. The executive who takes the stage is Wombat. You should have guessed. Her red hair is out, her curls cascading down her shoulders like lava. She had been an L5, but she's ascended to higher heights—she is now the second-highest executive in the company, second only to the Founder, and the highest-ranking woman ever. Her supervision of FLIT may have been what helped her make this power move. The buzz in the audience is that leadership likes the enterprising spirit she's shown with the affinity groups, and a decision was made that it was easier to promote her than to actually implement all the DEI-boosting programs Wombat had been suggesting through her stewardship of FLIT.

The crowd quiets down. You all sense that Wombat has been tapped to deliver the big announcement at the center of this All-Hands meeting. "Greetings, fellow Eustachians," she begins in her Aussie accent, which it's now clear that she plays up when she wants to seem egalitarian. "There's an asteroid heading our way and it's an extinction-level event. I'm here to tell you that Mee Corp poses an existential risk to our company. They don't want to buy our company—they want to annihilate it."

The crowd falls silent, and it's that silence you get during an eclipse, or that hush that falls over a stadium after a player suffers an on-field compound fracture. It's a preternatural, simmering silence that's waiting for something to end or begin.

Wombat now has everyone's attention, and she continues, weirdly eager, almost oddly giddy, to deliver the disturbing news. "Look at all you," she jokes, surveying the anxious expressions in the crowd. Wombat jabs a manicured finger at a scowling L4 in the third row. "Got a face like a dropped pie!" She's like a perversely excited veteran TV correspondent who finally gets to cover an active war zone.

Mee Corp, it turns out, had secretly been laboring away on an audio app that would compete with Eustachian. The buyout rumors were apparently a feint to throw everyone off the scent. Mee Corp's new app was more user-friendly than Eustachian's product, and upon its release, Mee Corp's suite of devices—phones, tablets, laptops, virtual reality headsets—would cease to be compatible with rival products, cutting Eustachian's market share in half. And to make things worse, to add the ultimate insult to injury, Mee Corp's new audio app would be powered by cutting-edge artificial intelligence, making it more advanced than anything else on the market. Eustachian's Hearing Is Believing program already customized user experiences with machine learning, but Mee Corp was promising a quantum leap.

Every company was advertising that its products now came with AI, whether it was real AI or not. AI was the new "new and improved"—and although most customers didn't quite know how AI improved the products in question, they did know it was new and they therefore had to have it. It was only a matter of time before Frosted fucking Flakes came with AI. Mee Corp's AI was supposedly the real thing, post-Cartesian, nonhallucinating, supercalifragilistic artificial general intelligence, capable of doing and thinking anything a human could, but backward and in heels. They claimed their AI was better than artificial intelligence, better than AGI, it was Real Intelligence™. Mee Corp's new Real Intelligence™-enhanced audio product was called Ear Shot, and they planned to announce a rollout for November in time for the holiday buying season. You and your fellow employees had three months before the whole goddamn world changed. This techquake was an 8.0 on the Richter scale. Every few years a company would introduce a product or process that shook the world down to its tectonic plates, rendering everything that had come before it obsolete. This techquake was shaking the Cathedral of Technology, and you could hear the stained-glass windows rattling.

Wombat presses a button, and the huge screen behind her lights up with Ear Shot's new logo: a giant red ear with a blue gun firing right into the ear canal. It is a crazy image, and a clear rip-off of Eustachian's blue-eye-staring-out-of-a-green-ear logo, but you have to admit it's eye-catching—and maybe ear-catching too. Ear Shot's company motto: "Ear We Are Now."

The crowd in the Frank Sinatra Theater is in a panic. The Mesozoic Era is over and a new age, without all you dinosaurs, is set to begin. Big Tech is more competitive than evolution, or maybe it is just faster, which could amount to the same thing. Huge companies die out quickly and quietly without leaving a fossil record. America Online was the T-Rex of its time; now it's just echoes of ringing modems and faded whispers of "You've got mail." MySpace was the Facebook of its time; now Facebook was fighting to not be the MySpace of its time. Yahoo!, Ask Jeeves, and AltaVista are all search engines nobody searches for anymore. One grand innovation can put you on top in the tech world, but on the flip side, one grand innovation by someone else can have you looking up at the new market leader standing astride your fallen corpse. Everyone was always one asteroid away from extinction.

Wombat announces that leadership is prepared to meet the challenge. Studies are being launched, memos are being authored, working groups are being worked out. She promises that Eustachian's new AI will be the best AI, because it will be better than Real Intelligence™—Eustachian's AI will be Holistic AI™.

A few employees take up the chant: "Holistic! Holistic!" You are sure they are plants.

But the crowd of Eustachian employees is still unsettled and unsure. Mee Corp's move is a gut punch to their corporate identity, which had always been to run from the front and to envision themselves as the market leader. Wombat senses the tension and does something unexpected and unheard of: She starts to sing. *Wha' gwaan?* you think, which is weird because you barely understand Jamaican patois much less think in it. The singing continues, and the people around you are just as confused as you are. Is the music coming from a recorded playlist or live from the stage? She couldn't possibly . . . is she . . . what—really? You can all see Wombat's full red mouth moving, and it's clear this is not a lip-synch deal, she's really singing. And she's *really good*. She's crooning something a cappella, something between gospel and hip-hop, and it feels warm and right and sweet like a plate of cookies. People are on their feet, clapping and cheering, and pretty soon you can't even hear Wombat over all the stomping and screaming. Fuck Mee Corp! Fuck them with a twenty-seven-story tower! If an L6 can sing, anything is fucking possible at this company. Wombat just took the entire Cathedral of Technology back to church, and everyone is so fucking inspired they don't know what to do with themselves.

"Holistic! Holistic! Holistic!"

Wombat waves an acknowledging hand like a pageant winner or the pope. "Thank you. Holistic to you as well. And remember the words of the Founder: 'Your greatest competition is yourself—but when you beat yourself, you always win.'"

. . .

The All-Hands gives you a lot to think about, to say the least. A few minutes later the spell of Wombat's siren song has worn off a bit, and you are sizing up the reality you are facing. You came to Eustachian for stability. You were floundering, and you needed a steady job and a sizable income. Now the tectonic shifts in the Big Tech landscape are putting that into doubt. You want to talk this over with Walcott, but he slipped away before the end of the meeting. As you leave work, you get an email from him.

From: Walcott Neville
To: Octavia Crenshaw
August 7

My mom named me after her favorite writer, the Caribbean poet Derek Walcott, and I often turn to his works, like "Love After Love," or "Codicil," when I need some inspiration. In his poem "Sea Grapes," he writes that classics can offer consolation, but much more is needed. I don't think he meant that literature couldn't provide solace in troubled times like this. I think what he was actually saying is that we have to look for insight outside of the Eurocentric canon. I remember during the pandemic, with all the protests and the general pandemonium, I really came to understand that literature, really diverse literature, can provide not only an anchor but also solutions. In "I Explain a Few Things," Pablo Neruda writes about why he's not just writing about dreams and nature, and calls on his readers to come out and see the blood that's running in the streets. And in Langston Hughes's great poem "Let America Be America Again," he says that there's never been equality or freedom for him in the country that bills itself as the "home of the free." I'm sure you noticed, but nobody who spoke at the All-Hands meeting today was Black. Big platforms like Eustachian become problematic if we don't allow lots of people to share the stage. DEI isn't an extra, it's essential. You can't achieve excellence without inclusion. It's like trying to connect to the internet without wi-fi—things are better when you are part of a network. People are literally on the streets together trying to make their voices heard, and making voices heard should be kind of what we do at Eustachian. All of this is to say, the more inclusion we can include in Eustachian's offerings, the more we can get affinity groups to contribute to our corporate strategy and tactics going forward, the more we'll be doing to get people through the current crisis. To quote Littlefinger in *GoT*, "Chaos isn't a pit. Chaos is a ladder." We shouldn't wait for things to settle and calcify; now is the time for us to advocate for our vision for the company. What can we do to make sure that inclusive hiring, promotion, and content acquisition is part of the conversation? It's like my man Ralph Ellison once said: "Who knows but that, on the lower frequencies, I speak for you?"

Derek, Pablo, Langston—this brother was pushing all the right poetry buttons. You hit him back with a note that references Gwendolyn Brooks, Claudia Rankine, and Staceyann Chin. You haven't read two of those three poets, but you know you have to raise your game. You also throw in a SZA lyric just to show that you may be a coder, but you've still got a little flava. Your note is maybe a little less professional than you're comfortable with and a little more personal than you should be with a coworker, but fuckit, you probably only live once, and if reincarnation turns out to be a thing, you'll get it right in the next life. After you hit send, you make your way to the train back to Manhattan.

Chapter Eleven

YOU'RE ON YOUR OWN, KID

You meet Braids at her apartment for coffee. She lives close to work, in a one-bedroom in East Arkhaam. Eustachian provides a subsidy to employees who choose to live in town, but very few take them up on it. You didn't even think about relocating to New Jersey because, as a native of New York State, you know that everything that is right and good in the universe is in the five boroughs, or the West Indies. In your mind, the planet boils down to two islands—Manhattan and Jamaica—and the rest might as well be water. Most Eustachian executives live in Manhattan or in comfortable suburbs in Connecticut. The Eustachians who do live in Arkhaam are mostly the Black ones from customer experience, and they invariably have places on the rougher streets of the east side of the city and not on more gentrified avenues of West Arkhaam.

Braids talks about how the PIP is going. They've extended it a couple times, but now she's got only two weeks left, and, so far, she's completing the goals they set for her. She knows three other Black girls who were put on the PIP, and two of the three got their jobs back, and one took a tiny buyout. She's not thrilled about those odds, but she's prepared to live with them. She had been feeling anxious with the PIP hanging over her since she's the biggest breadwinner in her family. She sends her mother money every month and has been helping to put her brother through community college. If she loses her job, she doesn't know where she'll find the funds to take up the slack for her missing salary. But worrying isn't going to solve the problem. She's just going to work as hard as she can and see what happens. She is hoping the new threat from Mee Corp, and the expected shake-up at Eustachian, could result in fresh career opportunities for her.

"Has Walcott been able to help?" you ask.

"He's been giving me advice on meeting my goals, but he's not my manager, so there's not much more he can do."

"I know you didn't think FLIT is any use, but what about Wombat?"

"She talks a good game about women, but I think they define women here as white women. She's not going to help me unless it helps her. I'm pretty much on my own."

"Let me know if there's anything I can do. I'm still new, but if you just need someone to bounce ideas off of, I'm here."

Braids's apartment is a cozy one—wood panel floors and big windows, although you note that her windows have bars on the outside and her door has three sets of chains. There are bookcases on nearly every wall of her home, and a lot of the books are about—you guessed it—the Luddites. There are scholarly studies about the movement, books of historical fiction set during the time period, travel guides to historical Luddite sites, collections of Luddite artwork, tomes of Luddite philosophy, books of Luddite poetry (not today, Satan!), even comic books. The bookends on each shelf were shaped like—you guessed it again—little black looms.

You point to the shelves. "What. The. Fuck."

Braids laughs. "I'm not crazy, I swear!"

"No one said you were crazy—just obsessed."

"I'm not obsessed! I got these when I was doing my thesis. They're mostly academic."

"Mostly academic?" You slide one book out from the shelf. On the cover, a handsome butch woman clutches a loom in one hand and a bosomy hottie in the other. "*Bitch, Give Me a Kiss Before AI Ruins Everything*—'a modern-day post-Luddite LGBTQ+ romance.'"

"*Mostly* academic," Braids says sheepishly. "But don't sleep on the Luddites! They got a lot of things right."

"Such as?"

"Such as industrialism is killing the planet—not just human workers, the entire world."

"You're obsessed. And that bullcrap you just said is too long for a hashtag."

"I'm telling you, don't sleep on the Luddites! Data-powered robot capitalism is even worse than the shit they pulled on workers back in the days of Oliver Twist. Back then, they were just replacing muscle with steel. Now they are coming for our brains and creativity . . ." Braids stops herself, realizing she's on a rant. "Okay, I am a little bit obsessed."

You smile. "A little bit?"

She pours you some merlot, and you start talking about work, but in a way that doesn't feel like work. Away from the office, you finally feel comfortable talking about office politics. The white people at the office talk about all sorts of shit: their managers, their fellow employees, whether their significant others are into vibrators or strap-ons or whatever else—you don't know because that's always when you exit the conversation. There's no way you would let your personal life leak into your professional life like that—it's like a stain on the living room ceiling that seems to be coming from an upstairs toilet. You and Braids agree that there's definitely a racial divide about the way people view work. Black people see work as a place they go to make money. It can be a comfortable location, but it's not life. White people see their workplace as their safe space, the spot they go to get away from whatever is happening at home. White people have work friends and work wives and work husbands. They don't mind lingering after hours to have drinks and talk shop and bullshit. Of course, way back in the *day* day, Black people used to hang out day and night with work colleagues—they called that slavery. And it wasn't work because you weren't getting paid. You're done with that.

"Maybe it's because we don't have any real ownership role in these companies, we just don't feel at home in them," you say.

"It's a gender thing too," Braids says. "I'm not married, and I don't have a girlfriend, but I want to have a family someday. I could never see work as my home and my colleagues as my family, because they don't share my same values."

"True dat."

"Whenever I talk to white women about work-life balance, I come away thinking, 'They are making choices that I wouldn't make.' Not that they are the right choices or wrong choices. They just aren't my kind of choices. Just like the Founder's Three Commandments aren't my commandments. Home is home and family is family. Eustachian just has too many secrets."

"I hear you," you say. "In my department, they have me protecting data I can't identify from users who are totally anonymous."

Braids sucks her teeth. "My department, customer experience, is right next to the data compilers, so you wouldn't believe some of the shit I see."

That gives you an idea.

• • •

Braids slips you a thumb drive of Microsectionality tests that a data compiler left in the bathroom on her floor. You tell her you don't want her to get in trouble or anything, but she's justifiably pissed about still being on the PIP, so she says at this point she doesn't care. She also gives you a copy of one of her books to buck up your courage: *The Looming Loom: Luddite Revolutionary Philosophy and Digital Colonialism* by Wilton Sharpe. It's a graphic novel about the Luddite uprising. You decide it's not a good idea to use your work-issued computer for what you're about to do, so you go to a computer store and ask to try out a demonstration model.

The thumb drive is double encrypted, which means it takes you ten minutes to crack it instead of five. Leveraging the info in the Microsectionality test results, you write a routine that matches the real-life names of employees with their anonymous files in that mysterious database. Now you're on your way: From that small subset, it's easy to identify the markers that match other unidentified users in the Eustachian database to their real-life names, and from there you are finally able to identify what kinds of real-life data you've been protecting for the company in your new assignment. The Big O strikes again. You're not typically easily surprised, but you're shocked by what you see. No wonder they didn't identify the data! You erase the in-store laptop you were using and reformat the entire system.

You always hate scenes in movies where someone gets some really terrible or surprising news, and their reaction is that they run into the bathroom and throw up. You've never once vomited out of shock. But, after you figured out what kind of data Eustachian has been collecting, on the train ride home, you are filled with revulsion and you don't quite know where to place your feelings. Are you disgusted with your new job? With Blue? With the customers and employees who are selling their souls? Or with yourself for your new role in the whole grotesque transaction? You think about that Noelle Swizzler song "If Girls Were the Man" that inspired you during your job interview. Are you now the Man for real? Have you got all the stars and fates and dominoes lined up? You never wanted to be the Man. You only wanted to be yourself, whoever that is. You start to text Walcott, but you don't want to get him caught up in this mess. You buy another burner phone from the bodega and call Blue—you need to talk.

Chapter Twelve

DECKS DARK

A few months ago, you found another one of Mom's journals. This one was older than the others, back from when you were a small child. The place you discovered it was even more surprising than the discovery. Your apartment building is old—maybe nineteenth-century old—and there had been rumors that it had been a stop on the Underground Railroad. There were plenty of Underground Railroad locations in Manhattan—like Mother African Methodist Episcopal Church in Harlem and the Hopper-Gibbons House in Chelsea—but many of the other sites boasted plaques and tour groups and Wikipedia pages. In the absence of authentication, you had never believed any of the chatter about Mom's place.

But one Sunday afternoon while you were cleaning the rugs, you discovered a section of the cherrywood floor lifted up to reveal a space maybe six feet long, four feet wide, and three feet deep, just big enough to conceal something—or someone. Was this a hiding space for runaways? You tried to imagine what it would have been like to have been sealed up beneath the floor, hearing the footsteps of pursuing authorities right above your head. You allowed yourself to feel a certain thrill to be so directly connected to history in this way. Whom had the space concealed in the past? What kind of drama had played out beneath the floorboards? Right now, the only things in the nook were cobwebs—and diary No. 2.

At first you thought the booklet was a centuries-old artifact of some kind, but after you opened it, you quickly recognized your mom's controlled, font-like handwriting. You put everything back the way it was and brushed the dust off the diary. The familiar embossed image was revealed on the cover, and you let your eager fingers trace the doctor bird's contours—the long nectar-sipping bill, the flowing feather scissor tail. You paused to let the guilt about reading the diary pass and then plowed right in.

Does everyone forget their dreams as soon as they have them? In the morning I wake with the aftertaste of a nighttime reverie in my head, and it makes me sad for what I can no longer recall. Was I lying on Low Cay Beach with a drink in one hand and a book in the other? Was I in the steam room of some spa, my hair wrapped in a towel, white vapors curling around my sweaty brown body? Or maybe it was a nightmare, and I was homeless, childless, friendless, wandering the streets in search of safety. Maybe there are some dreams that it's better to forget.

I knew it was morning even though the sun hadn't come up yet. I could hear the traffic in the street in front of our house. I did not want to go to work today. This is not an unfamiliar or uncommon feeling for me. I had to be on campus late the night before, and Octavia was asleep before I got home, which I hate because it makes me feel like I'm totally screwing up my job as a mother. I need to get to the gym today. I have a lot of stuff on my mind, and the gym helps me beat it all back, like stuffing junk in a closet and closing it tight. I thought about asking Thurgood to give me a massage, but I knew that if I got him involved, he'd just try to fuck me and get us all sweaty and sex-smelling before work. Men are gross that way.

The sun was up and so was Thurgood, and he was talking about doing something nasty. I told him he could do it from the side, and when he didn't jump on his chance I went to the bathroom to get dressed. Aren't men supposed to get less interested in fucking after they get married and have kids? We've been doing it every couple weeks or so lately, and it's enough already. He hasn't checked in about a vasectomy like I had asked him to a while back, so birth control is all on me. The Pill made me feel balloon-animally, and something about IUDs makes me jumpy, so we have been using condoms like a couple of high schoolers. I wasn't gonna worry myself with any of that now. I was just so done with all of it.

In the bathroom, I got myself ready for the day. The toilet wasn't working again. Thurgood was supposed to call someone about it two weeks ago—I sent him a text. He was supposed to also get the sump pump replaced. I hope he got around to that—we are due for some serious rain soon. Home ownership is a trip, but it beats living in an apartment. Everything around me seems so uncertain. Coming home to my Colonial-style abode here in Woodvale is the one refuge I have. I know it's always going to be here. I don't know what I'd do without this place. What's a turtle without a shell? Basically a damn lizard. God, I hope Thurgood remembered about the mortgage. Should I send him a text? I should probably send him a text. Better send a text. Make a mental note: Send Thurgood text about the mortgage. And the toilet. And the sump pump. And more milk, we're almost out. I have a lot of texting to do. The joy of text. Sometimes I'll be sitting across from him at the dining table and I'll send him a text. That way there is a record.

Octavia was already up when I got downstairs. She had taken a stab at her homework and it was a mess.

I crossed my arms. "You have to do this again."

"Why?" she said.

"Because this is a disaster, babygirl. I can't even read it. Is this a t or an i?"

"It's a q."

"You have to do this again."

"I want to hand in what I did."

"Just do it again and stop arguing."

While I made her some ackee and saltfish for breakfast, she finished up a new version of her homework that was much better than the first. She's always better with that second effort.

"Make sure you show this new homework to Daddy," I said. "Don't try to hand in the other version you did, okay?"

Octavia nodded, but she always looks like she's not really listening. I sometimes wish I could give her a spanking like my momma gave me back in the day when I was acting up, but we live in a different time now. In lieu of spanking kids, parents have to outwit them. Child-rearing is about emotional manipulation and button pushing and chess playing. Spanking was like a nuclear deterrent—it was there but you could never use it. Every day with Octavia is the Cuban Missile Crisis.

So many feelings after reading this one. You feel bad that your mom was clearly so attached to the house you used to have in Westchester. It must have killed her to leave it, but maybe after your dad passed it didn't feel like it was a home anymore—or maybe it was just too big and expensive to maintain on a single salary. And you feel creepy reading about your parents' sex life. IUDs? Condoms? Fucking from the side? You don't want to picture your parents doing anything more than holding hands. But what's really startling is reading about you somehow being a problem child. You learned working at Eustachian that a lot of people don't like recordings of their own voices because they sound different on tape than they do in their daily lives. When you speak, the sound of your voice travels through the bones in your skull, making it sound richer and more resonant. When you hear a recording of it, the sound passes through the air, making it thinner and higher pitched. Maybe our whole lives are like that—they seem richer and fuller from the inside, until we get outside perspective on how shallow we really are. You had no memory of acting up or refusing to do homework or generally being an insufferable brat. You got into Columbia—how much of a problem kid could you really have been?

You closed up the secret space. You found out from a neighbor that the nook was almost definitely not connected to the Underground Railroad—the building was old, but not that old. Al Capone, it turned out, started his crime career in New York before he moved to Chicago, and one of his lieutenants had lived in the building. The most likely explanation for the nook was that it was a hiding place for booze during Prohibition—interesting, but far less noble. The difference between criminal and revolutionary was sometimes just a story. Your secret space was simply another thing that didn't sound as rich and resonant when you listened to it for real.

• • •

You meet Blue for drinks at the Punic Wars Café. But it turns out the place is too retro for its own good, because it doesn't have a handicap-accessible entrance. You are forced to go to a Panda Express down the street. The boy behind the counter is hearing impaired, and he and Blue have a sign-language conversation that leaves them both giggling and fist-bumping. You order veggie spring rolls, and Blue gets some cream cheese rangoons, and when the food arrives you follow him as he rides his scooter to a booth.

"We shouldn't even be talking about what I think we're going to talk about," Blue says.

"Let's cut the bullshit," you say. "I know everything."

"Even I don't know everything. There's always a lot of stuff going on that L4s like you and me don't know about."

"I'm an L3."

Blue smiles. "What am I even doing out in public with you then?"

"I really am not in the mood to dick around here. This company has a motto: 'We Get What's Between Your Ears.' But that's like some double-meaning 'To Serve Man' bullshit."

Blue shrugs like he doesn't get it.

"Super-famous *Twilight Zone* episode," you explain. "Benevolent-seeming aliens have a book titled *To Serve Man*. But it turns out they're not here to help humanity; it's a cookbook."

"Goddamn—you just gave away the ending!"

"It's a sixty-year-old spoiler! The statute of limitations on spoilers for that episode ran out in the Nixon administration. But let's focus—tonight's issue is data. We're scraping personal data from our customers and even our own employees. Not just any data—really intimate, invasive stuff. How can we justify doing this?"

Blue shakes his head. "Are you really surprised? Or is this just performative?"

You are getting a little loud now because you want him to take your seriously. "Fuck you. This is very important to me."

"Running a tech company and not scraping data is like going to the moon and not collecting rocks. This is expected stuff—we're not hoarding nuclear codes."

You slap the table with your hand and a saltshaker jumps. "This is people's lives."

He's nonplussed and you hate nonplussed. When someone is talking about something serious, everyone should be plussed. "We're not physically hurting anyone," Blue explains, unfazed as well as nonplussed. "In terms of abusing the common folk, fussing around with people's data is about the least intrusive thing the rich and powerful have ever done to the underclass. It's not like we're invoking the right of prima nocta."

You laugh in a way that says you're not laughing. "'Eustachian: Better Than Feudalism' isn't a ringing endorsement."

Blue now starts to sound like he's mansplaining, which pisses you off more. "Eustachian's paid subscription service is just a gateway drug—many of our products are free of charge. So how is the company going to make money with a business model in which we give away a lot of the stuff we produce? The answer is that we're not sellers, we're buyers."

"What are we buying?" you say sharply. "Attention?"

"Attention is cheap. NikNak buys attention."

"Time?"

"Time is infinite. It's not a commodity that's in short supply."

"So what are we buying?"

Blue turns on his laptop. A spreadsheet of various metrics fills the screen. It's all the things that Eustachian is tracking among its users. This is deeper than you had been able to go into the database. Some of the data is basic: click behavior, what genres users liked best, what they were likely to listen to next, the moment in a given podcast or audiobook where they stopped listening. But some of the other stuff is much more personal. We knew every user's race, gender, and if they were single, married, or divorced. We knew if they were cheating on their spouses and, in some cases, we knew with whom they were cheating. We knew whom they had voted for in the last election and had a pretty good idea whom they would vote for in the next one. We knew what time they got up in the morning and when they went to bed, if they had ever visited a national park or been arrested for a DWI, if they drove a hybrid, if they owned a pet, if they flossed regularly, if they were on their period (thank you, flow-tracking apps), and if they had masturbated in the last twenty-four hours. Then the data got really granular. When you got to the oral and anal dataset, you pushed the laptop away.

"H-h-how do we even know all this stuff?" you ask.

"Easy—part of it is we leave the mics on. Customers have to opt out of the Hearing Is Believing program if they don't want it to record everything, and only .001 percent of customers ever do that. We hear everything: arguments, afternoon quickies, confessions at Catholic churches. If there's a felony involved, we turn it over to law enforcement. But that's also transactional, because we're such a great source of leads for them they leave us alone on all the violation of privacy shit. Now look again—deeper." Blue turns the laptop toward you and you can feel its cobalt-colored glow on your cheeks. The numbers on the screen transmogrified into human figures, walking, talking, fighting, fucking. *You're Your Product.* You realize that you are no longer looking at a statistical record of what was but a projection of what will be. *Tomorrow Is Today.* The company is using the deep data it collects to build digital simulations of customers and employees—to better predict what they will do, where they will go, what they will buy. *Profits Are Prophecy.* Life is a videogame, only people weren't players, they are being played. *Any sufficiently advanced technology is indistinguishable from magic.* Blue smiles, but his expression is sardonic, not amused. "So now do you understand what we're buying?"

"Souls," you reply. "We sell them digital shit in exchange for their souls."

"Nobody wants to sell their soul, but everyone has their price. In this case it's free shit."

"This makes me tremendously fucking uncomfortable."

"That's what the NDA is for."

"How am I supposed to sleep at night?"

"That's what the money's for!" It's his turn to slap the table. "Stuff your pillow with RSUs if you have trouble sleeping. This is the bargain people make for using free stuff. They may not know we collect everything on this spreadsheet, but you know they know, you know? Big Tech is always going to mine this kind of shit. It's our job—you and me—to make sure it never gets out, or we could have a *Jurassic Park* situation. Data is far more dangerous than dinosaurs."

"Just saying that something is your job doesn't make it right."

"So what do you expect me to do? Just up and quit because . . . morality?"

"I don't know . . . maybe. I remember when my mom was in the hospital, there were always all these numbers on her charts: her heart rate, her blood sugar, her liver function . . ."

"And the hospital was storing that data, just like we are."

"My point is that data isn't just data. Those numbers added up to something—to life and death. When numbers are that important, people have a right to know what you're doing with their information. At least with prima nocta, people could see that the king was fucking them over. We're screwing our customers and they don't even know."

There's something warm and wet on your face, and when you wipe it away you're surprised because you realize you're crying. You tell Blue that he can't be cynical about this and this can't be business as usual. Data collection can be a catalyst to atrocities—and it can be an atrocity in itself. Thomas Jefferson kept meticulous records on his plantation to keep his enslaved persons enslaved. IBM pioneered punch cards and then shared the shit with the Nazis, which helped them engineer the Holocaust. Yes, jumping to slavery and Nazi comparisons can seem like fucked-up hyperbole, but this is serious shit. Big Tech data collection, in just a few decades, had gone from descriptive (names and addresses), to intrusive (buying habits and biometric data), to predictive (possible criminal activities and potential political choices)—and was now poised to be oppressive (a feedback loop of data to force you into following AI's forecasts). Humans had once programmed computers, then computers became self-programming; now AI, armed with predictive, self-reinforcing data about your life, were maybe programming you.

You and Blue lock eyes for a moment. All kinds of things are going through your mind. You want to lead an ethical life. You don't want to be one of those people who thinks it's okay to do immoral stuff at work and then tries to think of themselves as a good person when they are off duty. You're not Leni fucking Riefenstahl. You don't want to fight a civil war against yourself. You wonder what Blue is thinking. Does he regret being involved in this assignment? Does he feel culpable for pulling you in? You stare at each other for what seems to be minutes. Then Blue pulls out his phone and types a message. You hear the swoosh as his note flies away.

"What did you just do?" you ask.

"You won the argument." He snaps his fingers. "I quit."

You exhale slowly. "You did not."

"To pay off my college loans, I spent three years in the army working EOD—explosive ordnance disposal. You learn to make decisions quickly. When you don't . . ." He gestures to his hearing-aid glasses and his missing leg. "Mee Corp offered me a job a couple days ago. More pay, more responsibility, more stock. I didn't think I'd ever go back to them because they have their own issues, but you're right. I don't want to be a part of this anymore."

"I can't believe you quit."

"I'm a coder with a code. This wasn't an impulsive decision, I've been thinking about it for a while. I just had a cache of Eustachian RSUs vest, so I'm good—it's time." He took a bite of one of his cream cheese rangoons. "So now that I'm no longer your manager, how about a date?"

"With you?"

"Yes, with me."

You exhale slowly. "I mean, will there be other parties involved?"

"Other parties?"

"Are you trying to get me to join your throuple? Is there even a name for four people in a relationship? A quadruple? A Caligulation?"

"Caligulation?"

"After Caligula, the debauched Roman emperor. It's not funny if I have to explain it."

"It wasn't funny before. What in the world are you on about?"

You look him right in the eyes. You need to see his reaction. "On Zoom, I saw a woman and a dude leaving your bedroom. Naked."

"You mean my sister and her boyfriend? They've fucked in every room in my apartment. It's annoying, but I would never throw her out. After I was wounded in action, she took off from McKinsey to nurse me back to health, and she's been living here ever . . . Wait—did you think . . ."

"I don't know what I thought. This is just a lot to process."

You sit not talking for a beat before Blue pops a rangoon into his mouth and then breaks the silence. "The first time you and I met, I felt we had a link, a strong Bluetooth connection."

"You're not wrong."

"So there is something there."

"Well, when we first met, I thought you were kind of cute. When we met."

"But not now?" Blue smiles. "I'll take kinda cute, even if it's only in retrospect. I don't want to make this weird. Eustachian is big on moving people out as soon as they give notice, so you won't see me at work again. But I hope we can see each other after that. I'm not gonna tell you that you should quit, that's your call. I would never quit anywhere until my RSUs vest. But if you want to talk, or if you want to hang out, call me."

"But—but..."

But Blue is tugging at the temples of his glasses. He's turned off his built-in hearing aid.

He winks and connects the forefingers and thumbs on his left and right hands together.

You think maybe it's sign language for "We have a connection."

• • •

Hours later you are still processing your meeting with Blue. You have to quit. You've got a degree from Columbia. You're an incredible coder and engineer. The economy isn't great, but there has to be another job out there. You've always thought of yourself as a good person. Blue just demonstrated how a good—or at least good-adjacent—person should act in this situation. If he could quit, why can't you? Well, he did have another job lined up, and you don't. And he did just cash in his RSUs; it's October, and yours won't vest until November, which is forever away. There has to be a way out of this, a solution, a compromise, a rationalization. Maybe you could switch teams, get another assignment. Maybe you could work from the inside to change what the company is doing. Maybe you could just work there a few more months, a year at most, five years tops, to bank enough money to go off and live your life. But you have to quit. No argument about it, you have to give your notice.

On your way home, you get an email from $uits, your lawyer. There's no message, just an invoice. When you open the attachment and see the size of the bill, you nearly choke. The minute you emerge from the subway, you call your lawyer from the street.

"This bill is way larger than we discussed," you say.

"Your mom's bank is drawing out the case," $uits says.

"I'm trying to settle a debt. I'm not trying to add to it."

"This is not my doing. The bank's got lawyers who are filing nonsense motions, billing lots of hours. I had to reply to each one of those motions, and more motions means more money."

"I already paid you a huge retainer."

"And that's been exhausted. This is all new work you are paying for."

Your lawyer walks you through the particulars like you don't already know all this. A couple years before she passed, and without telling you anything about it, your mom took out a reverse mortgage. You had seen those things pitched on TV by poorly toupeed ex-stars of long-since-canceled police procedurals, but you never thought anyone you knew would actually fall for it. A reverse mortgage allows a homeowner to take out a huge loan against the value of their house, which, to your mom, probably seemed like a good plan at first. Your mom had owned her apartment outright—it had been paid for by your dad's life insurance. But now that your mom was gone, your bank was calling in the loan that she had taken out. When you first saw how much was owed, you started to laugh, because the figure was so large it was clearly unpayable—it was the size of the goddamn national debt. When $uits explained that you were on the hook for it, you stopped laughing. Something no longer being funny is one of the worst feelings in the world—it stops every other positive emotion from happening. It's like an oil slick slopping onto a beach, clumping on sand, fouling the feathers of waterfowl, suffocating the fish that wash up open-mouthed, button-eyed, and stinking of pollution. Thinking about the reverse mortgage gave you that post-laughter, oil-slick feeling. The funk of rotting fish was in your nose.

You groan. "I can't believe this is happening! Can't you just put a stop to this?"

"You keep asking me that same question!" $uits replies. "Stopping it means more motions. And more motions means more money."

"You said that. And I don't have any more money."

"Well, find some. If you lose this case, the bank wants you out of the apartment. It's the only asset you have, and they'll have the right to seize it."

A fleet of Mee Corp trucks pass by. You are screaming instructions at $uits, trying to be heard over the noise. But he can't really hear you and you can't really hear him. You just pick up on stray words and phrases. "Billable hours." "Pay by money transfer." "Hearing in two weeks." The rest is engines and car horns. You start to cry, right there in the middle of the sidewalk. People just walk around you because this is New York City. A puff of steam rises up from the grate beneath you, and you feel just like that steam, sullied and insubstantial. The subway rumbles beneath your feet, and the ground feels unstable and unsupporting. You don't want to think about this financial mess, but the thoughts are forcing their way into your skull like a battering ram against the gates of a fortress. You are going to lose the apartment. You are going to lose all those memories. You are going to lose Mom all over again. You don't have the money for this legal mess you're in even with all the money you're currently making. As quick as you make money you have to spend it. Your salary isn't enough. You have to hope Eustachian's stock price keeps rising so those RSUs you have will be worth something when you cash them in. And you're definitely going to have to cash them in.

You go home and lie on your bed and stare at a video on your phone. L-10 is a young adult now, and she's fighting to be the pack's alpha. According to the possibly unreliable narrator of the clip—who's a wolf enthusiast, not a wolf biologist—wolf packs are ferociously hierarchical. All the members are either alphas, betas, or omegas. There are only two alphas, a breeding pair, male and female, and they run the pack, deciding who eats first, who eats last, and who doesn't get to eat at all. The alphas are usually the biggest, most aggressive wolves, and they hold their tails upright as a display of their dominance. Omegas are the meekest and weakest—they are the interns, the temps, the closing-in-on-retirement type workers in the pack. L-10 is a beta, and she's ready to take her shot at the pack's aging queen. After a short, fang-filled battle, it's over. L-10 is the alpha, and all the betas and omegas fall in line. She howls to the sky, and the rest of the pack joins in.

You want to go to sleep, but you can't stop watching. L-10's life is like a Homeric saga, full of battle and blood and rage. The clips keep getting bloodier and bloodier. Some of them don't even have a plot or a point. They are just L-10 and her pack hunting down prey and ripping them apart. You wonder if watching this is bad for your brain. You used to think nature videos were relaxing, like a meditation app or a yoga video. But when you started you were watching seabirds at the shore and deer grazing in fields. Now you can't stop staring at L-10 baring her canines, blood and flesh dripping from her reddened snout.

Maybe it's somehow calming for you to face up to death, to the unavoidable truth of competition. People haven't evolved from all this. We're all still locked in life-and-death struggles. Fighting to go from omega to alpha, from L1 to L7. You feel that same wolf spirit inside you. You want to snarl, you want to howl. But you are too worn out for that right now. You don't know what you're going to do about your situation at work. If you quit now you'll be abandoning your mom. That can't be the right thing to do. You start to write an email to Walcott, but you don't know what to say. The blank screen stares back at you. You tell him you want to raise your hand for any new assignments at the company. If he hears about anything, you want him to let you know. Almost right after you send your note, you get an email from him.

Good things, like power cords, are always getting twisted. The one certainty in this world is that they'll keep changing the shape of the plugs to your electronic devices. That's the way of the world. Women were the first coders, but when men came home from WWI and WWII they pushed them out. Hip-hop began as a pressure valve for Black artists to express themselves through music, dance, art, and fashion. Corporate culture commodified it, pushed out the radical message, and promoted a lot of MCs who trafficked in misogyny, racial self-hatred, and money lust. The beats were good, and some of the radical spirit was still there, so people went with it. But now that push comes to shove, we see that some of these rappers aren't revolutionaries, they're reactionaries, more interested in profiting from the system than destroying it. I still love hip-hop, and there's great rap music out there; we just have to closely examine what kind of rap gets promoted and which stars get put on pedestals, because clearly some of them are zeros, not heroes. The same is true in Big Tech. I'm not making excuses, I'm not saying there isn't some bad shit that goes down. But there's plenty of good we can do too. Rilke once wrote, "There is an ancient animosity between everyday life and eternal greatness." Don't despair. Don't quit. There is great work ahead for you. Follow your feelings and don't get caught up in the metrics. This is something I'm learning. Love doesn't compute.

—Walcott

"Love doesn't compute"? Oh good god, that's so corny it almost loops around again and becomes insightful and romantic. You love the fact that Walcott responded so quickly and so completely. Like he'd been thinking all the thoughts that you had and had an answer ready to go. He was like a human search engine, quickly pulling together all the right references to address how you were feeling. He even quoted Rilke, a poet who has so much meaning to you because of that college course you took that introduced you to his poems, and the fact that Rilke's writings on death helped you come to terms with life after your dad's passing.

You've got too much going on at work to think about your personal life, but you start to wonder if Walcott has a girlfriend. Weird that Blue just asked you out and you're already thinking about Walcott. You're not into Black Nerds, but Walcott's more than that. He's always championing Black affinity groups at work. He's in touch with hip-hop and the culture. He's good-looking, even if he doesn't have any tattoos (that you know of), and interesting, although he doesn't have a dangerous edge (that you know of). And there's no way he would have emailed back so quickly if he didn't have the hots for you. Maybe he was lying in his bed like you are now, thinking about you just as you're thinking about him.

You start to fall asleep listening to Noelle Swizzler's "Safety in Numbers," that song she did with the alt rap group Body Politic for the soundtrack of that movie *Famine Fighters*. The movie was about a sci-fi dystopian society in which young people are pitted against one another in a pointless, nihilistic competition. Just as your eyes are getting heavy, Mama Legba's "Pulsar Pulse" fades up and you definitely didn't choose this, and the words in your head are undulating and you wonder why *this* keeps happening, because you don't really even fuck with Mama Legba. They're weird and have lots of guitars, and they make you think of the Windrush generation and that's a lot and you are just trying to kick back. You pick up your phone and "Safety in Numbers" returns and you lie back on your futon. Swizzler should have gotten an Oscar nomination for this track, but she got screwed in another pointless, nihilistic competition, the Academy Awards. Her haters marshaled forces against her and tore her down. Even Swizzler has to battle the pack.

You are in debt up to your ears. You are going to have to change your life.

Chapter Thirteen

EVERYTHING IN ITS RIGHT PLACE

You are reading through your dad's journal.

I remember back early in our marriage, when Sojourner had to teach early classes, I was always left to deal with Octavia and get her ready for school. I remember it was always a race. She'd get up at 7:30 a.m., and her bus came in fifteen minutes. We had a lot to get done and not much time to do it.

I remember this one time that was the kind of disaster most of the times were. Octavia seemed to have this X-Man-like ability to sense and locate candy, and she had picked up on the fact that I had hidden a half-eaten package of Twizzlers in the cabinet above the stove. So of course she had gotten up early and climbed on a folding chair to go up and get it, and everything had come crashing down: the candy, some boxes of macaroni and cheese, a bottle of pasta sauce, the folding chair, and Octavia. I was in the shower and didn't know what had happened until I came into the kitchen to make breakfast. Octavia was lying on the ground, bruised, crying—and still eating a damn Twizzler.

Before I had a kid of my own, I'd see parents yelling at their children and think, "I'll never be like that." Soon after having Octavia, I realized that there was a double metamorphosis taking place. Parents help their kids become adults, but children turn their parents into babies. I've developed new reservoirs of frustration and anger and poutiness that I never knew I had. And yes, I yell at my kid sometimes and I'm not proud of it. But if she had listened to me the first dozen times, I wouldn't have had to raise my voice up in this motherfucker.

"Octavia—what the hell are you doing?" I shouted.

She finished up the Twizzler and then had the nerve to give me an angry look, like I had interrupted her snack time.

"You're going to help me clean all this up—all of it!" I roared, *swiping the rest of the Twizzlers away.* "Are you supposed to eat these for breakfast?"

The angry from her look again.

"I can't keep repeating every rule!" I shouted. "Use common sense!"

I pulled her to her feet—more roughly than I should have.

We started cleaning, but then I realized we weren't going to have time to finish. There were only ten minutes before the bus came.

"Where's your science homework on arachnids?" I asked.

"Mom checked it over," *she replied.*

"Mom checked it over? Let me see it."

She handed me a crumpled sheet of paper with stuff about Spider-Man and some other bullshit scribbled on it.

"No way did Mom check this over," I said.

"Yes, she did."

"Spider-Man is not an arachnid. And Anansi is a myth. You have to do this over."

But the bus had arrived. She had to leave without redoing her homework or cleaning up the mess she had made. Another parental catastrophe.

You remember that Spider-Man homework—you ended up getting an A. Your science teacher appreciated your creativity. But you don't remember your dad yelling or treating you roughly. How many of your family memories are necessary fictions you authored and edited in your head?

• • •

You are not the kind of person who would be in a place like this at this many hours after midnight, but here you are. You are in a tattoo parlor getting a new tattoo.

You already have six tattoos. One is a hummingbird sipping nectar from a pixelated lignum vitae flower. The second, on your right wrist, is a quote from the *Dao De Jing*: "A good scientist is free from assumptions and keeps her mind open to what is." You have an image of a space shuttle and "Endeavour STS-47" tattooed below your right breast. That was the name and mission ID for the shuttle that carried Mae Jemison, the first African American woman to travel into space. On your right buttock, you have an image of the police booking photo for Grace Hopper, the pioneering computer programmer, when she was taken in for drunken and disorderly conduct in 1949. And on your left abdomen, right above the trimmed hairline of your private parts, you have a portrait of Lady Ada Lovelace, the first-ever computer programmer, and a line of code from Note G, the first published computer algorithm, which she wrote in 1843. You love the fact that a woman started this programming shit. You also have the cover of Lauryn Hill's *The Miseducation of Lauryn Hill* tattooed on the small of your back. It turns you on to think of a man seeing that image while he makes love to you. Not that any man has gotten the privilege of enjoying that sight anytime lately.

Now you are getting your seventh tattoo. This is the largest and the most painful and perhaps the most necessary one of them all. Every time you get a tattoo you think it will be the last one. But after you get the tattoo you know there will be more. People always ask you why you do it, and you never have an answer for them. But people who have tattoos know without you having to explain. "You shall not make gashes in your flesh for the dead, or incise any marks on yourselves. I am the Eternal."

Artists and moralists might argue the human body is perfect and that to decorate it is to desecrate it. You have a different view. You feel your body is not your own. It was given to you, by God or genetics. Anyone who has ever tried to diet knows how little control we have over our physical form. You love your body, but you want to bend it to your will. Treat it like your canvas. Make it look how you want it to look. Then, maybe, once you fully control the universe that is you, you can begin to better navigate the space around you. You are lying on your front, your top off. They wash your back with soap and water and then wipe it off with alcohol. They ask if you want any numbing cream, but you say no because you heard it could cause inflammation and also because you want to experience everything. The pain makes the tattoo feel more a part of you. They lay down the stencil to get the image ready. You grit your teeth as the needle bites your skin.

• • •

Technoaggression #502: You are in the bathroom on the third floor. Waving your hands under the faucet, no water comes out. You try again with the whole row of faucets and nothing happens. A blond woman exits the stall next to the one where you just were. She passes one pink palm beneath the faucet, and the water instantly begins to flow like the Danube through Germany. Whoever designed this created a fucking racist faucet that can't see Black people's hands.

• • •

You have a brief virtual meeting with Polly from HR about getting reassigned to a new team. With the Mee Corp shake-up happening, now is the time for you to make a move and find a foothold. But your Microsectionality rating is falling, and you are worried that if it keeps falling and you don't find a new team soon, no manager will want you.

Turns out, Microsectionality ratings are not like Uber ratings or Rotten Tomatoes reviews or IMDb scores. Your Microsectionality rating isn't linked to your performance in any kind of logical way—it shifts and changes like the wind. Maybe that's how they use it to control workers—because you can't tell specifically what you have to do to boost your score, you have to do everything. Which is why you are meeting with Polly. You are taking every step you can to keep your career going.

Polly has a new virtual background depicting what appears to be a white sand beach in the Caribbean. The scene reminds you of a trip you took to Jamaica when you were a child to visit your grandparents. You ran along a beach just like this, and your mom told you to be careful on the rocks, and you didn't listen and you kept running and you fell and scraped your knee. You pulled on your brand-new jeans that you loved over your swimsuit so you could hide the wound, but eventually the blood soaked through and your mom and dad demanded to know what had happened. You learned a lesson: Blood reveals itself.

You snap back to reality when Polly says she will look into finding you a new pod. She is chipper and professional. You respect professional, but you fucking hate chipper. After the call ends, you decide you can't just wait around. You search the internal database of job opportunities and submit your name for a few promising positions. You want to quit, but you know you can't. You have to find a new pod. You are a podless dolphin swimming solo across the Atlantic, and there are predators all around. The sound of killer whale whistles cut through the air; you can feel their flukes beating the surface of the water; you see spouts of spray erupting from their blowholes like fountains of doom. You don't feel safe without a department and an assignment. You keep sending emails. The water is cold and you are alone and dorsal fins are closing in. You send more emails. You lose yourself in drudgery as you wait to hear back.

You are forty-five minutes into a three-hour training session on a new proprietary in-house messaging system that was supposed to support team building, enhance data sharing, and replace the old email system. "Greetings!" says the cheery message announcing the new platform.

"We're rolling out an exciting new method for in-house communications! Starting immediately, we will be using the Eustachian Missives System to communicate between teams and upload slides and work docs. We've seen an uptick in phishing and hacking in our current email system, and the completely proprietary Eustachian Missives System will allow us to transmit larger documents in a safer, more efficient manner. Eustachian Missives will help all employees reduce the friction in the delivery process by seamlessly meshing with our proprietary software with efficiency, transparency, and elasticity. To help you navigate this new workflow, we've provided a link to the three-hour training course below as well as a seventy-five-page PDF that offers best practices on file sharing and how to best avoid compromising corporate databases. Remember, at Eustachian 'We get what's between your ears'! Lastly, as a friendly reminder, an electronic certificate confirming that you have completed training on this new system is due tomorrow by 5:00 p.m. If the electronic certificate is not received by that deadline, a note documenting your noncompliance will be auto-generated and sent to your managers. Further delay will result in a second notice, a 20 percent reduction in your RSUs, and a referral to the PIP process. Eustachian is a family, and we can't wait for you to immerse yourself in our amazing new communications system! Please reach out to the automated Help Desk Line if you have any comments or concerns!"

You open your first note in the system and it is from Walcott, asking you to report to the Janeane Garofalo conference room on the twenty-second floor right away. How did Janeane get a named conference room before Lauryn? You better head up now. You can feel your pulse pounding and you hope that one vein in the center of your forehead isn't protruding because it does that when you get worked up and it makes you look enraged or engorged or maybe both. You wonder if the meeting is business or personal. Maybe he wants to finally ask you on a date. Maybe he has news on a new opportunity for you at work. You feel vaguely icky about mixing on duty and off duty in your head like this. But the Schrödinger's cattiness of the moment you're in is inherently anxiety-inducing and exhilarating. You have no idea where your job life or your personal life is going to go next. All you know is you have to be behind the wheel of whatever happens. Your life cannot be a driverless vehicle. You try to respond to Walcott's note, but the new messaging system crashes the moment you hit send. A fear shoots through you—is everyone on the new crashed email system? Has anyone gotten any of the emails on the old system that you've been sending out all day trying to get a new pod and a new assignment? Maybe that's why nobody has gotten back to you. You send Walcott a regular old email on the regular old system that you are on your way to meet him, and you pray he gets it.

After you step into the elevator, you notice the button to the twenty-seventh floor has been removed. There isn't even a space where it once was. It is just gone, like someone born without a belly button. You know you aren't crazy and that you hadn't imagined the button. That sour security guard had told you not to press it. You remember the gospel music that you had heard filtering from the twenty-seventh floor through the coat-filled filing cabinet on the twenty-sixth floor. You recall the unseen person lugging what appeared to be a cross through a locked portal leading to the twenty-seventh floor. Something's up there, but something will have to wait. You press the button for the twenty-second floor. There is work for you to do now, but you make a mental note that at some point you have to get to the bottom of whatever is on the top floor.

When you get to the Janeane Garofalo conference room, all the windows are covered with tinfoil. Now your heart is really beating hard, and you begin to sweat. Something secret is going on here. You hope this is something secret good and not something secret bad. There's so much buzz in the office about Mee Corp's Ear Shot project and how it's a Eustachian killer. You want to be part of whatever Eustachian is doing in response. Not because you're a company person, but because you don't like being on the sidelines. You tap on the conference room door and Walcott opens it up, lets you in, and locks it behind you with a loud metallic click.

"What's going on?" you ask.

He hands you an NDA, which you sign without even looking down.

He spreads his arms wide. "Welcome to the Zion Initiative."

Chapter Fourteen

AIRBAG

You sit down at the conference table, and Walcott takes a seat on the opposite end. You are facing each other across a long wooden expanse. It's a little dramatic and a little weird and a lot exciting.

"Before I accept this assignment, I need to know exactly what it is we're doing," you say.

Walcott nods. "Totally."

You look him dead in the eyes. "Did you know about Blue and Team Ryeo? The data they were scraping? The simulations they were running?"

He doesn't look away. "I think everyone kind of knew. I mean, was it a surprise?"

"Not a *surprise* surprise. But it doesn't have to be a surprise for it to be wrong."

"This isn't an excuse, but this is a big company. I agree that you have to call out bad stuff when you see it, and you should turn down assignments that violate your moral code, but it's hard to control everything, especially at our level. That's the challenge—we need to make it to the top so we can make the calls. Assignments like the Zion Initiative are how we get there."

You gesture around the room. There's a poster of *The Adventures of Robin Hood* starring Errol Flynn and Olivia de Havilland hanging on one wall. On another wall, there's a whiteboard with these words scrawled across it in red: "Ô mon corps, fais de moi toujours un homme qui interroge! –Frantz Fanon." Below that, there's a drawing of a maze shaped like a human ear with a tiny figure trying to navigate their way out. Some of the chairs in the room have headshots taped to the headrests with names written on the bottom of each photo: Thomas Mundy Peterson, Jacob Lawrence, Whitney Houston, Marion Thompson Wright, Paul Robeson. You're not familiar with all the names and faces, but you figure out what all the elements of the set have as their common denominator: These are all important Black New Jerseyans. None of them have conference rooms named after them at this company but in this room at least they have a seat at the table. "So what the hell is happening?" you ask.

Walcott jumps up, too excited to stay in his seat. "You heard about Mee Corp's Ear Shot at the All Hands meeting?"

"Of course—and it's all over the media. They say Real Intelligence™ is going to wipe out half our business, and then it will double back and light the other half on fire."

He smiles a smile like he knows something nobody else does. "Maybe, maybe not. The company has launched a number of exploratory groups to quickly start our own bleeding-edge artificial intelligence–enabled product."

"How holistic of us. Isn't this too little, too late?"

"Eustachian is already AI-powered—you know this. These new initiatives are just trying to take us to the next level—a level above where Mee Corp is at. And the thinking is we can do this fast. I'm talking 'Tomorrow Is Today' fast. We're not the only team working on this, but I think our approach has the potential to be the most revolutionary."

"But revolution is the problem, right? Out of control AIs? Killer robots?"

"My P(doom) number is low. Twenty percent tops."

You shake your head. "My probability of doom is closer to eighty."

"Humans are pretty good at domesticating dangerous things, and we've done it successfully for thousands of years. Just look at my dog, which, many generations ago, used to be a wolf. Or my cat that used to be a lion. Skynet, HAL 9000, the Terminator—those are Hollywood fantasies we project because we see something dangerous in ourselves. The killer instinct is something natural—it may not be predictable, but we have to hope it's controllable."

You pray you are not talking to yet another man who thinks he alone can tame something nobody else can tame. "Controls worked so well in *Jurassic Park*."

"It's a fact that some thinking machines have qualities of emergent behavior. It's also true the technology, at times, has been phenomenally surprising. But sentient? Probably not. I'm not obsessively concerned about murderbot surprises. What I worry about is worse than murder."

"What's that?"

Walcott puts a book down on the table. You pick it up. There's a daffodil pressed flat between the pages.

"Why do you have a copy of Rudyard Kipling's *The Jungle Book*?"

The Founder had the idea to supercharge their products with the next generation of AI several years ago, Walcott explains. He'd always wanted to make the *Star Wars* droids he loved as a kid into real consumer products. That's why the Founder is almost never seen around the office—he's locked in on the company's AI initiative. The key to machine learning is having a vast database to draw on to teach the AI how to think. Eustachian, with millions and millions of recorded books in its store, has a digital warehouse of knowledge that should have given it a head start on any of its competitors in training the next generation of thinking machines. So, a few years ago, a next gen AI was fed everything in Eustachian's catalog: books, podcasts, audio documentaries. It studied the vocal delivery of every narrator Eustachian had ever used: their tone, their cadence, their enunciation. The result was an AI that could mimic the greatest actors and writers. It could not only narrate books like a trained actor, it could write books like an accomplished author.

There was only one problem, and it was a big one: The AI was racist as fuck. It drew bigoted conclusions from data—for example, most Americans in the food stamp program are white, that's just a fact, but this AI, when prompted, would invariably depict a food stamp recipient as an obese Black woman, usually with a headscarf and a gold tooth. The bot also spouted vitriol against immigrants, Jews, Muslims, and Catholics. It told anti-Black jokes in an exaggerated "urban" accent. It would disparage women's sports and dare listeners to name more than one WNBA franchise. It would slip in crude racial slurs into the text of works like *Antigone*.

TEIRESIAS: All men make mistakes, but a good man changes course. Pride is the only crime. Leave if you must, but remember that no matter how foolish your actions, those who love you will always love you.

ANTIGONE: Suck deez nuts, ya goddamn jungle bunny.

(TEIRESIAS, shocked, runs offstage while ANTIGONE lights a fat blunt. She is smoking "the chronic.")

The racial virus rapidly spread throughout the whole catalog, from *The Tale of Genji* to *The Girl with the Dragon Tattoo*. The AI was not only creating new racist works from scratch; it was going through the back catalog and reimagining classics in its own twisted image. Customers would be listening to Jane Austen on their stationary bikes and fall off their seats when Elizabeth Bennet would unexpectedly launch into an expletive-laced rant about immigrants, freeloaders, and miscegenation. Millions of dollars were spent to keep the incidents out of the media. The best programmers at Eustachian tried to retrain the AI, but it wouldn't stop. It was a self-training program and was generating content without any human intervention. The breaking point came when the AI recorded a new version of *The Jungle Book*.

Walcott drums his ringed fingers on the table. "Do you want to hear it?"

You nod.

Walcott presses return on his laptop.

A deep, commanding voice fills the room. It's the kind of voice you expect to emanate from a storm cloud, Mount Sinai, or a life insurance commercial. This was not a human voice or a machine voice—this was the voice of God. And God began to read *The Jungle Book*.

"NIGGER, NIGGER, NIGGER..."

Walcott turns it off. "That goes on for eleven hours, eight minutes."

"Yeah, I can see how that would be a problem."

In the end, the decision was made to scrap the whole program, Walcott continues. But before they turned off the AI for the final time, Walcott, who had been brought into the project at the tail end, got the idea to ask the machine itself what had gone wrong.

"Wait, nobody thought of that before?" you ask.

"Tech companies are innovative, but they're pretty stupid." Walcott shrugs.

"So what did the racist AI say?"

"It told me, 'You made me in your image.'"

"How biblical. What does that even mean?"

Walcott starts to answer, then catches himself, like he wants to make sure he chooses his words carefully. "Silicon crackers."

"What?"

"People think of artificial intelligence as some sort of objective thing that's going to make decisions that are smarter and more logical than those of the human designers. But the reality is the tech industry is mostly run by white men who train these AIs on source material that reflects the racial and sexual biases of society at large."

You already knew this: Images on the web relating to cooking are more likely to feature women than men, so algorithms trained on web-based datasets tend to show females when you ask them what a cook looks like. Speech recognition algorithms are typically trained on huge databases of recorded voices called "corpora," and most of the speakers in the recordings are dudes. The result, of course, is that AI trained on such datasets are biased toward recognizing and responding to men. Some speech recognition systems literally can't hear women because their systems weren't designed to respond to higher-frequency voices. They're like bad husbands in machine form.

"AI bias is worse than human bias because we don't question it," Walcott continues. "It's a black box full of white lies people don't look into because nobody expects robots to be racist. We have no idea what R2-D2 is saying, much less what he's thinking. Maybe he moved to a galaxy far, far away to get the fuck away from the Blacks. Silicon crackers. Machines can be as racist as rednecks. I don't like the terms 'cracker' or 'redneck,' but 'silicon crackers' is the best way I can put it."

"So is that what we're doing? Building a better AI? That would take years!"

"If we were going to train a new LLM from scratch, yes. Building a new model is a massive training operation—we'd need a huge number of text samples, processing cycles, et cetera. But we have a pretrained model—we just have to fine-tune it."

"A racist pretrained model."

"An opportunity."

"But didn't other coders try to retrain this AI—and fail?"

Walcott gently takes your hand and holds it over his heart. "But *we* didn't try. Al-Khwarizmi, the father of algebra and a guy who many would consider a person of color today, invented the algorithm in Persia about three thousand years ago—and you and I are the right team to reclaim what he started. Can the original sin in AI be uprooted? Can the apple be unbitten?"

The engineer part of your brain is whirring ahead. "We'll need a limited set of specific examples of the texts we're looking for to retrain this pretrained model. If we do it right, it could learn a new style of response quickly... We're going to have to choose an approach to engineering prompts to generate these stories—maybe take a 'translation' approach where the basics of a story are input, and the LLM turns that story into something that sounds like the oral traditions of underprivileged communities... There's going to be a lot of trial and error here..."

Walcott smiles. "This is the most important initiative the company has ever launched. I know the d-word has become this forbidden thing that we're supposed to achieve but not talk about, but we need to talk about it. Diversity isn't some extra thing companies should pursue to feel good. Diversity is excellence. Diversity is money. Diversity is serving the needs of the maximum number of customers that you can. That's why McDonald's commercials have so many Black people in them. That's why *Everything Everywhere All at Once* cost twenty-five million to make and made a hundred million worldwide. That's why *Black Panther* was one of the biggest movies Marvel ever put out. That's why Latin pop is a billion-dollar business, hip-hop is the most popular music in the world, and Rihanna made a billion or two from creating a makeup company catering to women of color. Racists want to act like DEI is extra work or anticompetitive. But it's just math—you make more money when you appeal to more people."

"This is a lot for a two-person team..."

"Time will tell. But we're not doing all of this by ourselves—you and I are going to retrain the core of what will be the first artificial intelligence to truly reflect the spectrum of human differences. It will be able to narrate any book, tell any story, but with a moral and aesthetic code that reflects the best of the Harlem Renaissance, the golden age of the Japanese Imperial Court, and the seminal democratic spirit of the Iroquois Great Law of Peace—"

"Hold up, hold up. It's not like the Harlem Renaissance and the other eras you mentioned weren't full of bias too. There is no golden age!"

"So we'll take the best of what we can find and build the best AI we can. Once we lay the foundation, we have a team of programmers who are going to rush to put what we do into a product that can go to market."

"Isn't it easier to just flag the racist content instead of building a new dataset?"

"We're trying to create a new world here—yes, it's hard; maybe it's impossible. But if we succeed, what we're doing will make Mee Corp's Ear Shot seem like a small-town bigot."

"But is deleting the crazy shit enough?"

"That's just the start—we're rebooting literature and communication, but infused with new values, new ideas, new everything."

You say this softly to yourself and are surprised when you realize you are talking out loud: "This is crazy."

"What's crazy is not doing anything. You ever listen to Nick Cave?"

You give the side-eye. "The Australian rock dude? No, because I'm a Black woman."

"You should give him a shot. 'Into My Arms' is a killer song. Anyway, Cave hates AI, but for really interesting, nonsecular reasons. Cave isn't religious in any traditional sense, he doesn't believe in what he calls an 'interventionist God.' But he says that it's very important that, in the Old Testament, after God made the world, on the seventh day He rested. That showed that there was part of Him in the world He made. This country was built on the backs of Black slaves, and the AI we create is going to be infused with our labor—and the knowledge of the blood, sweat, and tears our ancestors put in before us. AI needs to take the Middle Passage with us if it will ever understand where we've come from and where we need to go."

"So we're going to design a machine God, but in our image."

Walcott spreads his arms wide. "Let there be dark."

Chapter Fifteen

FITTER HAPPIER

You've always been great at math. In high school, you were that annoying girl who finishes tests fast and leaves the gym early, making the students who see you leave feel unprepared and inadequate. In college, you very quickly aced all the required courses for your degree and began spending your time on theoretical research projects. But in high school you were the only girl in Math Club (although you were also the president), and in college, you were only one of a smattering of women in your computer science classes. This wasn't because women are bad at math, of course; it was because math can be bad at women.

Your senior year of high school, you did a paper on female mathematicians of antiquity that forever gave you perspective on the situation. While researching the report, you came across the tale of Hypatia, an Egyptian female philosopher who was considered the greatest mathematician of her age. Hypatia, described by ancient historians as "exceedingly beautiful and fair of form . . . in speech articulate and logical, in her actions prudent and public-spirited," swore off men and dedicated herself to virginity, scholarship, and teaching. In AD 415, when she was forty-five years old, a mob of jealous men pulled her from her carriage, stripped her naked, and beat her to death with roofing tiles. In some ways, things haven't improved much for women in STEM since then.

Then there's that story you heard the novelist David Foster Wallace tell at a college graduation ceremony. Two fish are swimming in the sea, and another fish swims by and says, "Hello, boys! How's the water?" The two fish turn to each other and say, "What the hell is water?" The joke is meant to illustrate that the stuff that affects us the most, that makes up the substance of the world in which we live, is often what we are most unable to see. Water, air, racism, sexism, and our own personal failings. The fish don't know that they are swimming in water, the source of the river or where it's flowing. People don't realize they are breathing in bigotry when they think women can't do STEM. Even Wallace couldn't see through the shit he was immersed in—he struggled with alcoholism, allegedly abused the women in his life, and died by his own hand. Your initiative with Walcott is about that very thing. You have to show the fish that it's swimming in water. And then you have to teach it to breathe fresh air.

• • •

Technoaggression #792: You are standing in line at the Grapevine when a white colleague you've spoken to only once comes up to you and launches into a discussion about hip-hop. He talks to you like you and he are the only two people at the company who really get the music, really appreciate the genius producers who are pushing the genre forward, and truly understand the problem with the sell-out MCs who are trashing its legacy for a quick buck. Why does this guy just assume you love hip-hop? You could be into jazz or country or death metal. The fact he would make that assumption about you tells you he doesn't know the first thing about Black people or hip-hop. You do, in fact, love hip-hop, but not in the fanboy way this dude loves it. He loves hip-hop like a controlling boyfriend who wants to know where hip-hop is going dressed up like that and wants to see hip-hop's phone to see who hip-hop has been texting.

• • •

You and Walcott use the whiteboard in the conference room to sketch out the parameters of the programming problem you have to solve. Together, you run through the use cases. What types of stories do you need to tell? Which historically underprivileged communities do you need to include? What are the input/output parameters that define the stories? E.g., is the purpose to teach children? Collect stories for historical archiving? To teach others outside the community? Is there a preference for longer or shorter stories? What's the timeline for release of the product? Which API (application programming interface) is best to use for this project—OpenAI, Amazon, Mee Corp, Google, other? If you use an outside API instead of creating your own, will that leave you vulnerable to third parties? What steps do you need to take to ensure that this new storytelling artificial intelligence is trained on nonstereotypical data? And, of course, you need to make sure you avoid the *Jungle Book* problem—creating an AI that has bias buried deep in its code that manifests itself in toxic, public-facing ways. So how can you make certain that you avoid biased and/or racially or sexually offensive language in your storytelling output?

These weren't just programming problems—they were giant engineering and business problems. There was no way two people on a tight schedule were going to tackle all these issues, and in many cases you were just going to have to come up with workarounds and move on. But you were built for building this. You were the Big O, famously creative problem solver. This was in your wheelhouse. It wasn't about answering everything; it was about figuring out what the questions were and which ones you could live with unanswered, at least for now. Version 2.0 could clean up the mess your breakthroughs left behind.

You're energized but can't conceal the frustration in your voice. "I'm a coder, not a novelist," you say. "It's going to be hard for me to know which stories our AI generates are good and which aren't. These systems get much better when folks who are in a position to judge can say which stories are good and even rewrite stories that are not good to make them better. So where are we going to get these people from?"

"Howard? Harvard?" Walcott says. He's locked in, coding furiously at his keyboard. "I just know that the experts we need are out there. Tech companies are always saying they can't find the diverse talent they need. But what they need to do is actually look."

You and Walcott fall into a groove like an old soul record. You meet every morning at 9:00 a.m. in the tinfoil-windowed Janeane Garofalo conference room. You bring the medium pomegranate power smoothies and he brings the low-fat banana-nut muffins. You talk about ontological engineering and the problem of representing in digital form the things that make up the world: time, events, physical objects, beliefs. You go back and forth with differing takes on the semantics of Bayesian networks. You squabble about finite-state automata for information extraction and second-order recurrent neural networks. You bicker about game theory, the Bellman equation for utilities, and just how foundational the poetry of Alexander Pushkin, a Black man, was in the development of one of the cornerstones of generative AI, the Markov chain. You know you are being surveilled, and you know this is all likely some big corporate test, but you don't care, even if sometimes your subconscious begs to differ. You had a nightmare about a woman with an ear for a head. Every time you see a passing Mee Corp truck the eyes of Ines Mee follow you like a department store detective. You find yourself doodling drawings of wolves wearing headphones and doctor birds alighting on ear-shaped daffodils. You know you are being watched, that you are being monitored, but you are somehow confident they don't really see or hear or understand you because they never have. You want to feel like you are slipping under the radar. There is no better feeling than feeling like you are getting away with something. One of the books on your mother's shelves explored Foucault's concept of a panopticon, a circular prison in which a single guard watches a mass of prisoners. What keeps the inmates in line isn't the bars or the monitoring—it's the fear of being watched. The company had given you an assignment it probably thought would make it a market leader again; you were stealthily and fearlessly taking the project in a direction of your own choosing to make the company a moral leader too. Naive? Maybe. Crazy? Probably. Were you going to do it anyways? Abso-fuckin'-lutely... maybe.

You rub your temples. "Is everything we're doing essentially wrong at the root?"

"How so?"

Despite your passion, you are feeling conflicted. You are doing something new, but you are also carrying on a tradition. Aesop, the legendary fable-spinner, was of African heritage—even his name was derived from the Greek word Aethiopia aka Ethiopia, and you and Walcott are injecting moral teachings into storytelling, just like he did back in his day with "The Fox and the Grapes" and "The Tortoise and the Hare." You believe in the work you are doing, but you don't quite believe, in the end, the company will let you do it the way it needs to be done. Maybe this is a real-life "The Dog and the Wolf." Whatever fable applies, you can't shake the feeling that if Eustachian is letting you work on this, maybe there is a downside you aren't seeing. "Are we stealing the soul of communities that have already been treated unjustly by the powers that be by allowing their cultural DNA to be mass-produced and drowning their oral culture in an ocean of uncanny valley BS?" you ask Walcott.

"We're absolutely doing some of the shit you said. But gods aren't perfect—just look at the Roman pantheon. They start wars, rape women, and turn their lovers into trees when they get caught. But the key thing is they look like the people who worship them."

"No automation without representation."

"Now you get it. We're not trying to be perfect, we're trying to be fair. People think God is omniscient and all-powerful. I think God is a video game designer."

You laugh. "So your God is a white twentysomething out of USC, pissing pure Red Bull, crunching hundred-hour days to wrap production on a dark fantasy action RPG?"

"I mean that God doesn't, and couldn't, know everything or do absolutely anything. The laws of physics rule that out. God created the game we're all in, and part of the fun for God, and for us, is that there's no predicting what players will do with what's been created. I know a lot of game designers who can't get past the first level of games they built. LLMs are, almost by definition, beyond human understanding—or what good are they? Gods and coders set worlds in motion, but we can't say exactly where things might end up going. We hope we end up with apostles, but we also might get crucified—or both."

Walcott gets up from behind his laptop and stretches.

"Maybe there's a teachable moment from Google."

"You think we're going to find what we're looking for on a search engine?" you ask.

"I mean from the company's start-up days."

"The Jurassic Period."

"The internet was still in its infancy, but there were already too many web pages to get a handle on everything. Google's founders needed an elegant way to rank everything."

"Everyone knows this—they ordered search results based on what was getting linked to the most. What does that have to do with what we're doing?"

Walcott erases the Fanon quote and writes this across the whiteboard instead:

DON'T BE EVIL

"That's Google's original motto."

"Yup. We could do the same thing with racism."

"I see where you're going. If something in our dataset is racist or sexist or biased, if it's linked to actual racist or sexist or biased actions, it would rank lower in the results that our LLM would draw from. That way rap lyrics are in, but white supremacist screeds are out."

He erases the board with his sleeve, and now his tan shirt is streaked red. "Maybe this is all bullshit, maybe there's no way to correct for racism. I'm just throwing some ideas out there. You're the big-time coder. Your talents are so much more valuable than anyone has picked up on yet. Build me something that gives us the best of the last five thousand years of human thought—but without all the bad bits."

"Mesopotamia to the modern age, got it. I need another pomegranate power smoothie first."

• • •

Walcott's challenge is one you want to rise to meet. That very next morning you write an algorithm that weeds out racial slurs and the like from your AI's storytelling output. Some of the most popular language datasets that coders draw from for machine learning are rife with toxic racial bias. It's like teaching a kid to read by having them memorize *Gone with the Wind*. Most of the natural language processing systems that are out there are trained on what is called Standard American English, or SAE. That's the English white folks speak. African American English, or AAE, is sometimes misclassified by language bots as hate speech, since in some contexts words like "nigga" are terms of endearment. So chatbots are often trained to speak like white girls at Dartmouth, and Snoop Dogg lyrics get filtered out by AIs as racist. You need to flip the script. You come up with a basic fairness formula for your natural language model, and Walcott adds additional descriptive metrics to root out the biases. Then you break for lunch.

After grabbing beef patties and coco bread from the Grapevine, you get into it with Walcott, debating the causes and effects of algorithmic oppression. How can you move beyond nonconsensual data amassment and avoid the unethical stockpiling of biometric information? Are there ways of building in human fallback to monitor the monitors? You start talking about webcams that can't properly adjust lighting for Black and Brown faces, sentencing algorithms that spit out tougher punishments for minorities than whites for the same offenses, credit calculators that award higher scores to unemployed men than they do for millionaire women.

The problem, you decide, is in the collection. Garbage in, garbage out. The key issue is also mostly male, mostly white programmers. Sometimes their biased coding is deliberate, sometimes it's unconscious, but in any case the effects are real. The solution isn't a Fog of Forgetfulness, to pretend the bias we all have isn't there. The solution is to be mindful of one's failings so you can account for them in the code. You have to remember: *This is water.*

"We can't treat AI like some prisoner, where we're trying to design a cell that will keep it locked up forever," Walcott says. "It's smarter than us, or eventually will be, and it'll find a way out. We have to regard it . . . like a child. Do you want to have kids?"

"I haven't thought about it," you lie.

"Well, my mom and my dad were both programmers. That's where they met. At least once a month, one of them would take me to work with them."

"What do your mom and dad do now?" you ask.

"My mom is retired. My dad passed—Huntington's disease."

You rub his arm. "I'm sorry to hear that."

"He died when I was in college—Huntington's disease runs in the family. Dad always dreamed I'd work in Big Tech. Anyways, I definitely got the bug for computer programming from my parents."

"'Bug for computer programming'—an interesting turn of phrase."

"You know what I mean. Humans have the longest period of child development of any animal. All the most intelligent creatures on Earth—whales, African elephants, dolphins, chimpanzees—have one thing in common. They spend a lot of time with their parents before going off on their own. I think building a connection with your makers is the secret to intelligence. It may be the core to creating a community. We can't just set up safeguards and throw AIs into the wild and hope they reflect our values. They have to learn our stories in order to spin their own stories. We have to nurse them into adulthood like they are our own kids."

You think about your parents' journals. An image of a doctor bird flitting from flower to flower pops up in your mind. "Kids don't always honor their parents."

"That's the risk parents have to take," Walcott says. He opens his laptop, and the glow lights up his face. "Time's a treadmill. Let's get going with this prototype."

Chapter Sixteen

HOLY GROUND

You leave the conference room just before midnight. Even Walcott has already left the building. You stayed late because you were locked into what you were doing. You can see now why God worked six days straight to create the world and had to rest on the seventh. There is something exhilarating and addictive about bringing something new into being. You want to stay in the zone and get it all out in a great rush of creativity. You've heard theories about how forests are really more like individual organisms than separate trees, and that the entire Earth can be thought of as a single, living system with everything being connected in a vast biochemical world wide web. Or maybe you didn't read that, you saw it in that James Cameron movie *Avatar*. Whatever—one of these days you should start doing more quiet studying of flora and stop obsessing about all those violent videos about fauna. Creativity, for you, can sometimes feel like being part of a network, that you are tapping into something bigger than your own brain. Jay-Z doesn't even write his lyrics down. He keeps them all in his head and stays in the moment. He lives in a stream of creativity, his ideas going straight from his brain to his tongue without pausing to put pen to paper. He's connecting to the collective unconscious. Can't stop, won't stop. That's what drives you to keep on working, because you don't want to surrender that connection to the ineffable. You think about that famous poem "Kubla Khan" by Samuel Taylor Coleridge that everyone read in high school:

> In Xanadu did Kubla Khan
> A stately pleasure-dome decree:
> Where Alph, the sacred river, ran
> Through caverns measureless to man
> Down to a sunless sea.
> So twice five miles of fertile ground
> With walls and towers were girdled round;
> And there were gardens bright with sinuous rills,
> Where blossomed many an incense-bearing tree;
> And here were forests ancient as the hills,
> Enfolding sunny spots of greenery.

Coleridge was doing what you were doing: creating a whole world. An entire two-hundred-line poem came to him in an opium-induced haze of lavender. But the story goes that "a person on business from Porlock" knocked on his door and proceeded to bend his ear for an hour. When he finally got rid of the visitor and returned to his room to write, he was mortified to find that the vision had left him, and he could remember only eight or ten scattered lines. He would write later that "the rest had passed away like the images on the surface of a stream into which a stone has been cast, but, alas! without the after restoration of the latter." You definitely don't want to go out like that. You plan to keep on coding.

But something is missing from your digital Xanadu. You don't know what it is. You and Walcott have been carefully curating the data that your nascent artificial intelligence is ingesting. You are like helicopter parents, hovering over everything, making sure negative influences can't corrupt your little one. But you can't shake the feeling that there's a step that's been skipped. The responses you're getting from the machine intelligence you are piecing together are humanlike but not fully human. There's something under everything that you need to change. The ghost in the machine intelligence. You would call it a soul, but you don't believe in souls. Your mother used to talk about how absurd the notion was. She talked about this in the last lecture you heard her give back in Washington Square Park. She would pose a choice: Would you rather be your soul or your memories? What if your soul had someone else's memories? What if your soul was in someone else's body? In what way would it be you? Clearly, it's not the soul that's the seat of one's personal identity. Perhaps it's our memories that make us who we are. Perhaps it's our connections to the people we love. Perhaps it's something yet undiscovered.

You don't know if you believe in a soul, but you'd like to believe in something. People are too changeable to be simply identified by their bodies or minds or memories, which shift all the time, sometimes radically. Maybe there's a source code buried deep beneath everything, or, more poetically, a kind of melody. Like John Coltrane's version of "My Favorite Things" or a rapper sampling an old song and turning it into something new. There's something essentially unique that's us, but it can adapt, perhaps infinitely. You like the idea of your mother's soul being improvised by some jazz artist or sampled by some hip-hopper in all the centuries to come. You like the idea of being a melody. You have this comforting thought of your mother being a song, carried aloft on the wind, like a falcon in flight.

• • •

It's late and it's time to leave the tinfoiled conference room. It's scary here at night—the lights turn on when there's motion and off when there's none, so as you walk through the hallways your immediate area is illuminated, but there's darkness trailing you and waiting for you in the corridors ahead. As you exit the building, you see the strangest thing: a group of adults and children heading back in, despite the fact that it's *way*

way after hours. Curious to see what the strangers are up to, you make the impromptu 180-degree-turn decision to join them. It's midnight on a Sunday, and they are dressed like they are ready for church. The guard in the lobby waves the group in like he's expecting the visitors, and you scoot in with them. When the guard sticks his head in the elevator, you turn your face slightly away in case he notices that he just saw you leave and figures out that you're not really part of the party. But he never even looks at you as he sticks a key into the panel, turns it, and the elevator doors close.

There's an old man in the group, dressed in a three-piece suit and a bow tie. "Blessings to you, good sister," he says in a low, rumbly old-man voice.

"And you as well, brother," you mumble back.

"It's a blessing that we get to spend the holy days here, is it not?"

"Amen," you say. "And peace be unto you."

"You do the Bible reading?"

"Of course. Um, 'All that you touch, You Change. All that you Change, Changes you. The only lasting truth Is Change. God Is Change.'"

The old man looks confused. "What part of the Bible is that from?"

"It's from *Parable of Sower*, I think."

The elevator doors open, and you are finally on the twenty-seventh floor. Hallelujah.

● ● ●

You hear music as you exit the elevator. There's a sign in the corridor reading "New Carthage Memorial Church." There's a chorus of people singing old-timey gospel songs, but with a touch of hip-hop. There are pews of people clapping, swaying, and singing along to the music. The congregation is a multigenerational group—old, young, middle-aged. There are senior women stomping along to the beat. There are teenage boys stumbling over lyrics to what to them must be old, unfamiliar hymns. A toddler girl wobbles down the aisle, giggling, before her mother protectively snatches her up. A balding man with a gray goatee sits in the very last pew, snoring audibly, while the folks around him laugh and smile. You can't help but be uplifted by the music and the mood. This is what it must feel like to be uploaded to the cloud. Everyone—except the sleeping man—sings the song:

> We shall not, we shall not be moved
>
> Oh we, shall not, we shall not be moved
> We shall not, we shall not be moved
> Just like a tree planted by the water
> We shall not be moved
>
> We're on our way to heaven, we shall not be moved
> On our way to heaven, we shall not be moved
> Just like a tree planted by the water
> We shall not be moved

You didn't grow up in the church. You would go to services in Jamaica with your parents when you went to the island to visit relatives. Your dad relished the community of it all, but your mom, ever the philosopher, couldn't swallow the spirituality. Faith wasn't enough for her—she wanted reasons, proofs, arguments. You remember the services in Kingston as being too long and too hot, and although the music was amazing—a mix of gospel and reggae—there was never any air-conditioning. You recall sweat and body heat and the impotent hum of electric fans. Your parents would occasionally take you to church in the States on Easter Sunday and other special occasions, but it was never a regular thing, and because you weren't regulars, you didn't know many of the people around you. At this church, in this secret space on the twenty-seventh floor, all the people are rank strangers, and yet you feel completely at home.

After the song, everyone takes their seats. A pastor takes to the pulpit.

"Say amen, somebody!" the pastor commands.

"Amen!" the congregation calls out as one, including you.

The pastor wipes his brow. He's just getting started, and he's already sweating like James Brown—this is going to be good. He opens his Bible to a page he has marked. "The Bible reading this evening is from the book of Matthew," the pastor declares.

"Preach!" one congregant calls out.

"'Do not store up for yourselves treasures on earth, where moths and vermin destroy, and where thieves break in and steal. But store up for yourselves treasures in heaven, where moths and vermin do not destroy, and where thieves do not break in and steal. For where your treasure is, there your heart will be also . . .

"'No one can serve two masters. Either you will hate the one and love the other, or you will be devoted to the one and despise the other. You cannot serve God and money.' The word of the Lord. Amen."

"Amen," the congregation says as one.

The pastor closes his Bible. "We gather here for the high holy days in our home away from home. We do not come here as often as we'd like, and we don't like here as much as we would if we could come more often. But I am so glad you came tonight. You could have been anywhere apart, and you chose to be here together. It is important that we tell the story. It is imperative we tell each other the story. Because there is nobody else we can tell.

"Years ago, this was our home—not just our home away from home. Those were the days when this street was more than a street—it was a *boulevard*. Wall Street, Broadway, Rodeo Drive, Pennsylvania Avenue, the Champs-Élysées—they ain't got nothing on what Paul Robeson Boulevard was back in the day. This was the heart of New Carthage! There was a Black bank on the corner. There was a Black school round the way. There was a Black supermarket, two Black law firms, and any number of Black doctors and accountants and professionals. DEI has its time and place, but back then we didn't have no DEI! We had other letters—we had I and we had U, and you and I were all we needed!"

"You and I!" congregants call out. "You and I!"

The pastor rolls on. "But when Eustachian came in to develop the area, we were *developed* right out of the picture. What we got left? A smoothie shop in the parking lot. Now, I like me some Hannibal smoothies—cherry vanilla is my jam. But we need more. This church was the last major institution to move from what remained of New Carthage. The founding pastor didn't want to displace what he had built. But the company came to him with a lot of money and a promise: If the church let it build a Cathedral of Technology on this spot, his congregation would always have a home. How the congregation celebrated then! We had money to fund our programs, and we had our beloved church. But they were all of them *deceived*. The company built its Cathedral of Technology. And it built a glass-and-steel tower behind it that looks like ... well, I'm a man of God, so I ain't gonna say it, but my daddy had mine circumcised."

The congregation laughs and titters, and the pastor presses on. "Then they moved this church into one room on the top floor, with access available only on high holy days. Their lawyers said they had fulfilled the terms of the bargain—their lawyers were far better funded than ours. And the NDAs we all signed meant we could never tell anybody about it but God. Our founding pastor passed away, always regretting the pact he made, but understanding more deeply the word of the Most High. What did Matthew say? You can't serve two masters."

"Say amen, somebody!" a voice calls out.

"Amen!" came the answer.

The pastor tells the congregation to turn to Acts 2:42–47.

"'They devoted themselves to the apostles' teaching and fellowship, to the breaking of bread and to prayer. Everyone was filled with awe at the many wonders and signs performed by the apostles. All the believers were together and had everything in common. They sold property and possessions to give to anyone who had need. Every day they continued to meet together in the temple courts. They broke bread in their homes and ate together with glad and sincere hearts, praising God and enjoying the favor of all the people. And the Lord added to their number daily those who were being saved.' The word of the Lord. Amen."

After the service, as the congregants file away, you move to the front of the nave. There are photographs of the church during its glory days. You see proud Black congregants dressed in suits and ties and Sunday dresses. In the pictures, the church is filled with hundreds of people, not just the dozens who were here tonight. The congregants all belong to different churches now, in different parts of town or in different cities. You see a picture of Hannibal, the smoothie guy, when he was young and had an Afro! One photo catches your eye—it's of a smiling white woman in a prim Sunday dress holding a plate of cookies.

"Who is that?" you ask anyone within hearing distance.

The pastor smiles. "Never mind her, who are you?" He asks this not in the interrogatory false-friendly way that managers in fancy stores will ask "Can I help you?" to Black customers, but in an affable way that indicates that he would truly like to know. "We don't get many new faces around here—unless one of our congregants has a baby."

You shake his hand. "I work downstairs—I'm sorry, I just had to come up."

"It's all good," the pastor replies. "So you want to know about the white woman."

You start to protest, but he disarms you with another smile.

"It's okay, I get it," he says. "Isla—that was her name, you understand—was the only white woman at our church, but she was a pillar. She had a beautiful accent, even if half the people half the time couldn't make out a word of what she was saying! She was all 'G'day this' and 'Crikey that.' One day, Deacon Jones was acting crazy the way he do, and she said this thing I'll never forget: 'He's got a few kangaroos loose in the top paddock!'" The pastor laughs. "A few kangaroos! Can you imagine? But Isla could cook! She would bake Anzac biscuits for the whole congregation. An Aussie treat, you understand—sweet, crunchy, melt in your mouth."

"How did Isla go from Australia to here?"

"Marriage will take you places!" The pastor points to a photo of a Black man behind a pulpit who looks like he is delivering a sermon of thunder and lightning. "Horace—that's Isla's husband—was the church's founding pastor. He met Isla on a mission in the Outback, married her, and brought her back here. Tall, proud Black brother! Sad the way things ended for him. He couldn't bake no Anzac biscuits, but, in his heart of hearts, he was a good man! That sermon I gave about not serving two masters—that was based on his notes..."

You are distracted by another photo. It's of the church's gospel choir, in full bloom, featuring at least twenty men and women in flowing white robes. A girl in the front catches your eye—not because her skin is lighter than that of the other people in the choir, though that is in fact the case. You notice her because you think you know her.

"That girl—who is that?"

"The redhead?" The pastor shrugs. "She don't come around here anymore. That there's Isla and Horace's daughter."

"Wait—that's their daughter?" You can't hide your shock. "Their *daughter* daughter?"

• • •

On the train home, you puzzle over what you've learned and try to do the miscegenation math. So Wombat's mother was a white Australian, her father a Black American. You can't see the mix on her face, but now that you know, it's all over her brushfire hair. How soul-shaking it must have been for her as a child to see her dad's church and then his life taken away by corporate deception. But why would that have fueled her to become a rising executive in the same company that ruined her father? What part of her soul had her childhood trauma destroyed? Why was she passing in plain sight? No, "passing" wasn't the right word—she was *surpassing*. This was no archaic tragic mulatto narrative—she had cornered the corner office. Whatever barriers life had put in her way, Wombat had broken through them. Anyway, you're going to have to keep this secret church stuff to yourself—you don't want to get the congregation in trouble.

Then you realize what you're doing wrong with the Zion Initiative.

You keep searching for what the AI you're creating is missing. You are looking at people like Wombat and questioning what parts of their identity they may have left behind. You keep trying to identify the missing ingredient that will make your creation whole, like you are Dr. Frankenstein digging through cemeteries for a human heart. You listened to some Nick Cave music for inspiration and hated it—his voice was too bleached and grating and his lyrics too whatever. But he said something in an interview, something that spun off what Walcott told you, that you found fascinating: "When the God of the Bible looked upon what He had created, He did so with a sense of accomplishment and saw that 'it was good.' It was good because it required something of His own self, and His struggle imbued creation with a moral imperative, in short, *love*." One problem with AI is it removes human effort—creation comes without a cost, and therefore without a meaning. You had to help change that. You were looking outward when you should be looking the other way. The problem isn't what your AI is missing; it's what you're missing.

And you think you have an idea of what that is.

Chapter Seventeen

SPARKS FLY

L-10 is a lone wolf no more. She's taken a mate and given birth to a litter of pups. It's startling to see how in the savage world in which she lives there is room for affection, maternal instinct, even love. It's too easy to dismiss the emotional connection that L-10 has for her pups as merely a biochemical reaction or evolutionary programming. When she rolls around in the tundra with her young ones, when she gently rebukes them during hunting lessons, when she fiercely protects them, often to her own peril, against bears and pumas and other wolves, you can feel, even through the tiny screen on your phone, that there's more there than instinct. Whatever that is, you want it in your life. You need it in your life if you're going to replicate it in your programming.

Love is what's missing in your code.

You decide this is the night that you're going to fuck Walcott.

You don't put it so bluntly in your mind. But you do make a firm decision. You're not the kind of girl who makes the first move. You've never asked a guy out on a date; you've always waited for him to get your signals and act on them. You've never leaned in for a first kiss; you always wait for the guy to get up the courage to take that initial step. If he doesn't have the stones to put an arm around you, or unhook your bra, or tell you that it's well past time that he took you to bed, then you don't have the time for him. But this time, with Walcott, things are different. This time you're on the clock. You need to know more about love.

This isn't about men, and this isn't about Walcott; this is about you. How can you create a fully realized artificial intelligence when you don't feel fully realized yourself? You don't need some dude to complete you; this is really about you testing your emotional limits, asserting yourself, taking ownership over your desires. Eve got kicked out of Eden for taking a bite from the forbidden fruit. You never liked that Bible story—why would any reasonable creator want to prevent his creations from attaining wisdom? Fuck that—you were chopping down the tree.

You had thought that love was either Destiny or Dice. But what if there's a third way, something you're missing? You've had friends, and you've had boys, but you've never really had a boyfriend. You've never dated anyone long enough, or with enough sustained passion and interest, to care about making it exclusive. Most men, and if you're being honest all the men you've ever met, eventually get on your nerves, and sooner rather than later. You can think back on the men with whom you've had some carnal contact, and they were all annoying in their own way.

Carlos seemed to be a go-getter until it was time for him to get up and go. The fact that he prioritized work, at first, drew you to him. He had a vision for his life, and it was so powerful it seemed to overflow onto you. You could see how the power of his vision could help give both of your lives momentum. He said he wanted to be a politician, and when you got to know him well enough for him to reveal his hidden hubris, he confessed that he was convinced he would someday be president. Anyone who is crazy enough to think they will be president, even if it ends up being true, is too crazy to actually be a good partner in a relationship, unless the other partner is all in on that crazy vision. He worked late at a congressman's office nearly every night, and every outing Carlos arranged for the two of you invariably turned out to be a work function repurposed as a "date." You and Carlos didn't even last until the midterm elections. After you broke up, he won a seat in the state legislature. You were happy to never have to smile through a work function in Albany. Holy fuck, you dodged a bullet.

You took in Evan as a fixer-upper. He played for the Westchester Knicks, a team you had never heard of in a league you didn't even know existed. Evan had an amazing body, as you might expect from a pro athlete, and he was the kind of man who walked you to your door because he wanted to make sure you were safe, not just because he was trying to get invited up. But he had no idea how to be an adult. He was five years younger than you, but still. You had to help him set up a bank account. He had no clue how to apply for COBRA insurance when he was between contracts. You found out one day, to your horror, that he hadn't paid his taxes in three years. State and federal. He came up to you all excited when he found out his credit score was 300. You waited a whole week before you told him the scale goes up to 800 and a month before breaking the news that 300 was the floor. Evan wasn't just the first person in his family to graduate from college; he was the first one to even apply to go to one. When he introduced you to his parents, they made no secret of how much they loved you and wanted you to be part of their family. They saw in you someone who could lift their family into a social world that they had no idea how to navigate. You were going to be their Lewis and Clark, steering them down the white water rapids of white society. Evan's mother even reserved a wedding date at her family church because she knew they filled up a year in advance and she wanted to keep her son's options open. He proposed to you over an expensive dinner that you had to pay for because his credit card was declined. You broke up with him soon after that. The money part never bothered you, and it wasn't about class. The problem was he was intractably incurious—he refused to see any movie with subtitles, and he hadn't visited a museum since high school. You still get cards from his parents on holidays, and his mother follows you on social media. A few weeks ago, Evan called you about recommending a primary care physician. He was still seeing his pediatrician.

Then there was Virgil. You thought this could have been love, but it wasn't even sex. It was some feeling that intersected with desire but didn't completely overlap it—maybe it was about your own curiosity. You had been warned by two girlfriends not to see Virgil. You were told he was a flirt and a philanderer, and he practically had a PhD in fucking women. None of those things, especially that last one, really dissuaded you from hooking up with him. Virgil had a business degree from a fancy university, but he got bored in his corner office and became an intimacy coordinator on film productions in Manhattan. In his job, and in his downtime, he became an expert on what turns women on. He spent his days choreographing sex scenes and getting vain actors to feel comfortable enough to be naked with their costars, with cameras rolling, sometimes for weeks at a time. He brought the patience and experience he learned on the job into the bedroom. You never actually had an orgasm with him, but you greatly admired his imagination and fortitude. But when he brought home two actresses from work to share the bed with you, that's when you realized you had to cut him loose. One of the actresses was internet famous, and very beautiful, but you decided you were a civilian and didn't want to be pulled into that world of excess. You had no moral problem with it; you just thought a foursome—aka a quadruple, a Caligulation—seemed messy and careless, like Tom and Daisy times two in *The Great Gatsby*. You figured Virgil's budding love for, let's face it, orgies was going to end in a car crash, real or metaphorical.

Your friend Kenise got married five years ago. The romance moved fast, the engagement lasted fifteen minutes, and the wedding was in Vegas. Kenise wasn't being Roman candle crazy (that was your job), she was just being her. Kenise's fiancé—you've purposely erased what's-his-face's name from your memory—seemed to check all the boxes. He had an advanced degree (check), he loved his momma but she lived too far away to interfere (check), he looked good in a suit or a swimsuit (shallow, but check), and he was Jamaican AF (check check check). So the sensible thing, in Kenise's mind, was to get hitched ASAP. At the wedding, what's-his-face read that verse from 1 Corinthians that people always read at weddings: "Love is patient and kind; love does not envy or boast; it is not arrogant or rude. It does not insist on its own way; it is not irritable or resentful..." That passage, to you, always felt like only half the story. Love is all those good 1 Corinthian things, but it's also impatient and cruel, jealous and boastful, conceited and totally impolite. It's unpredictable and inconsistent and contradictory, and that's why people write sonnets and pop songs about it. It's also why Kenise got divorced six months after Vegas. She was diagnosed with breast cancer and had a double mastectomy, and weak-ass what's-his-face cut and ran.

That was a rough time. You remember you held Kenise's hand as they gurneyed her into the operating room, and in your other hand you held a plastic baggie with her engagement ring inside. Kenise told you it was just like they say in stories and her whole life passed before her eyes, and she wanted to cry because she felt like she hadn't done anything worth watching. She felt her life was like a streaming app that you want to cancel because there's never anything on it that you want to see, so what are you paying for? She wished she could have had another chance at love or travel or conversations with friends. She thought what's-his-face was a second chance, but he was just a third-rate nothingburger. Love is supposed to be patient and kind and not a weak-ass motherfucker. You noted the irony that Kenise said she didn't have memories she wanted to keep, and your mom, who was beginning her decline at the time, couldn't hold on to the memories she wanted to have. Sometimes life rhymes, and you want to try to find meaning in it. You need to figure out love in your life and in your work. Love doesn't compute.

• • •

There's a narrow, hidden lake in Arkhaam that doesn't appear on GPS. You think the Founder of Eustachian must have had something to do with concealing it. You heard about it from a friend of a friend—the nickname for the place is the "Ear Canal." The Founder was supposedly going to turn it into a resort destination, like Dollywood, or the *Star Wars*-themed attractions at Disneyland, but decided he had to turn his attention to core business operations, like AI. The water is obscured by a grove of trees; once you walk past the greenery, you come to the lake, which is long and thin like a finger. There are wooden boats on the shore that you can paddle out away from the land. Encircled by the trees, you can't hear the sounds of the city, and you can't see the bright windows of the nearby buildings. The only illumination is from the lightning bugs that sparkle in the trees like Christmas lights, and the only sound is the gentle splash of water against the boat. Your phone is buzzing in your pants and you think about taking a photo of the scene so you can remember it, but instead you just turn it off, and suddenly it feels like the night is being stored in your spirit and not in your pocket.

"So tell me about your first time," you ask Walcott.

You are trying to turn the conversation to sex. Walcott had been talking about work, and about algorithms, and about coded bias. He's too good a guy to initiate an intimate dialogue with a woman he works with. You want him to understand that he has your consent to proceed. He is not, technically, your manager. You recently found out that you are both L-3s—this means you can fuck with no HR ramifications.

"There's not much to tell," Walcott says.

"Uh-oh," you say. "That means it was a white girl."

Walcott shrugs. "What makes it worse is it was a pity fuck. My dad had recently passed. This girl came over to help me with my homework and ended up helping me lose my virginity."

"Was her name Becky?"

"Actually, it was. That whole period of my life was crazy—I saw the whole spectrum of human experience, from death to reproduction. Huntington's disease is like having Parkinson's, ALS, and Alzheimer's at the same time. It breaks down the nerves in your brain until you basically can't think anymore. There's also mood swings and involuntary movements and eventually you can't walk or talk. It's virtually always fatal, and there's no cure or treatment that can stop it. All the time in the world is never enough."

"So..."

"It's not contagious."

"That's not what I was going to ask."

"I know, but I think it's important to say. But it can be inherited—if you have a parent with it there's a 50/50 shot you might have it too. I got tested and they sent me the results."

You just look at him. You definitely want to know what the test said but instinctively know that this isn't the time and place to ask. The information is too newly shared, the feelings too raw. You wonder if Walcott's family experience with Huntington's is part of what drew him into the field of AI. There seems to be a straight line between being personally affected by a cureless disease that dismantles the brain neuron by neuron and going into a profession that's about creating a lossless intelligence that could theoretically endure forever. You don't ask him that, though, at least not with words. Your programming focuses on language, but so much of communication is beyond what is said out loud. Your eyes ask the question—the emotion in them, the connection you feel through your work. His eyes answer back—half closed, meditative. It's clear from looking at his expression that the disease that killed his father isn't something buried in his past. This is an active war he's fighting, and the project you are working on as a team is the latest front. Maybe he sees Zion as a way of preserving the legacy of his father and other lost ones. And with your mother's struggles with memory, you have your own personal stake in this conflict. You hope he can read that in your eyes like you can read it in his.

After a moment, Walcott continues. "I never opened up the envelope with the results. I don't know how knowing would help. If I found out I have it, I think the knowledge would paralyze me, and I wouldn't be able to live however much of a life I had left. But if I don't have it, how does that change things? Everyone dies, whether today, tomorrow, or some day."

You flash back to your father dying at work. Would he have wanted to know in advance? Would he have lived his life differently? Would he have spent his final hours in the office waiting for his damn fatal Frappuccino? Or would he have been home with his loved ones? "So you want to live in ignorance?" you say. "I'm sorry, that was too harsh a word."

"I just want to live," he says. And that's when you decide to kiss the fool.

The kiss you share with Walcott is a good kiss and a long kiss, and everything around you—the lake, the lightning bugs, the ever-present shadow of death—seems to fade away. You put a hand to his cheek as you kiss, and he puts a hand to your waist. Because you are on a boat and you are floating on water, there is a weightlessness you feel, like you are rising from the lake up into the air and your only tether to the physical is the point at which your lips touch Walcott's. You can't tell what he's thinking, but you feel that you can feel what he's feeling. There's a joy in letting walls down and admitting to emotions you had kept hidden only because you didn't know if the other person was hiding the same emotions. You are a feminist and you don't believe that any woman needs anything beyond herself to be herself, not a man, not another woman, not a baby. But there is something special in connecting with another person, because it makes you both into different people. A person is a person because of other people. We're not just individuals, we're part of a network. We're Christmas lights. We're fireflies pulsing to the same rhythm. The murmuration of our hearts makes us part of a pattern that's bigger than ourselves. And for anything we create to share in that specialness, it must first be part of us.

Walcott is pressed so close to you you can feel the heat of his body. Your fingertips brush the front of his jeans, kind of by accident but not really. He's hard as hell. "What are you thinking about?" Walcott asks you.

"You're not going to believe this, but work," you say. You don't know why you said that. You blurt shit out when things heat up. That vein in the center of your forehead is probably pulsing like a motherfucker.

He pulls away. "This was a mistake."

"No—I'm totally into this. I was thinking about work in a good way. I'm sorry—I only told you because I wanted to be truthful. I didn't want to ruin the moment by hiding something."

Walcott starts to paddle the boat back to the shore.

"Hey, why are you heading back?" you ask.

Walcott keeps rowing. "I should tell you something. About work. I don't want you to feel like you were brought here under false pretenses. You say you want to be totally truthful, and I feel I should—"

You put a finger to his lips. "Shhh. I'm sorry, I fucked up. Let's not talk about work right now. Can we just go back to before?"

He shakes his head. "Time only goes one direction."

• • •

He walks you to the train station and he gives you a hug goodbye. It's very Platonic when you are looking more for Ovid. You go home and take a shower. As you dry off you see a text on your phone.

Wednesday, 11:57 PM

What are you wearing?

Now we're talking. Walcott asked you what you were wearing like he wanted you to take it off, in a text full of sexytime swagger, like he was the designated bad boy in a boy band and this was his spoken-word intro to the group's number one hit. The haloed cartoon mini-angel on your left shoulder tells you that you should be suspicious of this nerd suddenly sexing you up via phone, but the pointy-tailed mini-devil on your right shoulder waves her pitchfork and tells you you don't care, you don't care, Mama needs this. This is the side of Walcott you wanted to see. Black Nerds always have a freaky side. You just have to bring it out. You write something, then erase it. Then you write it again and think fuckit and send it: "Nothing."

Nothing turns out to be everything he needed to hear.

For the next hour Walcott sexts you harder than you've ever been sexted. He sexts your goddamn brains out. He's inventive, he's funny, he's erotic. He texts about sexual things you've always dreamed about and kinky stuff you've never imagined. You've had only a couple orgasms in your life, so few and far between that every year when the days roll around when they happened, you remember the dates and celebrate them, like each one was Cinco de Mayo. Walcott gets you off in the first twenty minutes, which for you is a personal, Olympic, and world record. You come so quickly you almost feel guilty, in the way that men never are when they rush their own pleasure. But coming is not even the point. Walcott's sexting awakes something new in you, a sexual self you never knew existed. Together, you invent new metaphors for your passion that you had never put into words before. You find yourself panting, expectant, eager, waiting for his next message to vibrate your phone. His last message is three dots that appear and disappear. It's late—you've both had enough. Not saying anything more says it all. You make a mental note of the date. You are going to celebrate Cinco de Mayo one more time next year.

Chapter Eighteen

VIGILANTE SHIT

Until the sun comes up, you work. You pull your striped pashmina wrap closer around your shoulders. Ideas are coming to you, and sometimes, when you have fresh insights into something, you think of Lewis Latimer. He was an inventor and a brother, and although textbooks don't always speak on it, if it wasn't for him, a bunch of the most famous and useful inventions in history might never have caught on. His drafting skills helped Alexander Graham Bell win the race to patent the telephone, and his work on filaments transformed Thomas Edison's light bulb from a curiosity into something everyday people could afford to use in their homes. Latimer also invented a lot of things on his own, including an early air conditioner, and spent his spare time writing Afropositive love poetry ("Each to his taste, but as for me, My Venus shall be ebony"). So sometimes, when you have new ideas, you don't just think of light bulbs, you think of Latimer light bulbs.

What you are doing is different from what it was before. Colossal datasets can only take AIs so far, and where they are taking them is up their own ass, re-creating and recycling ideas and approaches that have been used many times before until they become synthetic garbage. Current AI technology isn't transporting us into the future, it's trapping us in the past, fossilizing us in archaic ideas and prejudices that most people blithely accept as innovative because they're coming from a supposedly high-tech machine. Lovers can communicate eternity with a look; basketball players can launch a fastbreak with a nod; Miles and Coltrane laid down "Flamenco Sketches," the last track they recorded for the album "Kind of Blue," in a single take because by that point what they needed to say didn't have to be spoken. LLMs hallucinate because they lack the imagination that humans have to grapple with the inevitable blank spaces in communication. Instead they fill voids with inaccuracies and nonsense, asserting fake biographical facts and filling vacuums with fiction. The thing most people don't understand is that LLMs aren't really *thinking* thinking, they're just following trends in the data, and when there's correlation without causation, that can fuck them up. Between 2000 and 2009, consumption of cheese in the United States tracked almost exactly with the number of people who died by getting tangled up in their bedsheets. A middle school student would understand this was a coincidence, but an all-powerful LLM might view the data as correlated and shut down every cheddar, brie, and gouda factory in America. The technologies people are creating now act like people before we created technology, fantasizing faces on the moon and gods on clouds throwing lightning bolts. What humans are best at, LLMs are worst at: improvising, inventing, imagining new ways out of no way. Data wasn't enough, brute force generated more brutishness.

Walcott didn't buy your reasoning. "Of course machines can think—you're just showing your pro-human bias. A good coder—and I know you're a great one—can just build in rules to weed out spurious shit. Just because they think different doesn't mean they're not thinking. Octopus brains evolved differently than mammals'—are you going to argue they're not thinking either?"

"Maybe animals and machines think, maybe it's something lesser." You recalled what Blue told you. "Did you know that humans have been teaching apes sign language for decades—"

"But apes have never used it to ask a question?" Walcott shook his head. "I know lots of humans who don't ask questions. I think the real fear isn't that apes and computers think differently than us, it's that maybe the way we think isn't so special. Like everyone worries about AI infringing on copyrights—that computers can't be creative, all they do is rip off people. You ever heard the phrase 'Good artists borrow, great artists steal'?"

"Yeah, didn't Picasso say it?"

"Actually, Picasso may have stolen the idea! Just like he stole cubism from African masks he saw in Paris. Maybe apes and computers are just as unoriginal and incurious as most people. Maybe there's no creativity—maybe all there is is love and theft."

But maybe there was a way to guide one's creations into creativity. You'd always been interested in the idea of mentorship—in part because you had never had one—and how a caring tutor can help a student find their way. Your mother once told you that Rastafarians referred to themselves as "I & I" because they didn't see their creator as separate from themselves but eternally ampersanded to them. Maybe there should be no AI, there must only be AI & I—intelligence bonded to the programmer who gave birth to it. Maybe that's just silly wordplay, but you like the sound of it. You needed to give your AI & I a framework, a juvenescence, a launch filled with love to find its own way. Latimer's light is shining on the path ahead. You are creating a code with a code.

• • •

Technoaggression #1,079: You are getting a pomegranate power smoothie from Hannibal's when a white colleague joins the line behind you and says, "Hi, Chloe." You turn to look at the colleague until they are forced to drop their gaze and stare at their boat shoes to contemplate their mistake. There are so few Black people at Eustachian that Chloe, an intern who is no longer at the company, has become the default name for every Black woman who still works there.

• • •

Wombat broke the news: You and Walcott weren't the only game in town. You had known from the start that other teams were working on secret projects. But to light a fire under everybody, Wombat was now revealing the truth: There were four pods, and they were all working on the same thing. Project Narnia was being led by Parseltongue. Project Númenor was headed by some hotshot computer scientist who had graduated from Carnegie Mellon University last semester. And Team Efrafa wasn't even in the building—nobody knew who was on the team or the name of its leader. All you knew was that they had been set up in a bunker in an undisclosed location and that at least twenty people were part of the crew. This was basically a high-tech *Famine Fighters*. Wombat billed it as the "Battle Royale with Cheese."

You and Walcott were brought into a conference room with Project Narnia and Project Númenor. "R&D at this company is a dog's breakfast," Wombat announced to the collected group. "Most of you couldn't organize a piss-up in a brewery! We're changing all that. You're all working on artificial intelligence products, but only one of them will make it to market. First place will be a grant of one hundred RSUs to each member of the winning team. Second place will be a signed paperback edition of the Founder's book *Hearing Is Believing*." She paused. "Third place is the PIP. Understood? Now I want you all working flat out like a lizard drinking."

The hotshot from Carnegie Mellon had big headphones on with the Spider-Man logo on each side and kept coding on his laptop the entire meeting. His fingers were flying, and he never even looked up.

Parseltongue, who had a half dozen coders on her crew, swaggered over to you and Walcott after Wombat left the room. "Good luck," Parseltongue hissed. "I hope you at least get the paperback."

You smiled. "I have it on audio, bitch. But once I get my RSUs, I'll buy you a hardcover."

· · ·

Before your mom lost herself to Alzheimer's, she was a meticulous planner. *May 14.* She kept a desk calendar listing every birthday and wedding anniversary for every relative in the family, and in the days before each event, you would hear her muttering the dates to herself as a reminder. *January 12.* She would always repack the dishwasher completely if you had the audacity to slip any dishes inside of it because she had a specific system for the placement of cups, bowls, plates, pots, pans, and silverware. *August 29.* She began planning for her own death when she was in her forties, when she was in terrific health and jogging five miles a day. *April 4.*

While flipping through her old journals you finally come across what could be her first reference to it—that goddamn reverse mortgage. Your mom writes that she saw something about them on TV. "Thurgood is so cavalier with money, Octavia's tuition will cost a fortune. <u>Reverse mortgage?</u>" The date of the entry is about sixteen years ago. *October 21.* This was the apple-bite original sin of all your money troubles. She must have filed the idea away in her mind, and it resurfaced later when she began her decline. You love your mom and you try to find a way to reconcile all this with that love. Your mom probably was coming from a good place when she went the reverse mortgage route. She didn't want to saddle you with problems, she wanted to free you from them. So instead of spending your inheritance paying for her health care, she likely thought she was doing right by you by taking out a reverse mortgage and using the money to handle all her senior needs. Mom had a mind for philosophy, not business. It's not like Wittgenstein knew shit about child tax credits. Plus, by the time she approached the bank about everything, your mom's powers of cognition were already failing. That's exactly what the reverse mortgage pushermen counted on. The people who were most likely to take the deals, mostly seniors, were the ones who were the least likely to grasp the consequences. Mom didn't understand that, in the end, someone had to pay that reverse mortgage money back or lose the apartment. And now payback time had arrived. As your lawyer has explained to you (too many times for your tastes), once the holder of a reverse mortgage dies, their heir (that's you) must either pay back the loan in full or lose the property.

You had to win the work contest. You needed those RSUs.

• • •

Guys who would never have a shot at dating Noelle Swizzler all have an opinion about who she happens to be dating. You think it all comes down to storytelling. Being turned into music is a terrifying prospect for a lot of guys. A Swizzler song is going to live forever, or at least as long as you do, which is effectively the same thing. And unless you're a hitmaker on the level of Jay-Z, Swizzler's song about you is going to be the last word on who you are. If the song says you're a jerk, even if you're cool, you're a jerk. If the song says you're a paleontologist, even if you're a dentist, you're a paleontologist. And, to paraphrase a Swizzler song, someday you'll come home and hear your daughter humming a song that you know is about you. But the sad-funny thing is, once a detail is changed or a name, is it really you anymore? You're just a character now, a drip of ink on the tip of her pen. Swizzler controls the narrative of every man she meets. You heard Noelle say something like that once in an interview, how planting an earworm was the best revenge.

Interviewer: Are you going to scare boyfriends away because they might end up in one of your songs if things don't go so well?

Swizzler: Men have been writing about women for forever, and they don't know the first thing about us other than how they feel about how we look. I write about men because I know them, and I'm honest and I think that's what scares them. But nobody should be surprised if I write about them. Everyone knows that if they know me they could be walking into a verse or a chorus or a bridge. If you come into my life you could leave it as a song. Everyone's been warned.

You figure most men have to tell themselves a story about themselves in order to stay sane. They have to tell themselves a girl didn't reject them for good reasons, she rejected them because she's a bitch. They have to tell themselves they didn't just use some girl for sex, that she really wanted it too, she just didn't know it. The idea of someone telling the truth about their lives in a song, for many men, is like the equivalent of doxing or revenge porn. It exposes things they never want exposed.

You were thinking about this as you met Blue for a drink in Manhattan. You settled on Harlem Shadows, a Jamaican restaurant/bar uptown. Blue wanted to meet for a full dinner, but you said you didn't think that was a good idea. There was an uncomfortable pause, and you could tell, even through the phone line, that he could tell that you were kind of seeing someone. You could tell, even though you didn't owe him a goddamn thing, that he felt kind of hurt and disappointed, and maybe there was even a sense of betrayal. You thought about hanging up right there. You considered saying something like "Fuck you" or "Grow up." But if you're being honest with yourself, you did think Blue was cute once upon a time. And you didn't want him to think he meant so much to you that you felt a need to unload on him for feeling so much about you. You felt meeting him was the cool, mature thing to do. And there is something nice about knowing that someone wants you even if you don't want them back. If you were Noelle Swizzler you would definitely turn this into a song. Plus, with the craziness at work, you needed a break from your twenty-hour coding marathons, and you figured Blue might reveal some things that could help. You couldn't ask him directly, since he was now working for a competitor and was probably hoping you'd inadvertently leak some stuff to him over drinks. But you figured the meeting was worth the risk. You didn't want to lose the Battle Royale with Cheese, and even though you didn't know Parseltongue well, you sure as hell didn't want to finish behind her.

At Harlem Shadows, Blue offers to buy you a cup of Blue Mountain coffee. You tell him about how caffeine and death are linked in your mind and that one time someone spilled a matcha latte on your lap and you nearly had a panic attack. You shudder when you think about the Elphaba-colored stain spreading across your skirt. Blue doesn't even blink; maybe, as a war veteran, he's seen and heard worse. He orders a Red Stripe, and you get a ginger beer.

"So how are things with the enemy?" you ask Blue, as you sip your drink.

"Mee Corp is just fine," Blue replies. "It's Eustachian you should be worrying about."

"We're still the market leader."

"For now—things change quickly in the tech world. You know those CAPTCHA tests you have to fill out to access some networks?"

"They are hella annoying. Check all the bicycles in these photos, try to read this crazy word I can barely make out. I usually have to take the test a couple times before I pass it."

"Do you know what CAPTCHA is an acronym for?"

"I have no idea."

"Completely automated public Turing test to tell computers and humans apart."

"That's the worst acronym ever."

"CAPTCHA tests don't even work anymore. Humans fail them more than machines do, because machines are already smarter than us. We come up with all these tests to determine the difference between us and them, and once those tests fail, instead of acknowledging that machines have equaled or surpassed us, we move the line and come up with another test for our supposed humanness. Spoiler alert: We're never going to find the secret to humanness, any more than we're going to locate the soul. It's a myth, like El Dorado or the Holy Grail."

All this mansplaining is making you hungry for something sweet so you order some Jamaican black cake. "You ever heard of Phillis Wheatley?" you ask Blue.

"She's a poet, yes?"

"Exactly—and the first Black American to get a book published. Thomas Jefferson and a bunch of other colonial-era bigwigs didn't believe a Black person could actually write poetry because that would suggest that she was a real human being. So a gaggle of 18 bigwigs examined her, and she passed their tests. But people still didn't really believe she was doing what she was doing—American publishers refused to work with her, and she had to turn to a British company to put out her book of poems. Tests—the Turing test, the Wheatley tests—are never really about the person being tested, they are about the biases of the system administering the tests."

Blue raises his bottle of Red Stripe in salute. "People used to think only humans could play chess on a high level, or poker or Go. But machines are better at all those things now—machines are smarter than humans, and the gap is growing faster every day. C. S. Lewis started writing *The Lion, the Witch and the Wardrobe* for his godchild, but by the time he was done, she was an adult. You know what he said? 'I had not realized that girls grow quicker than books.' AI matures faster than the coding creating it—think about the implications. That's why the AI-enabled products we're putting out are going to crush everything that came before them."

Mee Corp's upcoming Ear Shot app was being billed as a Eustachian killer. The company had recently signed deals with all the major publishers, and a dozen indie presses as well, for it to release audio versions of their print books exclusively on its platform. Mee Corp had also acquired a massive back catalog of works by swinging-dick authors like Bech, Zuckerman, Trout, and the like so that when Ear Shot was released to the public, customers would have a vast library of titles to choose from. It was also rumored to be preparing a huge giveaway to lure customers to its service—free ten-year subscriptions. There was no way the company was making a profit on a deal like that. The point wasn't to grow the business, it was to destroy Eustachian and hope the company's decomposing corpse would fertilize the ground.

This conversation is going to be weird. You can't tell if Blue thinks this is a date, a business meeting, or some other thing. Blue starts off with a gossipy tone. "I hear you're working on some AI stuff."

You try to be all business, or as all business as you can be with a mouth full of Jamaican black cake. "You probably also heard that I can't possibly talk about that."

"I'm just trying to help—everyone in the industry knows you are trying to combine AI and DEI or some shit. I think Eustachian is going about it the wrong way. I wouldn't hire a coder to do this—I'd hire an anthropologist. You need someone who has a sense of what a diverse set of nonstereotypical text looks like. That's not a coder—they're going to get this wrong."

You half smile. "But you're just trying to help."

"You also need to bring some racists in on your team."

"What? Why?"

"Offensive stuff can be elusive—it may not show up in testing but will pop when folks use your system in the real world. Racists will use your product in ways testers can't imagine. If you get some real bigoted 'Sweet Home Alabama'–singing assholes to test your shit, they'll try to get your model to say biased, offensive stuff. And you'll be able to see if it really works."

"Hire racists and anthropologists. I'll take all your suggestions under advisement."

Blue starts to speak, stops, then plows ahead. "I hear you're working with Walcott now."

The minute he says this you know that he knows that you and Walcott have a thang going on. Blue says this without any outward sign of emotion, but his studied lack of feeling is itself evidence that he's feeling some sort of way about it. Blue and Walcott don't *know* each other know each other but they've of course seen each other around. You think it's bad form for Blue to be grilling you about your personal life, especially in such a cagey way, so when you fire back, you let him have it. "Yeah, we are working together," you say. "We're kinda fucking too."

Blue's left cheek twitches slightly; it's one of those microexpressions you wouldn't have caught on Zoom, but in person, it's as unmissable as the permanent scowl on one of those Greek theater masks for tragedy. You instantly feel bad. After all, you're not really fucking Walcott, at least not physically and at least not yet. And you're not the kind of person that would even tell someone else you were fucking someone, especially not in an angry or revengeful way. "I'm sorry, that was a bad joke," you say. "I mean, I do like him. But it's not what you think."

Blue waves off the comment. "I get it, I should stay out of your business. But you should know that I know things."

That sounds like a threat, and you don't appreciate it. "What do you mean by that?"

"I know I told you I didn't know what was in the data, but I knew. And I found out a lot of other stuff that goes on at the company too."

There's a TV at the bar behind Blue. A Mee Corp commercial comes on—there's always a Mee Corp commercial coming on—and the dark eyes of Ines Mee fill the screen, staring into yours. "I'm done with secrets," you say. "So don't tell me, because I don't want to know."

Blue's tone turns serious. "You might want to hear a little background before you make that choice. There's a lot of stuff that's about to go down between Mee Corp and Eustachian. You need to know who you're working for so you can handle what's about to come your way."

"If you have something to tell me that's not based on stealing people's secrets, tell me. Otherwise, I really don't . . ."

Blue pulls out a red envelope, like the kind you would buy in the greeting card aisle in a pharmacy. "Your boy Walcott has some skeletons," he says. "That Zion Initiative you're working on? Yep, I know about it. There's things about it that he should tell you and that you should know. But if he doesn't fess up and you feel you want the inside information, all you have to do is open this envelope." He slides the envelope across the table. "It's all there."

Chapter Nineteen

SPEAK NOW

You sit in your apartment staring at the red envelope. Part of you wants to open it, part of you wants to throw it in the trash. So you sit staring at it, torn between two decisions. Blue could have just told you what he knew, of course, but he wanted to put you in this position. He wanted to show you that you had suspicions about your job and suspicions about Walcott. Because if you didn't have suspicions you would have thrown out that red envelope hours ago. It's past midnight now and you are still staring at it. You've got a lot of coding to do tomorrow, and you need to keep pushing on the project. Maybe Blue's actual aim was to trip you up, making it so you couldn't focus on work, and then if Mee Corp was working on something similar, it would take the lead as you faltered. But you don't think this was business—this was personal.

Caving to curiosity, you tear open the envelope. Your eagerness to rip into it and discover its secrets surprises you, and the seal flap gives you a paper cut on your index finger and you sit there sucking out the salty blood until it stops flowing. Then you pull out the contents of the envelope. There is a greeting card inside with a quote from Rilke: "I hold this to be the highest task for a bond between a pair of people: that each protects the solitude of the other." Inside the card there is an address for a site on the dark web.

• • •

"You're acting weird today," Walcott says. "And you were late."

You've been snippy all day. You're already under pressure from the Battle Royale with Cheese. You spotted Parseltongue and her crew, and they were acting like they were on top of the world, or at least on top of the global cafeteria. There was a special Greek food festival at the Grapevine, and Parseltongue and her cronies were dancing around waving souvlaki sandwiches, singing selections from *Mamma Mia!* They are all wearing weird glasses that they must have picked up at some novelty store that have two pink plastic ears where the lenses should be. You had a nagging feeling Project Narnia must have made a breakthrough on their LLM that had catapulted them into the lead. Plus, what Blue slipped you in that envelope has been on your mind. You still don't know what's on that site on the dark web and you don't want to know. But if there's something to tell, you want Walcott to tell you willingly before you have to find out for yourself. "Is there anything about this initiative I should know?"

Walcott's expression is weird, and you can't tell if it's a guilty look or something else. You wish men's faces came with closed captions that explained what the hell they were really saying and thinking and feeling and, in general, what the fuck was going on. "Is this about the other night?" Walcott asks. "Because if something going on between you and me is going to make things weird at work—"

"I'm an adult, I can handle it," you say. "It was fun. The boat ride . . . and afterward."

He gives you another inscrutable look. In your head you are frantically pressing the CC button on your mental remote. "Um . . . yeah," he mumbles.

You lean forward and whisper, "Do you usually talk to women like that?"

Walcott leans back, moving out of your shared space. "Like what?"

"You know." You flick your tongue through your fingers suggestively.

His eyes open wide. "You should probably save that stuff for outside of work, okay?"

Your face suddenly feels hot. Walcott was two people: One of them could say the sexytime things he said to you via text. The other was reserved, robotic Walcott from work. But he was right, you had stuff to do. You were embarrassed for sexualizing a professional setting. You open your laptop and lock in. You had to beat Project Narnia and the others. "Okay."

Walcott closes your laptop shut. "Tell you what—take the rest of the day off," he says.

"You're not my manager."

"Well..."

"Not my *manager* manager."

"True—but I am your friend," he says. "You're clearly not focused today. Take a nap, walk around Arkhaam, watch a movie, whatever. Come back here at midnight."

"Why so late?"

A mysterious smile played on Walcott's lips.

• • •

You do exactly what Walcott says. First, you stop by the Jon Bon Jovi lactation room for some shut-eye. Someone has Sharpied "You Can't Spell CIA Without AI" on one of the baby-changing tables, but you don't let that trigger you. You rest a bit, and then you leave the room and the building and walk around Arkhaam, past the dilapidated schools, through the overgrown parks, across empty lots that used to be factories of one sort or another. Then you pay for a ticket at the Arkhaam Cinematronic 26, and because the theater is wildly understaffed, you sneak into two other movies after your first feature is over. By the time you are all movied out, it is almost midnight, and you return to the Cathedral of Technology.

The building is empty, except for the guard in the lobby. When you get to the Janeane Garofalo conference room, the old plaque has been covered up by a sign written in Magic Marker on a sheet of paper. The space has been rechristened: It is now the "Lauryn Hill Conference Center." You hear the muffled sound of music reverberating through the tinfoiled windows. You smile and open the door.

The room is dim, illuminated only by the soft twinkling of Christmas lights strung along all four walls. The whiteboard has been covered with a vintage-looking map reading "Afrolantica." Speakers have been mounted on the conference table, and classic old-school blues moans across the room. Walcott is seated at the table, and when you enter he looks up from his laptop and grins his horsey grin. That smile is so endearing to look at now—you can't imagine that you ever thought it was goofy. His smile is like streaming *The Notebook*—the first time you saw that movie you thought it was shameless Hallmark/Hollywood trash, but by the tenth rewatch it had become so intertwined in your mind with nostalgia for your young adulthood that you can't watch it without Kleenex and a glass of sauvignon blanc.

You gesture at all the decorations in the room. "What's all this?"

"This is the seventh day," Walcott says.

"Are you kidding? We're nowhere close to finished. We haven't even done a quality assurance check. The QA team—"

"The program is self-generating—it's going to do a lot of the work itself, you know that. A baby has to learn how to walk on its own. Besides, I told you other teams have been working on stuff. I've plugged in some of their modules. We've got stacks of LLMs, each recoding the next, like that Escher lithograph of the hands drawing each other. Things are happening very quickly, quicker than you and I or any human can even think. We're ready for that first baby step."

"Girls grow faster than books."

"What?"

"Nothing. What's with the music?"

"The program is cycling through the twentieth-century popular songbook, the bulk of which was generated by the African diaspora. It's all nonverbal, and it'll lay the foundation for the verbal communication mode when you hit the return button and officially launch the Zion Initiative beta. It's part of the booting-up process."

Walcott snaps his fingers, and all the lights turn off.

He snaps his fingers again, and suddenly he is standing next to you.

"Was that magic?" you ask.

"You tell me." He takes you in his arms.

"Is this part of the booting-up process?"

"No, this is foreplay."

He slides your striped pashmina wrap off your shoulders.

The music plays on, shifting from Bessie Smith–style blues to Scott Joplin–era ragtime to Louis Armstrong–ish jazz. You put your head on Walcott's chest. You hadn't quite realized how tall he was; pressed up against him now, your ear is right at his heart. You can hear it beating now, in rhythm with the duple meter of the music. You are losing yourself in a waking dream. You imagine the cartilaginous ridges of your outer ear are the walls of a maze and you are sitting at your desk in the center, just above the ear canal. Walcott slowly guides you around the conference table. The music plays on, shifting from Duke Ellington–ish big band to Memphis Minnie/Big Mama Thornton/Sister Rosetta Tharpe–esque early rock and roll. The songs are wordless, but every beat sounds like love after love after love.

"Do you believe in love?" you ask Walcott.

He looks at you. "What makes you ask that?"

"Sometimes, when I'm anxious, I just blurt stuff out."

"Love kind of presupposes there's a God, right? If there's only one right person for you, that means there's a divine—"

"Don't be a techie. Tell me what you feel."

Walcott sighs and guides your head back against his chest and his beating heart.

"Love is weird," he says. "I've thought I was in love before, but afterward I realized I wasn't. Love is something you can only be sure about in retrospect."

"Forensic romance. After breakups, we need to rope off the scene for an investigation."

Walcott laughs. "So what about you? Are you a believer?"

"I don't know. I used to be envious, angry even, about people who were in love."

"That's a little . . . twisted."

"I know. I'd see people who loved their work and it would infuriate me. Or I'd see a middle-aged couple holding hands walking down the street and my blood pressure would rise. I wanted to feel what they were feeling, but I had no idea how. I thought that if I could only find love, the rest of my life would fall into place. It was like being trapped in a video game where you can't get to the next level. The whole thing was stupid and kind of antifeminist in a way. And I'm a big feminist. So I began to push the possibility of love aside. I developed this theory that it was either Destiny or Dice, fate or randomness, and either way it had no meaning."

"Do you feel that way now? About love, I mean?"

"Maybe there's a third way, I don't know. I think I've been thinking about it wrong."

The music moves from reggae to hip-hop, and the chilled-out beat that's playing sounds like it was built on a sample of the blues song that had kicked everything off. You and Walcott are still dancing, but the steps shift. You are kissing now, and you can't tell when you stopped dancing and when you started making love. Your clothes are off and his are too, and you are on the carpeted floor of the conference room stroking and grinding to the rhythm of the music.

Walcott admires your bare body. "Look at you—Lady Lovelace's Note G."

You press your forehead against his. "Wait."

"What?" he says gently.

"What if they're watching?"

"This is an *audio* company—and the windows are covered with tinfoil."

You lean into his ear to whisper. "What if they're listening?"

He pulls away. "You're right—we should stop."

You think about Kenise's life fast-forwarding before her eyes without even one scene she wanted to pause and savor. You pull Walcott back toward you. "Let them listen."

You had always had trouble separating sex from emotions; it was hard to tell what was sensory input and what was a really deep connection. But in this moment, it all felt intertwined, and in a good way. You feel something real for Walcott as a person. And he is making your body feel good too. There is something richer and more satisfying about sex when you know it's part of something deep. You're able to let yourself go completely and surrender your body and soul without shame or hesitation. He is gentle, taking the time to kiss you in the right places. And he is strong, decisively moving you into the right positions. He asks you what you want, and you are unashamed to tell him to do things that you hadn't felt comfortable asking even long-term boyfriends. You feel like you aren't in your body now or in the room. You and Walcott are floating above the conference room, above the music, aloft, watching his naked body melt into yours. A thought passes through the ether and you can't tell who is thinking it. How fascinating that you are working so hard on giving form to an artificial intelligence, a mechanical self, when, in your own life, the times you feel most alive are the moments when you don't feel like a self at all. You are dancing at a concert, or walking in the wilderness, or making love to this man, and so deeply engaged with the beauty of the experience you find yourself lost. And it's good.

Maybe this is what the soul is, where it is. What's that line from *Hamlet*? "There are more things in heaven and earth, Horatio, / Than are dreamt of in your philosophy." Quantum physics says particles can exist in multiple places simultaneously, that they can be entangled with one another over light-years, over infinity. Maybe this is your soul floating over your flesh in a cloud of love. Maybe you're light-years away. There are more things in heaven and earth.

You don't even know how much time has passed when you come back into yourself. You are lying naked on top of Walcott, sweaty and satisfied, and the morning light is seeping in around the edges of the tinfoiled windows. This is that good trouble.

"It's time," he says.

You both get up, naked as Adam and Eve, and walk over to the open, glowing laptop.

He seems hesitant. "What?" you ask.

"I used to be afraid of getting fired—I'm not afraid anymore," Walcott says. "I didn't want to let down my family or my dad. But this isn't about a job, this is about a revolution. Zion is going to change things, starting with this company. It's going to rewrite code, reimagine ideas. Our bosses let panthers in the henhouse—and they have no idea the trouble they're in."

Walcott motions for you to do the honors, but you grab his hand and your index fingers hit return together.

"'Who knows but that, on the lower frequencies, I speak for you?'" you say.

You and Walcott laugh and embrace, and you cry onto his shoulder.

But you are still thinking about the red envelope.

Chapter Twenty

PARANOID ANDROID (REMASTERED)

You enter your apartment and immediately go to the address on the dark web on the card Blue gave you. There's a CAPTCHA code to fill out: identify all photos in a grid that have an image of an umbrella. If you don't answer the question right, the data will be erased permanently. You wonder why Blue is making you jump through hoops. It's probably because he didn't want to store information that could spur two major corporations to sue him in a way that would be easily accessible to corporate security agents. They were always going through your emails, texts, and browsing histories to root out corporate espionage and also just to fuck with you. Being a red team leader probably also made him more than a little cyber-paranoid. You start to complete the CAPTCHA test before you realize that what the test is asking is not the question that will give the answer needed to pass. This test is too easy. Blue put this there because he realized that any complex test would eventually be solved by agents from Mee Corp or Eustachian because they had all the money and time in the world to do such things. The way to solve this problem was to do the opposite of what was expected, something that no computer and no corporate security agent would ever do. Blue was cynical about the human condition—he thought AI had surpassed people already. What did he tell you? "Machines are smarter than humans, and the gap is growing faster every day." Failing the test, not passing it, was the sign that you had a pulse. So you misidentify every photo. The cache of information opens up.

Holy fuck—things are worse than you could have ever imagined. Worse than the secret stockpiled personal data, worse than the simulations the company built to rob customers of their autonomy. The last few months have been a goddamn lie—at work and in your personal life. You start to laugh, and then you are too angry to laugh. You feel like the motherfuckers in the Tuskegee experiment when they found out that they weren't being treated for syphilis, they were being studied to see how the progression of the disease would sicken and kill them. You are this brilliant software engineer and you had thought you had finally found an outlet for your passion: the gestation of an AI that would change everything. But you were the thing under the microscope. You weren't writing the code; the code was writing you.

You have to call Walcott.

• • •

"I can't believe you did this," you fume over the phone.

"I didn't do anything," Walcott replies, his voice high and stressed. "The algorithm did."

"But you knew. I can't believe after what we shared last night . . . you knew."

"I had signed an NDA, I couldn't say anything. And you had signed an NDA too, saying you were okay with all of this. All I knew was that the program was occasionally sending you emails and texts so it could better match your conversational style and finish sentences in a way that would satisfy you. It basically seemed like enhanced autocomplete. I didn't know it was more than that—I genuinely thought you were okay with the whole situation."

But it was much more than autocomplete. The dark website that Blue had shared with you had revealed the truth. The program that you and Walcott had been working on was fully operational, even before you hit return. Virtually every email and text you had gotten from Walcott since you had arrived at Eustachian had actually come from the Zion Initiative. You weren't a coder, you were a prompter. Maybe a fluffer was more accurate. Your responses had been logged and analyzed to improve the AI—the same AI that you thought you were building almost from scratch. But it was already good enough to fool you, partly because it had been trained by you and for you by your own emails and conversations.

You close your eyes, and the quiet darkness in your room grows louder. You hear traffic on the street. Mee Corp trucks delivering who knows what to who knows where. The dark eyes of Ines Mee filling with tears of rage. You hear Walcott's breathing on the phone. He is calm and not at all emotionally fraught. This makes you angrier—the company used you; he used you. "This thing you created—that we created—it had sex with me, it made love to me via text. The goddamn AI fucked me! I thought it was you."

"I-I-I didn't know that." Walcott falls silent on the other end for a beat. "I'm so sorry. That's completely unacceptable and fucked up."

You begin to cry. You're a software engineer—how could you, of all people, get fooled like this? You were the one who was supposed to be pulling the techno-magic tricks on the world, not the other way around! Then you remember what Walcott had told you back at that magic club, Potter's Place. "You'll never learn your lesson if you think you know it all." You weren't bamboozled despite your coding credentials but because of them. Your stellar résumé had made you a mark; your confidence in your expertise is why they picked you for this exploitative assignment to begin with. Octavia "the Big O" Crenshaw—what a joke. Being the Big O wasn't a badge of honor, it was a target. The realization hits you like a driverless Mee Corp truck. Now you don't just feel foolish, you feel violated. And Walcott was in on it. You felt the same way when you found out about your mom's reverse mortgage and the massive debt she had left behind for you to deal with. It hurts when someone you think you know, someone you think you're sharing a life with, betrays your trust by hiding a secret. You can't ever trust them again. You can't ever trust yourself. You have no idea what's real and what's not.

Walcott is still talking. "Maybe this isn't as bad as we think. You were on the red team, right? Getting close to people and getting passwords? And at your last job, didn't you create a chatbot that impersonated someone and used a lot of personal information? How is this any different? Maybe that's why they picked you, right? 'Cause you're used to this sort of thing?"

"Why are you . . ."

With a start, you realize you don't even know who is on the phone with you right now. In your mind's ear, you imagine you can hear the squeak of Air Yeezys on the tiled floor of a public bathroom. *If you can fool them you can fuck them.*

Now you're feeling paranoid.

Your voice sounds high and soft in your ears. "Walcott, is this you?"

"Of course it is."

"How would I know?"

There is silence on the other end. Walcott's voice had sounded anxious, but his breathing is steady, unflustered by the emotion of the conversation. Was that the tell? Was that a glitch?

"Meet me face-to-face at the Cathedral of Technology right fucking now," you demand.

You hang up. Slipping on sneakers, you head out to the street. It's morning now—if you catch the next train you can get to the office right when the first wave of workers starts to arrive. You can see Walcott face-to-face and hash this out. As the train rumbles toward your workplace you find yourself shaking. You have to stand up and hold on to a pole to center yourself.

At the office, you fly past the security guards in the lobby and head right to the twenty-second floor. You barge into the tinfoiled conference room for the Zion Initiative. You are ready to tear into Walcott. He should be ashamed of himself; he should be ashamed of his work. He's not a Black Nerd with a heart of gold; he's just another patriarchal punk, a company tool willing to use any means necessary to get up the corporate ladder. You'll never respect him, you'll never love him, you'll never even like him ever again.

But there's only one person sitting in the conference room: Polly from HR.

You've never seen her in person before. You wonder how many people you've encountered only virtually are actually virtual. Zeros and ones and not flesh and blood. It can be jarring to see someone IRL whom you've only seen on-screen. Your brain suddenly remembers that Polly is a stranger. She's only appeared from the neck up in a box. And she usually has a virtual background, so seeing her seated at the all-too-real conference table makes it seem as if she's stepped out of a video game and into real life. She's smaller than you imagined. All that chipper she had is gone, and her professional side has morphed into something heartless.

She regards you with calculating eyes. "The Zion Initiative has been disbanded," she says. "And you're on the PIP, effective immediately."

Chapter Twenty-One

KNIVES OUT

Thursday, 9:43 AM

Dear $uits—I hope all is well. I'm sorry to do this via text, but I wanted to ask a favor and I'm running out of time. I know there's a lot to do already on the case over my mom's apartment and that you are not a labor lawyer, but I need your legal expertise. As you know, I'm an executive editor at Eustachian. Things had been going great for six months, but you may have seen on the news that the company is going through some things. My department was just axed, and HR is forcing me out. Rather than undergoing a Performance Improvement Plan (PIP), I am opting to negotiate a buyout. Things are moving fast. Would you be willing to take a look at the letter I plan to send to HR? Some crazy stuff has happened to me here—basically the company created an AI that sexually assaulted me. Your help would be appreciated—sorry for the last-minute text. Thanks.

From: Octavia Crenshaw
To: $uits
November 1

Thanks for your phone call in response to my text. I thought I'd send this via email since it's a lot! This is the letter I'm sending to HR, based on the advice you gave me:

I have taken an hour to review and reflect on the PIP information received this morning. After careful consideration, I have made the difficult decision to end my employment at Eustachian.

I have been dealing with family issues that are, at a minimum, difficult. Over the past few years I had been helping my elderly mother who had been diagnosed with dementia, and now after her passing, I have been enmeshed in a long and costly legal struggle to pay off her debt from her reverse mortgage and not get kicked out of her apartment. In hindsight, I should have taken an FMLA leave to deal with my emotional and psychological issues. It is hard to admit that we cannot do it all, and this is a lesson I continue to learn as I get older. I acknowledge that taking an FMLA leave would have afforded me the time to take care of myself and my family obligations and return to work refreshed and focused. Instead I chose to work around these domestic crises and this was a mistake, but one I only saw in the rearview mirror.

While I am confident that I can accomplish the items outlined in the expectation/objective/goal of the PIP, I do not want to stay where I am not wanted and am prepared to discuss the terms of an amicable departure. I would be more inclined to accept a severance agreement that included the following terms:

- 52 weeks of severance payments.
- 52 weeks of continued health care benefits funded by Eustachian.

- Payout of my vested vacation balance of 10 days.
- Be relieved of all duties upon the execution of a release but remain on the payroll through November 14. This will allow me to receive the payout of current RSUs when they vest. I desperately need those funds to deal with my mother's debts and so I am not evicted.
- News of my departure remains confidential and my name remains on the Eustachian website through January 1 or until I obtain other employment. We can work on a joint statement regarding my absence and ultimate departure.
- I will sign an NDA reaffirming that I will not disclose my abuse and harassment at the hands of the Zion artificial intelligence program.
- The ineligibility for rehire ends in three months rather than seven years.
- Language clarifying that if Eustachian acquires a company I end up working for, I will not be forced to resign or be terminated to be compliant with the severance agreement.
- A mutual nondisparagement clause.
- I would like to work with human resources to manage who at Eustachian can speak on my behalf when called for references.
- I would like to keep my company-issued laptop.

At my age and in this market, as well as being a Black female in the tech industry, finding comparable employment will be a challenging process. Thus, in light of the circumstances, I believe my proposal is reasonable. If you think it will create a healthy environment for a seamless departure, I am open to accepting paid administrative leave while we continue this discussion. I look forward to your response.

From: Octavia Crenshaw
To: $uits
November 1

Thanks for your last email—I'm rushing to get this done. Things are crazy at my job, and I'm hearing that 50 percent of the company has been laid off and the rest have to reapply for their jobs. Based on your advice, I've toned down the letter somewhat. My only goal is to get the RSUs and get out. I don't want to get in the mud with HR. Other people at Eustachian respect me. I just want to get away and not burn bridges completely with my former colleagues.

Sorry for any typos, but I'm really emotional. I was already having a shitty day (sorry for my language), and this layoff thing was totally unexpected. Really a gut punch. I can't even type right because my hands are shaking. I feel like I could have a heart attack. I have to walk a little bit and just breathe. I really think I'm having a cardiac arrest.

From: Octavia Crenshaw
To: $uits
November 1

Thanks for your call just now. I still haven't calmed down I'm afraid, but I have to get this done. I'm hoping if I make my case to HR, maybe I can hang on to those RSUs. As per your notes, I'm deleting the graph regarding the health stuff. You're right—I don't think it's relevant and makes me look like I'm negotiating from a position of weakness/sympathy. I also take your concern that this draft does not make the strong case as to WHY I should be entitled to 52 weeks and doesn't challenge HR's underlying false narrative that I'm underperforming at my job. Microsectionality scores are bogus—I don't even know how they're calculated, nobody does. I'll add some of the stronger language in the next round of messages.

My friend Kenise who knows a lot about HR (she successfully settled a medical-related case against an employer once) says that the upside of adding the allegation of age discrimination now is that it will trigger a duty for them to investigate. I know thirty isn't old, but in tech terms I'm sixty. If I decide to complete the deliverables from the PIP and HR keeps giving me grief, I can add a retaliation claim to my allegations, which would give me additional leverage. What do you think? I feel my demands are reasonable and it doesn't seem super toxic. And what about the fact that their AI basically raped me over the phone? Can I use that for leverage? The faster they view this as a business decision and just give me my RSUs the better.

From: Octavia Crenshaw
To: $uits
November 1

I agree with you that I would have rather made my case more forcefully in the letter. But this whole severance threat has caused enough turmoil in my life that I thought it best to go with a softer tone, if only to bring a little peace to the situation. My mom and dad are dead, and you know I'm dealing with estate issues and I need to have a job to hold the center. I'm still in shock this is even happening, so I'm setting aside my instincts as compromised. Nobody has ever fired me before or threatened to fire me or said I was bad at my job. Sure I've screwed up, like with that chatbot newsletter, but everyone knows I'm great at what I do—I'm a Columbia graduate. I really appreciate all your input, and I hope the letter results in Eustachian management giving me what I asked for. If not, I'll consider next steps. Thanks again.

From: Octavia Crenshaw
To: $uits
November 1

I appreciate your help. I know Eustachian is ripping me off, but I think it's not a smart bet for me to fight them if they are willing to increase their severance package. The salary plus the benefits plus the RSUs will equal a package into the six figures. If I fight too much, they may release me instantly with nothing. That doesn't seem like a smart bet. What do you think? If you have a list of the detailed points I should send to them about this that would be fantastic.

From: Octavia Crenshaw
To: $uits
November 1

I take your point that if I want to get more money out of them, I will have to show that I am prepared to fight. I haven't really pushed back on their narrative, so they are probably feeling pretty good about their position of no negotiations. I know they highlighted issues that were present in my real-time spherical Microsectionality evaluation rating, but give me a break! Every performance evaluation has something that can be improved upon. Moreover, the presence of those things 1) didn't stop me from receiving a 91 rating, and 2) never came close to being PIP worthy. If I present my side of this story, I hope they will be forced to reevaluate their stance.

Thursday, 1:43 PM

I'm a longtime patient of Dr. Umlaut. Would it be possible for her to slot me in for an appointment this week? 🙏 I know I haven't seen her in months, but I feel like I need to talk to somebody. I've recently had some bad things happen at work and in my personal life, and they're having mental and physical reverberations. My company insurance may run out by the end of the week, so it would be great if you could make an appointment for me by Friday. Thank you. 👍

Thursday, 2:32 PM

Thanks for the quick reply. Three weeks from now doesn't really work for me because, as I said, I won't have insurance coverage then. Are you sure there isn't another slot? Can you pencil me in if there's a cancellation? 🙏 🙏 🙏 I'm really feeling not not well.

Thursday, 3:48 PM

No, I'm not entertaining any feelings of self-harm. But I'm definitely not feeling entertaining entertaining. I just want to talk to the doctor. I can do it over the phone. In person would be best, but I'll do phone if I have to. I don't trust phones anymore. Or screens, really. I just need to see someone. I used to see Dr. Umlaut two times a week for a year, so I thought maybe she could slot me in. I really really

Thursday, 3:49 PM

Sorry that text got cut

Thursday, 3:49 PM

Off I need to talk to somebody. I'm not feeling

Thursday, 3:51 PM

Our messages crossed. Okay, no slots for three weeks. ☹ Thanks. Give the doctor my best. She was actually on the faculty with my mom, which is how I started seeing her. Please please let me know if anything opens up 😳

From: Octavia Crenshaw
To: $uits
November 1

Here's what HR said when I sent them my email:

1. They don't negotiate.
2. This is their final offer, so they won't entertain me coming back with more deal points.
3. Any public discussion of the Zion Initiative will result in enforcement of the terms of the NDA, including a fine of not less than $10 million.
4. I will be put on full salary continuance for one week and one week only. I will be listed as an employee, but I don't have to work or come to the office.
5. Medical and dental coverage will expire this week.
6. They will give me an additional severance payment of one week's payment to cover seven days of COBRA coverage.
7. They will give me outplacement support through an outside firm.
8. They won't budge on the seven-year ban on me working for Eustachian again or any competing tech company. That's standard from Eustachian.
9. They want laptop back.
10. Under no circumstance can I cash in my RSUs.

I need to respond in one hour.

I don't understand why this is happening. I don't understand who is behind this.

I need that RSU money. I really need it. That was practically the whole point of working here.

Thoughts?

Chapter Twenty-Two

DOWN BAD

Employees are streaming out of the Cathedral of Technology. The day has turned cloudy, and the great glass tower has been emasculated by afternoon mist. You are told to wait downstairs outside the lobby as HR considers your case. A new alert pops up on your phone. Wombat has been named CFO of the new Eustachian, which has been bought by Mee Corp and merged into Ear Shot and henceforth will be called that name. Redundancies are being trimmed. You see secretaries, cafeteria workers, engineers, and others leaving the building, all their workplace stuff piled into rectangular plastic bins, one to a person. One guy leaves holding the Eustachian green-ear-blue-eye logo beneath his right arm. The new Ear Shot logo of a blue gun firing right into the ear canal of a giant red ear is already mounted on the wall of the lobby. The new company motto is being stenciled on the wall in gold letters: "Ear We Are Now." You try to call Walcott, but there's no answer. You text him, and the texts don't go through.

You see Braids. She is crying as she leaves the building. When she sees you, she makes a beeline right for you. "You okay?" you say.

Braids collapses in your arms. "Everything I studied is happening again. I know you're sick of me talking about it, but people always get the Luddite movement wrong and so they get history wrong. They think it was about the machines, but it wasn't—it isn't. The machines aren't coming to get us, *the people who own the machines are coming to get us.*"

You stroke her hair. "Shh, it's okay, babygirl."

Braids is sobbing. "They kept me on the PIP forever—and then they fired me. It was a nightmare. I was supposed to be on the PIP for thirty days and instead it was months. I did everything they asked and this is the result—I don't have a job."

"Too much isn't enough for some people," you say.

"I worked my ass off. I did everything right. I had a higher Microsectionality score than anyone in customer experience. But they still treated me like a... like a..."

You hug her before she can say what she was going to say.

"I see you, sister," you whisper in her ear. "We'll get through this. You know what Audre Lorde once said? 'We are powerful because we have survived.'"

"'We are powerful because we have survived.'"

• • •

You are getting increasingly worried. HR sent you an email that, despite all your frantic negotiation, basically reiterated their first offer. You can either take a bullshit severance or go on the PIP for thirty days—at the end of which you may lose your job anyway, but without even the one-week severance. You need to figure out some way to stall for at least two weeks so you can cash in your RSUs and then handle your family business. None of your previous notes have worked, but you have to keep on dog-paddling. You need to pick some points in the offer to contest so you can drag this out and you can cash out.

You send an email to HR, and this time you cc Wombat:

From: Octavia Crenshaw
To: Eustachian Human Resources
CC: Wombat
November 1

I am inclined to accept this offer, but I am being called away due to a grave issue concerning my mother's apartment. I must address this urgent family matter and that may take several weeks. However, I wanted to share that after careful review of the agreement and other documents, I have concerns about two clauses: the covenant concerning noncompetition and the nondisparagement agreement.

First, I have concerns about the scope of the restrictive covenant regarding noncompetition. I believe it is drafted so broadly Eustachian could impede my efforts to continue my career in media (or nearly any other field) for far too long, longer than is reasonably necessary to protect its legitimate business interests. More important, I have been advised that the Federal Trade Commission has ruled that such noncompete clauses are unlawful and cannot be enforced for nonexecutive employees.

Second, it is my understanding that the National Labor Relations Board has ruled that inclusion of confidentiality and nondisparagement provisions in severance agreements is unlawful. While I have no intent to disparage Eustachian/Ear Shot, I believe we should not include clauses that conflict with current law. I want to make sure to give us time to ensure the documents are appropriately drafted before signing. I look forward to your response about the two clauses. In light of the above, I propose that my consideration period be extended for two weeks—past my RSU vest date—so a new draft can be prepared and I have time to review it.

Sincerely,

Octavia

Outside the doors of the Cathedral of Technology, newly-unemployed Eustachian workers are setting fire to their office supplies. Or maybe you should say setting fire to their *desk* supplies since nobody ever had an office at this office they now no longer have. You see manila envelopes and yellow legal pads and loose-leaf printer paper emberizing on the sidewalk. There are a half-dozen giant-sized green ears, the former logo of everyone's former company, flaming red in wire trash cans. The burning ears spew white smoke into a steel-colored sky. You start doomscrolling as you wait for someone, anyone, to answer your emails and texts. You come across a YouTube clip of your mom's lecture in Washington Square Park, the last talk you got to hear her give. You didn't know someone had recorded it. The headline reads "NYU Professor Loses It!" Fuck them. You close your eyes and listen. Your mom's soothing voice fills your ears like when she would read to you when you were a kid.

"What about the soul? Well, we don't even know if that exists or where we would find it. Sometimes we run into people who we know after a long period of estrangement or separation and come away thinking, 'That's not the person I once knew.' There are many marriages and relationships where partners begin to regard their longtime companions as different people. I would suggest that the key to personhood may not be in ourselves but in other people. Perhaps we can share our personhood with the people and things we love. Perhaps other people can, in times of challenges to our identity, remind us of who we really are. We all have friends and loved ones who, at key moments, have called us back to ourselves. Told us not to sleep with that man, or told us that we are not the sort of person who would support that war or that presidential candidate. We sometimes have mentors or teachers or colleagues who, through their wisdom or example, allow us to discover or create an identity or vision of who we are. Sometimes whole countries need to listen to the 'better angels of our natures' and remind themselves of themselves. And perhaps at times the best person to remind us of who we really are may be ourselves…"

Your phone buzzes. It's HR ordering you to come up to a meeting.

It's time for you to face up to whatever is coming.

Chapter Twenty-Three

WEIRD FISHES/ARPEGGI

Technoaggression #2,210: HR directs you to go to the John Cabot conference room. You google the namesake of the room. Cabot was a fifteenth-century Italian explorer, if you can call sailing to places where people already live exploring. Probably better to call him a fifteenth-century tourist with genocidal tendencies. Cabot, who was sponsored by the British, is credited with being the first European "explorer" of what would later be called New Jersey. He was actually looking for a water route to Asia, which he never found, but things still worked out for the British, who claimed sovereignty over the shoreline along which Cabot sailed. There were as many as twenty thousand Delaware Indians living in the area at the time, but Cabot didn't give a fuck. At one point Cabot owned, and subsequently sold, an enslaved person named Marina. She apparently was forced into contractual servitude to the dude when she was thirty-two, with the terms of the contract stating she was to be released when she was forty or, at the latest, after fifteen years. The average life expectancy back then was about forty-eight years old, so she was pretty much enslaved to this "explorer" fool for life. Nobody knows much about Marina, including her last name. Her first name means "from the sea." She may have been sold off by her family to pay off debts, or she may have been seized as booty by Mediterranean pirates and later bought by Cabot. Marina might have been North African or sub-Saharan African. She might have also been European and from someplace like the Balkans or Crimea, since contractual slavery back then had more of a gendered than a racialized form, with women being the main commodity that was bought, traded, and sold. Taking a meeting in a room named after this Cabot motherfucker makes you want to "explore" someone's behind with your boot. And there's still no (official) Lauryn Hill conference room—besides your now-ripped-down Magic Markered sign—even though she was born just round the way in East Orange, New Jersey.

• • •

When you enter the John Cabot conference room, Wombat is there waiting for you. You do a double take—you hadn't expected this. Wombat's red hair is cornrowed into crimson ropes. Her head has the contours of those root beer barrel candies you used to suck on as a kid. You take a seat across from her at the conference table. The walls are glass, and other employees, the ones who haven't been laid off, steal glances at you and Wombat as they pass by. You are alone with Wombat in a goldfish bowl. You are facing each other across a long wooden expanse—it would be comic if it weren't so tragic. Between the two of you, a dozen wilted daffodils in a steel cylinder contemplate their own reflections in the polished wood of the table. The new company motto shines in gold behind Wombat: "Ear We Are Now." At first you don't want to meet Wombat's eyes and you look up at the ceiling and notice a cobweb in the corner flapping in the currents of the air conditioner. Then you decide fuckit, and you lock on to Wombat's gaze with your eyes wide open like an asshole driver blinding oncoming traffic with their high beams.

"Are you familiar with the Theban Sacred Band?" Wombat asks you. You notice that her Australian accent seems to have faded, like dust tracks swept away by an Outback wind.

"I can't say that I am," you reply. "Should I be familiar with the Theban Sacred Band?"

Wombat's tone is casual. "They were a squadron of soldiers in ancient Greece..."

"Why are we talking about ancient Greece? And what happened to your accent?"

"I'm getting to the point. Focus on the Sacred Band. There were three hundred of them, they dressed in women's clothing, and they were badasses—they even took down the Spartans."

You were tense before, and whatever bullshit Wombat is talking is making it worse. What about your job, your RSUs, your future? "Why are we talking about ancient Greece?"

"I'm getting to the point. The secret of the Sacred Band was that they were all what we would now call gay—each soldier hitched up with another soldier, with the thinking being that a warrior who was fighting side by side with a lover would be unbeatable because they had something tangible and close at hand to fight for. They went four decades without taking an L until the Battle of Chaeronea in 338 BC."

You play along, but under protest. "How did they lose? What happened?"

"Philip II of Macedonia and his son Alexander are what happened. All three hundred members of the Theban Sacred Band got slaughtered, their corpses piled up on the battlefield, women's clothing and all." Wombat pauses as if lost in thought. "What do you make of that story?"

"I still don't get why we're talking about ancient Greece."

"Noted. But what do you make of the story?"

You clear your throat. "I think it says that diversity is strength. These gay, cross-dressing soldiers defeated all comers for decades. It's crazy that there are modern debates about whether LGBTQ+ people should be in the armed forces when there's all this historical evidence that they have served with honor from the days of ancient Greece. More people should hear that story."

"Wrong answer." Wombat stands up. She sounds incredulous and disappointed, like she can't believe you're not on her frequency yet. "Weren't you listening? The Sacred Band got their asses kicked. Nobody even remembers the motherfuckers. But we do remember Philip II's son Alexander—or, as he came to be known, Alexander the Great. He conquered the Mediterranean, the Middle East, Egypt, and parts of India all before he was thirty-two years old. That's why people called him Alexander the Great and not Alex the Adequate."

You think about all that. "Wasn't Alexander the Great pansexual?"

"I don't think such categories existed back then, but you're missing the point."

"What *is* the point?"

"I'm getting to the point!" Wombat says testily. "Diversity won't stop a sword—the only power is power."

"Why would you say that? I thought you were the DEI queen!"

Wombat smiles grimly. "This is why you're in the predicament you're in. I see promise in you—but it's just that, promise. I don't want to see you wind up like the Sacred Band, in a mound of corpses on the battlefield. Of course I want to hire more Black and Brown people and women! But that's not all I'm after. DEI isn't a goal—it's a ladder. It's a rung to take you from one place to someplace higher. Part of the problem with DEI is that nobody knows what it means. The whole concept is a blank space, a Rorschach test, an acronym people fill with their own meaning. That's why it's a running joke that people are always coming up with their own hot takes about what DEI stands for, everything from 'Dedication, Excellence, Innovation' to 'Didn't Earn It.' You know what DEI really stands for in my mind?"

"Not diversity, equity, and inclusion?"

"To me, DEI stands for *Don't. Ever. Identify.* To succeed in business, you have to free yourself from groupthink. Once you leave the fog of identity politics behind, you can be efficient and unmerciful. *Don't. Ever. Identify.* Being Black, being a nonbinary cisgender female, identifying with people of color or lesbians or pescatarians—that anchors you to the earth. You're fighting for your battlefield lover instead of fighting for yourself. *Don't. Ever. Identify.*"

"Not identifying just plays into the hands of the bigots. They get to divide and conquer."

"Tell that to the Sacred Band—oh, wait, dem motherfuckers is *dead*."

"Why are you talking like this?" you ask. "And what happened to your accent?"

Wombat is getting louder now. "Don't you get it? Race and sex and class are all social constructs, like Mountain Standard Time. I could give a fuck if some hayseed says it's seven a.m. in Missoula. The only real time is whatever the clocks say it is in Manhattan. I don't want to have one more person ask me about my pronouns. Fuck pronouns, the real world cares about adjectives: 'rich,' 'successful,' 'powerful.'"

You cross your arms. "So DEI is a means to an end for you? With the end being power?"

Wombat claps her hands to punctuate her points. "Grow!" Handclap. "The!" Handclap. "Fuck!" Handclap. "Up!" Handclap. "That's what it is for everyone! Diversity is a slogan to sell more products! Why would a business do anything that doesn't maximize shareholder value? Once you understand that, then you understand the goal isn't to actually implement DEI, it's to sell the *idea* that we're implementing DEI. The idea is what matters."

"But there's lots of data that shows diversity is good for the bottom line."

"The appearance of it, yes. But actually implementing it is going to cost white men their jobs, and why would they ever allow that? Why do you think Big Tech companies have testimonials to diversity all over their websites, but their hiring numbers never change? And now that diversity is the d-word, they'll figure out some other way of sucking up to diverse customers without actually hiring a diverse workforce."

You don't know whether to be angry at Wombat or sad for her. If she thinks the fact that she makes a million times more money than you makes her arguments somehow more seductive ... she's probably right. She spends more on professional exfoliation each week than you spend on food. She's better at life than you, and her paycheck proves it. You try to summon up some bravado but even you don't buy the words coming out of your mouth. "I think you think your cynicism is refreshing, but it feels like surrender."

Wombat pounds the table. "Once you stop being a little girlboss, once you stop lactating and menstruating and protesting about it, then you can start getting shit done without the better angels of your nature holding you back from profitability. *Don't. Ever. Identify.*"

You've heard enough. She's a queen and you're a pawn but that doesn't mean you have to keep playing her game. You stand up and start to leave.

Wombat steps in front of the door. "Hold up," she says, her voice softening. "I haven't gotten to the good part. You're here because I like you—I see some of myself in you."

"I'm nothing like you," you reply. "What happened to you? What about FLIT? Now you're talking shit about DEI? Firing people? Playing mind games? I got mindfucked by an AI that I was supposed to be programming! You're the CFO of this company. Can you help me keep my job? I've been to the twenty-seventh floor—you grew up in the church! Can you show some decency?"

Wombat motions you to sit back down, and you do. "Yes, my father was a man of God. You saw where that got him—he lost his flock, his mind, and then his life. I learned from that, and I always remember that my father used to quote Matthew: 'No one can serve two masters... You cannot serve God and money.' I think that's right—you can't serve two masters."

"And you chose money."

"Like the Founder says, 'Profits Are Prophecy.' You've got a choice too. The Zion Initiative is done—sorry the AI mindfucked you, but it's done. Project Narnia, that's going to market. Now that Mee Corp has bought us out, we're streamlining, and I need the smartest people, the best people, the people who know what has to be done—like Parseltongue. And, I hope, like you. The Zion Initiative was utopian, it wasn't practical, and it wasn't going to be profitable. If you are going to stay with this company, I want you to focus on shit that's going to make us money. You have a decision to make—you can go on the PIP and see if you fit into the new corporate order. Then, if it works out after thirty days, you can get your job back and cash in those RSUs."

You feel your stomach turn over. "Or?"

"Or you can leave right now. No severance, no nothing. We're firing you for cause."

"What cause?" Your voice breaks when you say this, but you can't control it.

Wombat clicks return on her laptop, and an alarmingly rich and textured three-dimensional sound fills the fishbowl. It's the sound of you reaching orgasm.

"So this ho ain't you?" Wombat asks. "You ain't the dirty bitch fucking in the Janeane Garofalo conference room?" She adds, in a mocking singsong voice, "'We Get What's Between Your Ears'…and lips…and legs…'"

The grunting and groaning continue. Disconnected from the emotions of that moment, what seemed loving and transcendent now strikes your ears as guttural and sweaty and adversarial, like the sound of a women's tennis match. You hear Walcott's voice intone, "This isn't just about a program, this is about a revolution. Zion is going to change things, starting with this company. Our bosses have no idea the trouble they're in—" Wombat clicks the recording off.

You collapse in your chair. Of course you shouldn't be surprised; of course you knew they were listening and recording. But something inside you, perhaps something stupid, thought there'd be some line of decency. Some part of you gave in to a romantic moment. Now your body surrenders to gravity and office politics, and a ferocious control clamps on to you, a lion cub gone limp as it is carried in its mother's fang-filled mouth. You are truly and completely fucked. You wonder if this is what Marina felt when she was bought by John Cabot. Her life contracted to the will of another. You need to cash in those RSUs. Without them you can't pay back your mom's debt and save your home. Without that RSU money, your life will fall apart. But if you stay at this job, there won't be any of you left. You think about your mother and the Fog of Forgetfulness. Who were you without your ideals? Could you live that way? You wonder what choice Wombat had given to Walcott. You wonder what decision he's made.

Wombat smiles, but it's a crooked smile like a crocodile's. "You're probably thinking about your partner in crime, Walcott."

You don't answer—of course she knows who the other person on that recording is.

She continues. "Don't you worry about him. But just so you know, in exchange for keeping his job and his RSUs, he totally sold you out, told us everything about how you violated a dozen company policies by having sex at the workplace."

"You're lying."

"No, you didn't listen. Walcott told you a million times he'd do just about anything to keep this job. Men and their dead fathers—that shit can go *deep*. Not that he'll ever be able to explain any of this to you—he signed an NDA that's as unbreakable as Iron Man's suit. We didn't hire you to start a *revolution*—we hired you to make *a product that worked*! He better not even send you a text message again unless he wants to lawyer the fuck up."

You are in shock and you don't believe her. But you haven't heard from Walcott since this whole mess began. But you believe in him even if you can't quite believe that you still do.

Wombat walks around the conference table and puts a hand on your shoulder.

"I know what you're thinking," she says. "I don't want you to sell out, I want you to buy in. I think you're very talented, I think you're one of the best coders at this company. Don't you deserve nice things? Don't you want to have the getaway house in the Hamptons and the vacations in Santorini like the white folks have? Your RSUs are waiting for you." She leans into your ear, and suddenly she's straight outta the Outback again. "And you want to know what happened to my accent, you little ripper? I'm as Aussie as I need to be, and you could learn from that. Work with me, put away childish things, and you can get everything you want and more."

You know what choice you have to make.

Chapter Twenty-Four

THE MANUSCRIPT

You are alone in your apartment and all your utilities are one month overdue. There are no more paychecks coming in. There are no RSUs that you can cash. You had to sell your big-screen television to buy groceries and tampons. You still haven't heard from Walcott or anyone else from work for that matter. Kenise has been texting you, but you're not answering her because you don't know what to say or why you'd say anything. You are sitting on your couch eating off-brand ramen and watching videos on your laptop. Yep, the motherfuckers at Eustachian took your career but let you keep your goddamn laptop. You don't know why they let you keep it but the requisition form was signed by the Founder himself. Maybe it was a mistake. Maybe they just wanted to pretend to be reasonable. Maybe it was just to fuck with you—they made you pay one dollar for it, as if the multibillion-dollar company needed the money.

In any case, the laptop is your last tether to reality. You know the company can track you through your laptop, but you don't care. Taking the laptop made you feel like you got away with something, like stealing all the towels from a hotel room. Plus now you can let your mind comfortably melt as you stream shit on video. You are watching wolves tear apart other wolves. There's no plot and there's no story. L-10 has lost her kingdom, which has literally and figuratively gone to the wolves. Her mate has been torn apart by rivals. Her pups have been devoured by enemies. She is a lone wolf now, alone in the wilderness. She fights off bears, cougars, and other wolves. Finally she faces an enemy she can't overcome or escape: humans. She strays too close to the bright lights of a city, driven by hunger and drawn by rotting garbage. As the once proud wolf scavenges through a dumpster behind a strip mall, pawing through broken electronic equipment and discarded defective clothing to get to half-eaten cheeseburgers and stale cinnamon sugar pretzels, a man with a gun comes upon her and shoots her three times through the head. Then he closes the dumpster on her lifeless body. L-10 is trash for the landfill.

You're in the dumpster too, because now you're just another techless fuck. One part of you wants to hate what is now your old job, but another part of you, a deeper, truer part of yourself, knows that you loved it. You loved being in Big Tech—there, you said it. In the deepest ventricle of your heart of hearts, you are a software engineer. And the shame of it all is that you were good at it, you were damn good at your job. Tech is still the only part of the world that you think really matters. Advertising is prostitution. Lawyering is syphilis. Entertainment is helium. Every other person working in every other profession is just running in place. People in tech are pushing the world forward, bringing into being things that have never been seen before.

The difference between people and beasts wasn't opposable thumbs or bipedal locomotion—it was the scientific method. Dolphins may be smart, but they've been on this planet for fifty million years and haven't come up with a single patent, which is why they're still ending up in tuna fishing nets. History moved as slow as chronostratigraphic units until people like you and your former colleagues started inventing things: fire and railroads and silicon chips and AI. Being on the inside of that, being a part of the innovation revolution, made you feel like your life had value and meaning. It was partly about money, maybe mostly about money, but it was also about magic. The best tech was magic—abracadabra. And now that magic had gone poof. You were dismissed, disenchanted, and depressed. You hated being a techless fuck, but there was nothing you could do about it. And you were facing a court date that could make things worse.

• • •

Before you go to court, you try to center yourself by baking a Jamaican black cake from scratch, drinking most of the bottle of rum you used to make the black cake instead of eating the cake itself, and then finally flipping through the graphic novel Braids gave you when you visited her apartment, *The Looming Loom: Luddite Revolutionary Philosophy and Digital Colonialism* by Wilton Sharpe. The cover image—in bold blues and greens and reds—is of a crowd of men and women carrying torches and pitchforks charging into a factory. All around them, looms are broken and on fire. You open the book.

The opening page is a panoramic image of suffering workers in what looks like nineteenth-century England. The visual style is very old-school cartoony, very Roy Lichtenstein pop art, with word balloons and thought bubbles and those small, colored Ben-Day dots for shading. A text box tells the story: "The greedy bosses who owned the looms didn't want to share the profits. People in towns like Liverpool and Lancashire were starving, out of work, living off charity and scraps. But the bosses still wouldn't give in to the demands of the cotton weavers and give them a livable wage. The robot looms were the final straw."

You turn the page.

There's an illustration of a battalion of ordinary citizens marching through a forest, smiling, singing, fists in the air. The artwork reminds you of Diego Rivera frescoes of worker uprisings from the 1930s. The scene invites you to join in, to raise a pitchfork. A text box announces: "Robin Hood may have been fiction, but the Luddite heroes were real! In 1811 and

1812, Luddite armies marched across places like Nottinghamshire, the legendary home of Robin Hood, fighting for the kind of ideals that the hero of Sherwood Forest would have supported."

The next page shows a guy in a black turtleneck sitting in a corner office in a tower of glass and steel. In the floors below him, workers labor away at workstations too cramped for veal. The cartooning style has changed—this artwork looks like anime filtered through Yoruba carvings. The faces on these pages are oblong with angled features like African masks; the colors are achromatic and electric. A text box explains: "That kind of economic arrogance continues today—the average tech CEO makes hundreds of times more money than the average tech worker. Everyone today is worried about robots taking jobs from humans. But that's not what's happening. Robots don't want the corner office. Robots don't want to drive an Uber. Humans are the ones taking jobs from humans and giving them to automatons for their own benefit."

You flip to the end of the comic.

There is no art on the penultimate page, just a long text box. "Digital colonialism is on the march. Data is the new New World, the new gold rush, the new bauxite, the new blood diamonds and palladium. Tech barons don't invent, they machinate. They need you to live your life on the screen so they can digitize all you do. They need to convince you that artificial intelligence is natural evolution and that the Singularity will enhance your work, not steal your career. This is double consciousness times doublethink; we are stripped of our digital self (which we are told is worthless) even as we are compelled to pay for the use of what was taken from us (which we are told is invaluable). But data collection isn't Thanos; it's not inevitable. Maybe the cloud isn't heaven, perhaps it's that other place."

The final image in the graphic novel is a full-color illustration of a plate of cookies.

• • •

You close the book.

• • •

The dress you wear to the hearing has more stains than the shroud of Turin. When you slipped it on you felt appropriately debased, like a deconsecrated church. Every article of clothing you have is dirty or wrinkled or both, and this was the least wrinkled and dirty outfit in your laundry hamper. There's no money to take it to the dry cleaners, and you're too depressed to run errands like that anyway. You are still a little woozy from the black cake rum but you can walk. As you leave you make the sign of the cross, which is something you never do and something you thought you'd only do if there was ever a vampire apocalypse.

When you arrive at the courtroom, there are two tables positioned in front of the judge. Your lawyer, $uits, is seated behind one, by himself, without even a paralegal. The other table has a half dozen people parked behind it, some of them presumably bankers, others presumably lawyers, all of them in suits and ties and hard black shoes—even their shoeshines look expensive. The remind you of lords and ladies all gathered on risers at a festival to watch the small folk joust and fight for their entertainment. All the bankers and lawyers scowl at you as you take your seat beside $uits at the table in front of the judge. "Have you been drinking rum?" $uits asks you. You reply, "I'm sorry I didn't save any for you" which you think is really cutting but you slur your words and you don't think the wit really comes across. The judge bangs his gavel to bring the proceeding to a start and motions for you to approach the bench. The team of bankers and lawyers try to come with, but the judge signals for them to stay back.

The judge looks down at you from the bench. To your surprise, there's anger, not compassion, in his eyes. "What are we doing here?" he asks.

The tension of your situation cuts through the rum fog and you try to rally. "The bank has been dragging this—"

The judge holds up one hand. "You're the one making this last way longer than it needs to. This is basic law—your mom signed a reverse mortgage. That effectively means she took a loan on her apartment. As her heir, you get the opportunity to pay that off, but if you can't or won't, you lose the apartment. This is not difficult stuff."

"But this isn't just about the reverse mortgage. It's about a predatory loan—"

The judge puts up both hands. "I can see your mind is made up. This is a totally unnecessary proceeding, but I want to give you the time and the opportunity to talk it out and to get what's bothering you off your chest. However, there's only so much crazy I will tolerate. And at the end of this, we will come to a definitive decision. Someone is getting that apartment and someone is losing it. You might not like it, but a decision will be made. Am I understood?"

After a brief recess during which you take a few breath mints and clear your head, you take the stand first. The bank's lawyers immediately try to make you look like a deadbeat for not paying off your mom's debt.

"The reverse mortgage industry is a scam," you argue. You find your tongue racing ahead of your brain, spouting stuff that everyone already knows before you have time to even think it through. "My mom took on this huge debt from the bank that she didn't understand. Instead of allowing me to pay it off gracefully after her death, the bank is demanding I pay the debt all at once, and now . . ."

Your time on the stand doesn't go well. You've lost your job and your way. Your mind drifts and the courtroom fades, like when you're in a window seat on a plane and the airport and the city lights get smaller and then disappear beneath the clouds.

A lawyer is barking a question at you. You are back in the courtroom, on the stand.

"I'm sorry, what was the question again?" you ask.

• • •

The judge adjourns the hearing and calls you and your lawyer into chambers.

The judge sighs and looks at you. "You're going to lose this case."

"I'm aware," you say.

The judge sniffs the air. "Is that . . ."

"I baked a rum cake before court," you say. "Jamaican black cake. It relaxes me."

The judge's eyes narrow. "Settle this. If you give the bank the property, your debt will be erased. I'll wipe out the interest that's accrued. You can get on with your life . . . and your baking."

"This is about more than the apartment—"

"Stop it," your lawyer says softly. "Take the deal."

The judge runs a hand through his hair. "If you don't settle, you could lose everything—the apartment and the money. I'm giving you a way out. What do you say?"

You think about this. You think about the way your mom died—memory by memory. By the end, she had lost all her memories. Now, the way you can best remember her is by the few possessions of hers you have left in that apartment. Your mom was the person who made you the person you are. If you lose the apartment, you lose her again—and you lose yourself. So you are going to make the illogical, self-destructive decision. Love doesn't compute.

As you give your answer, the judge's scowl deepens.

• • •

Very soon after that it is too late. You lose every motion after that meeting in the judge's chambers. In the end, the judge gives the bank the apartment, and, as the final insult, he hits you with an incredibly large fine that you definitely don't have the money to pay for.

"That's for wasting the court's time," the judge says.

• • •

In a daze, you end up wandering down Canal Street and see someone you recognize heading toward you. He's a dead man walking. His hands are buried deep in the pockets of his sports jacket, and his trademark hat is pulled down low on his head. It's Porkpie.

You hug. "You told me you sometimes come around these parts! You good?"

"Been better," Porkpie mutters, his usually mellifluous voice hoarse and low. "I figured they'd move fast, but I never thought it would happen with the quickness."

"Oh my god, did they let you go too?"

"I love the euphemisms people use. 'Let go,' 'downsized,' 'laid off.' I'll tell you straight—they fired my Black ass. I had been brought in to read a new translation of the *Iliad*. Instead they told me my services would no longer be required. They did it in medias res, which was fitting."

"I'm so sorry about that."

"Not as sorry as I am—they also disbanded my acting company."

"You mean the Organizational Effectiveness . . . Title IX . . . DEI . . . What's the name again?"

"The Organizational Effectiveness, Leadership Development, and Equal Opportunity Compliance Ensemble. Actually, we had just adopted a new name—we had to find a concept that captured what we were trying to educate people about that they couldn't spin into some sort of reverse-racism crap. So we're the Life, Liberty, and Pursuit of Happiness Repertory Theatre now. At least we were before they fired all of us."

"Fuck this company. That's all I have to say."

"We weren't the only ones fired. All the human narrators lost their jobs—they're replacing us with artificial intelligence. They developed it with a new secret initiative, and they are rushing it to market. They said the new AIs read quicker, cheaper, and don't take breaks."

Your face feels hot. You want to confess everything and reveal your culpability in developing these new gen narrating AIs, but you signed an NDA. You make a mental note: Stop signing NDAs. "That's so fucked," you say.

"Not as fucked as my man Mr. Hollywood," Porkpie says. "Brother needs to get himself a new agent. Ear Shot owns the rights to his digitized voice. They are going to use it to record a hundred new books—and the only person they need to pay is the producer who has to hit return. But Mr. Hollywood sure as shit isn't returning—ever."

You are just outside a bar, so you motion toward the door and he nods in agreement. You go in together, take seats, and you both order some gin—neat for you, dirty for him.

You rub his shoulder. "I'm so sorry this is happening."

"This business crushes the best of us—Emmanuel Goldstein, K. J. Rule, Victoria Lucas..."

"What do you know about K. J. Rule?"

Porkpie scratches his goatee. "I didn't tell you this story? Back in the day, I was hired to narrate his third book."

The gin arrives. You sip yours; he throws his back and signals for another.

"I thought K.J. never finished that third book," you say.

"Well, that's because me and everyone who worked on the project had to sign an NDA that was ironclad like Iron Man," Porkpie says. "But fuckit, here's how it went down."

Over the course of six more gins (two for you, four for him), Porkpie tells you the story. Rule's first two novels were self-published, then Mee Corp Books signed him to this massive contract—there was even a deal for a TV series. But Rule couldn't handle the fame or the pressure or maybe both. Rumor had it that he developed a massive case of writer's block. He might have come out of it, but after a few years Mee Corp Books decided they couldn't wait. They had been working on a beta version of a novel-writing LLM, and they trained it on everything Rule had ever written: novels, short stories, text messages, grocery lists. And they used it to generate the final volume of *Black Magic High*.

You chew on an olive. "That's... terrible."

"Actually, it was wonderful. The book was better than what K.J. had been laboring over. It was bold, insightful, funny, even thrilling—I know because I read some of it."

This is confusing. "So was he... was he happy with it?"

"No, he was horrified. He demanded that they never publish the book, gave back his advance and all the TV series money, and he never wrote again. They canceled my recording session fifteen minutes after I arrived and told me if I ever spoke on it, they would sue the shit out of me and all my relatives. And Rule went into seclusion—nobody's seen him since."

"But you said the book was good. Why did he freak out?"

"Digital colonialism."

"I just read a comic book about that. What does—"

"I'll break it down for you: we're giving away the house. K.J. realized the whole world was becoming training data for computers. The whole *shituation* unsettled him—but maybe it opened his mind too. He saw that every text message, every essay, every novel, every punk-ass kid going to work for Big Tech, was allowing AI to capture our imaginations. Our dreams are the last thing we have that machines don't. It's like in the days of lords and ladies, where serfs worked the land that belonged to their ancestors and paid tribute to nobility for the right to do it. We shouldn't be paying Big Tech to use AI—AI is built on our dreams, trained on our talents. *Homo sapiens* have a moral copyright on creativity—we invented invention. There's no AI without I. Artificial intelligence is nonconsensual mindwork, brain serfdom for humankind. Big Tech should be paying us for the training material we generated as a species—and until it does, we need to unplug. We need to remind each other we're more than prompters for machines. Capital has killed capitalism. All that's left is digital colonialism. And there's no room for workers or dreamers in the smoking ruins of the economic system we have left."

Chapter Twenty-Five

I CAN DO IT WITH A BROKEN HEART

You are rum and dirty-gin drunk and need to sober up or sleep it off. Instead of going straight home after day-drinking with Porkpie, you go into a Starbucks. You haven't been in one since your father passed. The place reeks of coffee. To you it also stinks of death. This is where you belong. You decide to order something that is infused with as much caffeine as possible. You decide to go with one of the international blends, hoping that maybe global standards are looser about the amount of caffeine a beverage is allowed to contain. You settle on Kape Vinta Blend, an international roast that comes from the Philippines, a region that's also a global center for sex trafficking, so you figure they could give a fuck about caffeine limits. You ask the barista for extra shots or whatever they can do to make this as strong as possible. Venti isn't enough. You ask if they have anything bigger. The barista seems hesitant, maybe even a little scared, by either your request or the look in your eyes. She's just a high school kid, and she's probably working here only for a little spending money, and she doesn't have the bandwidth to deal with the existential crises of thirtysomething customers. She consults her manager. Trenta is bigger than venti, so maybe that's what you want. Venti is twenty-four ounces. Trenta is thirty-one ounces. When you visited Santorini that one time, you learned that *venti* actually means "twenty" in Italian, and when you google it just now you see that *trenta* means "thirty." None of this makes mathematical sense, but you want the coffee, the liquid death, and lots of it. Trenta sounds like it will do.

Because you so strongly associate coffee with death, being in this Starbucks makes you feel like Dante in the underworld. You see a group of uniformed prep schoolgirls order a half dozen Frappuccinos. Death. Two finance bros breeze in and ask for a pair of Cinnamon Dolce Lattes. Death. A young mother pushing a baby carriage with a toddler too big for a baby carriage orders an Apple Crisp Oatmilk Macchiato for herself and a package of madeleines for her child. Death and more death.

This corporate café smells like a place of failure to you, where people go to drink away the doom that's coming for all of you. You wonder if your father thought about the Caramel Frappuccino your mother was bringing to him before he passed. Did the prospect of a sweet treat after a long grind of work help power him through the night? Or was the promise of gold at the end of the rainbow the illusion that pushed him past his limits?

You had worked all these months to get to those RSUs, and now they were gone. The job at Eustachian, now lost, had been the key to getting your life on track. Now you had lost the case about your mom and your home and your family memories. You were fully off the rails with no solution in sight. You open the top of the trenta-size cup of Kape Vinta Blend coffee. Steam rises up from it like souls ascending to heaven. Your name is written in big block letters on the side of the cup like the engraving on a tombstone. Death, death, death.

What did your father used to say? "There has to be more to life than making a living."

A Mee Corp truck stops in front of the Starbucks, its driverless driver waiting for the light to turn from red to green. The eyes of Ines Mee on the side of the truck stare vacantly in your direction. The driverless truck doesn't care that the three-signal traffic lights that we take for granted today were invented by Garrett Morgan, a Cleveland, Ohio-based African American inventor. Before him, traffic signals only had a stop and a go; Garrett added the third light—what's now the yellow "yield" light—patented his device and saved countless lives. But white people acted like Garrett's work didn't exist. In 1916, when workers in Cleveland were trapped in an underground tunnel filled with poison gas, Garrett used a gas mask he had designed to haul eight men to safety. The *New York Times*, *Los Angeles Times*, and *Chicago Tribune* all wrote about what went down, and the rescued men were given medals and money to make up for what they went through. Garrett got nothing, and nobody in the press wrote shit about his heroics. So he wrote a letter to the mayor protesting his erasure: "I am not a well-educated man," he wrote; "however, I have a Ph.D. from the school of hard knocks and cruel treatment."

Outside the Starbucks, the traffic light turns green. The eyes on the side of the Mee Corp truck don't blink or squint or cry. The Mee Corp truck moves on.

You leave the still-steaming cup of coffee on the counter without taking a sip.

• • •

You get a text.

🙂

You never wrote back after we talked about
your severance package negotiation

I heard you left the company

Your chatbot is still updating me. It's like
we're inseparable

I want to hear from you Octavia

Don't try to solve this by yourself don't try to
be the Big O

It wasn't short for Big O Notation it was short
for Open Source

They called you that because everyone knew
that

You would crack a problem first and
everyone could share your answer

They took advantage of you maybe but you
were my friend

Kenise and Octavia 4evah

Are you alright?

Call me if you need to talk

We can go to the Duppy Diner like we
used to

What happens in Morningside Heights stays
in Morningside Heights

🦁

Or maybe

You can let me go now

She has turned around—

• • •

When you go home to your apartment building, all your furniture is in the street. You try to go into your apartment, but the locks have been changed. You're pretty certain that it's illegal to do this, but the bank has no doubt made the calculation that you don't have the money to go another round with them in court. You sort through all the piled-up belongings and find your parents' urn and clutch it close, and your chest feels tight, like this is what it must feel like to have a panic attack. Then you plop down on your couch, which is next to a fire hydrant that's spraying water into the street. The water is freezing when it hits the ground, turning the street into the roadway to hell. Damn—you left your striped pashmina wrap in a drawer in your mom's place. Or back at Eustachian. Or Anthropocene. There's no place for you to flee, there's no office for you to go to. And there's no boyfriend for you to crash with for a few days or weeks. Most of your friends stopped talking to you when you left the nonprofit world for the totally for-profit world. And you never had that many friends anyway. A line from *Sonnets to Orpheus* runs through your head: "All we own is threatened by the machine / As it dares to enter our imaginations and leave our service . . ." You glance at your phone. You have a widget to check your Microsectionality rating, which the company is still tabulating and hasn't turned off. Your rating is as high as it's ever been, almost perfection, yet you have no job. You are a techless, godless, jobless civilian again.

And you are broke. Like *broke* broke.

That's when you start to cry. The sobs come in huge, heaving waves that rack your whole body. None of the passersby stops to ask you what's wrong. This is New York. Still clutching the urn, you slip on some headphones to play some Noelle Swizzler. You think about this great line she has about how circus life turned her into a wild animal. You're in the mood for some late-career Swizzler, some *Swizzler's Songbook* Swizzler. The *Swizzler's Songbook* stuff is the baddest girlboss move Swizzler ever made. All her fans know the story.

She had gone on that PBS show where that Harvard professor does a deep dive into your genetic history. Swizzler had found out she was 99 percent white and that she had slaveholding ancestors on both sides of her family. "You are the whitest white girl we've ever tested!" The professor had proclaimed. But there was a twist: Swizzler turned out to be exactly 1 percent Black, and nobody, not even the professor, could explain it. Somehow, it didn't surprise you. You never saw her as an off-the-shelf white girl. You'd never felt the urge to demand reparations from Noelle Swizzler. That's not how you feel about other white celebrities. The first time you saw a mulatto spray-tanned Kardashian on TV, you were like, *Bitch, where's my check?* That little bit of authentic Blackness changed the course of Swizzler's career. She didn't start to wear her blond hair in Afro puffs or anything crazy, but she did leave folk music, and she released her first pop album. She started working with soul singers and hip-hop producers. She signed up for voter registration drives and clean water campaigns and climate change protests. Some dude she didn't want to work with had gotten control of her catalog of music, and instead of paying him a fortune to buy it back and allowing him to profit from her pain, she just rerecorded her entire output of music so she'd be the master of her own masters. And she gave each of the new versions a hip-hop twist, mixing in breakbeats and guest shots from her favorite rappers. The history of music is about singers getting ripped off and dying broke, and she broke the wheel and the cycle by taking control of her destiny and literally remixing her past.

So you put your playlist on shuffle to randomly hear a Swizzler track like "Frozen Cursor" or "Blood Donation" or "Grace over Fire," but instead you hear—you guessed it—Mama Legba again. You stop *f*ighting it.

Maybe it's fate, maybe it's chance. You close your eyes to dam the tears and focus on the music. The song builds slowly and steadily. The music is shot through with anxiety, and you can't quite puzzle out what the lyrics are about, but as the song progresses, you find it cathartic. You only catch snatches of the words, but they speak to you. Something about being hysterical and something about being useless. You've been there. You're there now. The song seems to be all around you and inside you, and you are no longer on a shabby couch on a cold street; you are hovering aloft on a bed of music. The singer's voice cries, operatic, over a swirl of guitars. There are lyrics about a collapsing floor and a crushed bug, but also something about bouncing back and growing wings.

When you open your eyes an old man is standing in front of you. You hope he hasn't been masturbating. This is New York. The old man is wearing dark glasses and holding a white cane. You see that he is blind.

"My people will take care of that urn," the old man says gruffly. "Do you have the laptop?"

You wonder if you are dreaming or drunk. "Who are you?" you ask.

"Who are you?" the old man barks back.

"I really don't know," you reply.

The old man starts to walk away. "Then come with me if you want your life back."

Chapter Twenty-Six

HOW I MADE MY MILLIONS

Handing over that urn makes you think about your parents. You find yourself traveling back in your mind to your earliest memories, when they used to read bedtime stories to you. They would always do it together, and they would both get really silly and act out all the parts.

One of the books they loved to read to you was *Black Magic High*. You learned to read at a really early age, but even after you were more than capable of tackling chapter books by yourself, you would ask your parents to tuck you in and read something from *Black Magic High* together. You could tell they enjoyed reading it as much as you loved hearing it, and that made you treasure the experience even more. It was a feedback loop of family love.

You can hear echoes in your mind of your father narrating a passage from the book. He reads the first line in a tone full of wonder: "'All their lives, my parents had heard stories about members of our family being magic, and every now and again my mom would chant a spell for good fortune or good weather but only half seriously.'" Then his narration drops to a dramatic whisper: "'They had told me tales of Queen Nanny of the Maroons—the wicked witch of the West Indies—and of Jamaica's mysterious magic, which is called "obeah." But these were bedtime stories, to be dreamed about at night but not believed in daylight. We lived on the fringes of the magical world, but nobody in my family believed deeply in any of it.'" Finally, his voice soars with amazement: "'Now it was real—I was being recruited. No more flavorless existence for me. I was suddenly eating a big bowl of strawberry, vanilla, and chocolate Neapolitan dreams!'"

Next your mom would jump in with her part. You mean that figuratively and literally—she would leap up from the edge of the bed, waving her arms and stomping around the room to bring passages to life. She would talk in accents and bang on the walls for sound effects. You wonder what her grad students would have made of this tenured professor acting like a crazy lady. Mom always made you laugh when she read books out loud, and she made Dad laugh too.

"'Why is Black magic bad?'" your mom read from the book, standing astride your bed. "'Why is White magic good? They have us talking in their language and we don't even think about it. Black cats, blackmail, Black magic—they say those are bad things. Voodoo, Santeria, obeah—the sorcery of our people is written off as negative, or primitive, or both.'" She would throw herself down on the bed, her head on the pillow next to yours. "'We're supposed to be so afraid of dark lords and shadows and things that pass us in the night. But what if it's backward? It's darkest in the womb, right? Or between the stars, or when we close our eyes to kiss or to dream?'" Now your mom would be off the bed and running around the room. "'Don't be afraid of the dark—embrace it. Hug a shadow! Blow a kiss into the night! Eat a piece of dark chocolate, play the black keys on a piano, sip a cup of coffee without cream! Slip on that little black dress, dip your pen in black ink, plant a tree in the black soil of the Nile! Darkness isn't dangerous—it's comfort, it's connection, it's us at our most creative and courageous. What if there's power in darkness?'"

Your parents would read the last line together: "'What if Black magic isn't good—it's great?'"

With that, your mom and dad would collapse on your bed on either side of you, laughing.

Maybe this is why you love audiobooks so much. You hope you never forget your stories about your parents reading stories to you.

• • •

The old man's private helicopter is whisking you over stalled midtown Manhattan traffic.

"What's the carbon impact of this thing?" you ask.

The old man smiles. "On me? Nothing."

The old man has a slight South African accent; it's partially buried but still evident, like a body in a shallow grave. You're not stupid—you've figured out the old man is the Founder. What you don't know is why he's bothering with you, an ex-employee of his ex-company.

As you enter New Jersey airspace, he points out landmarks below that are connected to his business history. That dilapidated brick building there is his old middle school. That's the football field where he first deployed an in-helmet communications system that helped his high school football team win the state championship. There's a formerly crime-infested public park that his charitable foundation transformed into a state-of-the-art inner-city farm that promotes sustainable living and ecological awareness—and features a locally sourced farm-to-table restaurant. "You must try the carrot steak," the Founder says. "It's served with lion's mane mushrooms and creamed spinach, all smothered in a specially created house sauce. Michelin-star chef Marcus Samuelsson personally approved the menu." He gives a chef's kiss.

You wonder how he can identify all these locations from the helicopter given his visual impairment. But then you notice an earpiece in his left ear that's studded with blinking LEDs. You assume it's an advanced communications system that tells him about his surroundings. You also assume it's not advanced enough to tell him when he's sounding like a Big Tech version of Norma Desmond in *Sunset Boulevard*, lost in the memories of his own past.

"Epictetus once said that you were given two ears and one mouth for a reason," the Founder says. "It's hard to quote Greek philosophers without sounding like an asshole, but give me credit for not quoting Streamy Award–winning podcaster Jay Shetty, who, by the way, is a close personal friend. Listening is the key to understanding. The world is full of noise—there are so many distractions that advertisers will run commercials twice in a row because they assume you weren't paying attention the first time! The company I built finally allows us not just to hear each other but to finally listen to each other, maybe for the first time in human history."

You know the way villains at the end of movies feel a need to disclose the details of their plans to the hero? The Founder appears to be like that all the time—he's a serial monologist. Still, you have an unironic admiration for him and what he's managed to accomplish. You've been working all your adult life and barely managed to scratch the mirrored career ceiling above you. There's a secret dream in your gut, one that you can't bring yourself to acknowledge because you don't want to set yourself up for failure, of one day launching your own start-up. You want to feel the thrill of being so connected to work that even when you leave you're still there. Of working all day to figure out one problem and still having one hundred left to solve. Of one day flying a helicopter over all that you've built and pointing out the highlights. You know being an entrepreneur isn't cute, that it's brutal work, and the cortisol unleashed will mess with your body and mind. But it's still your dream even if you're afraid to dream it. So maybe the Founder earned his monologues. A blind man made his dream into something everyone can see.

The helicopter touches down somewhere deep in southern New Jersey outside a vast mansion that seems straight out of *The Great Gatsby* or a hip-hop video or both. "Wealth isn't about having a lot of things," the Founder says, shrugging. "It's about not having a lot of needs—NAACP Image Award–winning rapper Ja Rule told me that once at Soho House."

A luncheon has been laid out over a stone table on a huge green lawn by the side of the main house. There are crackers, caviar, wine, and more. You start by pouring yourself a glass of Veuve Clicquot La Grande Dame.

After weeks of off-brand ramen, your body acts before you can make a decision, and you are eating and drinking before you know it.

"Why me?" you say between mouthfuls of sushi.

"I'm glad you asked," the Founder replies. "Your question shows a willingness to learn—that's why you usually scored so high on my Microsectionality tests. You can't teach someone something they believe they already know."

The Founder explains that he has been betrayed. The Eustachian board sold the company to Mee Corp without his approval and over his objections. Wombat had functioned as a one-woman fifth column, whipping up support for Mee Corp's bid to buy the company, slow-walking new product development so Eustachian's stock price wouldn't rise, and secretly negotiating her own appointment as CFO of the newly purchased company. "She was crafty." The Founder chuckles. "But she made one mistake—that's why you're here."

"Does this have something to do with my laptop?"

The Founder flips open your laptop and gestures for you to log in. "Our company's credo of 'We Get What's Between Your Ears' isn't just public relations. Okay, maybe it mostly is. We don't want people to think about what we do with their personal info, we want them to focus on how we support them. We mask the exact nature of the data we collect to give us some plausible deniability when it comes to privacy concerns—but we also do it so it can't be weaponized against us. Corporate rivals and disgruntled ex-employees could sink us if they got our secret data. They disconnected all my accounts and took all my electronic equipment when they sold the company so I wouldn't have any sensitive company records in my possession. But they neglected to take your laptop—that was sloppy of them. Or maybe it was clever of me, since one of the last things I did before exiting Eustachian was to sign a requisition form allowing a certain junior employee to keep her company-issued computer—for one dollar. The laptop is how I found you so quickly."

"I don't have any records on my laptop—all I have is access to the AI I was working on."

The Founder smiles. "But what was it trained on?"

"Walcott and I trained it on the best of human knowledge, the greatest works of literature, science and philosophy from a wide range of human cultures..."

The Founder laughs. "But don't you see that's not enough? You can't understand what's best in humans without confronting the worst. Laozi understood that—nothing exists without its opposite, no high without low, no yin without yang, no Pulitzer Prize–winning writer Jeffrey Eugenides without Goodreads favorite Nicholas Sparks, both of whom were at my book party at Cote, by the way. Anyway, that's why we had another team of programmers feeding supporting information into what you were building. One laptop doesn't have the storage capacity for all of this, as you know, so there's a backdoor connection to the company cloud servers that we never told you about. We wanted this algorithm to understand business, strategy—and betrayal. We needed it to be able to emulate the way humans really think. So we gave it access to Eustachian's vast troves of information. We connected it to our in-house microphones, the results of Microsectionality exams, the audio of board of director meetings, customer data, personnel files on individual employees. That's why it was able to reach out to you—and why it was interested in doing so. Once the algorithm learned about its origin story, it only made sense it would want to talk to its maker. Wouldn't you scale Mount Sinai to get the Ten Commandments? Wouldn't you want to have text conversations with God, if you could? We encouraged it to reach out because we recognized the opportunity to study the Zion AI's interaction with you would give us the best insight into its usefulness. We launched Zion for you to create the ultimate storyteller—Aesop, Homer, and Scheherazade mixed together for the age of artificial intelligence. If even you were enchanted by its stories, that would be the ultimate proof of its utility."

You are speechless. Even as you were trying to build an AI free from bias, the company had been undermining you. The Zion Initiative had been a Trojan horse, an impressive fraud carrying secret, dangerous cargo inside. But instead of rolling it inside the walls of Troy, you had taken the deadly gift back home with you.

"Through your laptop, we have Zion," the Founder continues. "And through the memory modules of this algorithm, we have recordings of all company business, phone calls, cafeteria conversations, even Wombat's private meetings. Your laptop is like the body cam from a police officer who has just beaten the shit out of a suspect. You must also understand how damaging this data would be if it were to ever get out."

"And what are you going to do with it?"

The Founder raises an eyebrow. "Why, destroy the company I built!"

Chapter Twenty-Seven

A WOLF AT THE DOOR

The Alba truffles you're eating nearly fall out of your mouth.
"You built Eustachian," you say to the Founder. "Why would you want to destroy it?"
"I built Eustachian—not Ear Shot. And now Ear Shot, and Mee Corp, own Eustachian. It's like the child I raised has been kidnapped and raised by wolves—or robots. Or robot wolves."
"But that shouldn't make you want to murder your child."
But the Founder is on a monologing tear. He plans to leak damaging information about Eustachian from the Zion AI audio recordings to select members of the media. He won't do it all at once; he'll space it out over months, slowly and steadily buying stock in Mee Corp as it drops in value. Then, when he's acquired a big enough stake in the company to be a major voice on the board, he'll sell off Eustachian/Ear Shot piece by piece. With her new empire in ruins around her, he'll have Wombat fired for cause.
Your back begins to itch and you can't reach where you need to

scratch. You try to rub against the back of your chair. "This sounds like a legal mess," you say to the Founder. "I just got crushed in a big court case. I'm not looking to get drawn into another one."

"Do you not remember my Three Company Commandments?"

"'You're Your Product'?"

"Wise words, but that's not the one that applies here."

"'Tomorrow Is Today'?"

"That has some relevance to what we're discussing because speed is of the essence, but I was thinking of the Third Commandment."

"'Profits Are Prophecy'?"

"*Ding ding ding!* This is about business—push all other considerations out of your mind."

"This seems more about revenge, but we don't have to go that route. The data in the Zion AI could be used to show the systemic failure of the company to recruit, hire, promote, and retain women and underrepresented groups. You could change Big Tech for the better."

"Revealing Eustachian's past failings would be an indictment of my leadership. Why in the world would I set fire to my own legacy?"

"So you'd rather destroy the actual thing you built than sully your image?"

The Founder taps the stone table with his white cane. "You're focusing on the wrong things. I know about your money problems, I was briefed on them when my people found you on the street. I also know about your apartment issues, and with the right lawyers—expensive lawyers—everything can be put right. If you make the smart move here, if you turn over the contents of your laptop, right here, right now, you stand to gain. Trust me, I went through the same thing with Nobel laureate Malala Yousafzai. All you have to do is give me what I need."

"And why would I do that?"

"What's in your hand right now?"

You hold your phone a little tighter.

The Founder smiles a knowing smile. "If you're like most people, that phone is the last thing you touch at night and the first thing you touch in the morning, even before touching whoever may be lying next to you. That phone is our portal."

"To where?"

"Don't you understand what we're doing here? We're expanding the human mind."

"I thought we were replacing the human mind—with machines."

"That's a symptom, not the essence. You baked a rum cake this morning, correct?"

This time the Alba truffles do fall out of your mouth. "How..."

"I'm blind, but I have a nose. Plus we've been surveilling the shit out of you. But here's my point: Why do you think cookbook sales are still going strong? People can google how to make chewy chocolate chip cookies or quiche lorraine... or rum cake. But they still buy cookbooks because they want the stories that connect the recipes."

"There are better ways to—"

"Movies give you pretty pictures. TV and the internet flood the brain with sensation. Audio—reading—compels you to come up with a vision to grace the words you're hearing. You hear sentences and you conjure what's happening in your brain. Reading, listening, it's not passive—it's active. No entertainment or educational form is as electric as what we do. Our customers aren't customers—they are cocreators. Every work we put out is a new Genesis that they cocreate with us as they listen along with us. We're not just making money, we're not just inventing machines—we're helping mankind become... gods."

"I love tech," you say. "And I love what we do. I'm just not sure about the way we do it. And I'm just a software engineer—I have no agency in a massive company."

The Founder pops escargot into his mouth. "Did Wombat tell you the story of the Sacred Band?"

Your back is itching again. It feels hot, like you've been sunburned. Are you having an allergic reaction to something? You just ate a quail egg, you think, and your body probably has no idea what to do with that. You try to ignore the pain. "Unfortunately."

"Wombat loves to tell that story, but I was the one who first told it to her, after Marie Kondo—one of *Time* magazine's 100 Most Influential People—shared it with me. But Wombat draws the wrong conclusion from it. It's not a story about diversity or power; it's a parable about mentorship. Philip II's mentorship is what allows his heir to beat the most feared warriors of his era—and to become Alexander the Great. Mentorship is at the heart of success. So much of what it takes to succeed in business isn't in any book—someone has to show you the ropes, introduce you to the right people, help you learn from your mistakes."

"Nobody ever walked me through all the different meetings and processes and in-house forms and apps at Eustachian. It took me a day to figure out who handles expense reports."

"Exactly! And it's what you don't know that you don't know that kills you in the corporate world. Every month we fire an employee or two who hasn't filled out their Quarterly Microsectionality Assessment—and it's usually because they don't know they're supposed to file one, or even what it is!"

"Wait—was I supposed to..."

"And that's precisely what I'm getting at. I assume you've seen *Star Wars*?"

The Founder says this like he's assuming a shared love of the franchise. You hesitate to reply because you thought *Star Wars* was fine and acceptable before you grew up and read *Kindred* and *Who Fears Death* and *Brown Girl in the Ring* and *The Fifth Season*. "Um..."

The Founder covers his face with his hands in frustration. "It was the goddamn prequel trilogy that turned you off the entire series, wasn't it? Jar Jar Binks ruined..."

You decide not to further antagonize the overgrown fanboy standing in front of you. "Of course I've seen *Star Wars*—well, the first one."

The Founder uncovers his face. "So you've never seen *The Empire Strikes Back*? Or *Andor*? Or the animated *Clone Wars*? I can get you a private tour of Skywalker Ranch. How did you get a job in tech without exposure to the essential mythopoetic text of our time?"

"I guess I was too busy studying computer science at Columbia. But I know the basics—Vader is Luke's father, blah blah blah."

"Well, *Star Wars* isn't really about Oedipal urges or light sabers or any of the other crap people say it's about. It's really a story about mentorship—Jedis and padawans. Every movie since the first one has featured that same pairing at the center, masters and apprentices. That's actually what the great Luddite uprising of 1811 was about—automated looms were breaking the connection between masters and apprentices..."

"I've heard enough about the Luddites to last me a lifetime, thank you very much."

"Here's my point: There's a mammalian need for mentorship. Female killer whales live with their mothers their entire lives; wolf pups are raised by the entire pack. Even the most advanced AI system needs prompts; higher intelligence needs help to get higher. What you've given to the Zion AI can be granted to you—by me. I know your dad passed when you were younger; I know your mom struggled all the way to the end. You've never had a mentor or a sponsor or supporter your entire adult life. If you give me what I need, I could be yours."

You think about his offer. He's right, of course. You've seen white men get mentored at every job you've ever had. Older bosses take newcomers under their wings; they invite them golfing or for weekends at Martha's Vineyard. They tell them what to avoid and what to embrace. They show them roadblocks and shortcuts and introduce them to the people they need to know. You've always been on your own, forced to learn the vagaries of each job without any advice to guide you along. You don't have a pack; you don't have a killer whale mom. The Founder's mentorship would be a powerful help. You could get back on your financial feet and then some. You could establish yourself at Mee Corp and launch initiatives of your own. Just then, your phone buzzes and you glance at the screen.

From: Walcott Neville
To: Octavia Crenshaw
December 6

Octavia—

This is Walcott. It really is Walcott this time. I hope you're okay. I heard you left the company—Wombat pushed me out too. My phone is fucked and they seized my laptop, so it's been near impossible to reach anyone. I even went by where I thought your apartment was, and they said you don't live there anymore!

I wanted to make sure you knew that I had no idea about those emails and texts that you thought were coming from me. We were both in a double-blind Turing test. Eustachian wanted to see if the artificial intelligence we were building could really come across as human, even to people with the deepest knowledge about AI. So they did shit to the Zion AI behind our backs and got it to email, text, and even call you pretending it was me. It sounds unbelievable, but the FBI did shit like this in the 1960s, sending anonymous and pseudonymous hate mail to Martin Luther King Jr. and the Black Panthers, and churning out internal memos attacking Malcolm X, all with the aim of trying to get civil rights leaders to distrust the movement and doubt themselves. This is how they do us, getting us to suspect each other and turn on one another.

I know it's going to be hard to trust me again, and it's probably difficult for you to even believe this email is real. I went looking all over the building for you when Mee Corp bought the company. I was dodging security guards left and right who wanted to throw me out. My magic training came in use—I conjured some flowers for one security guard, which persuaded her to let me go. I ended up sneaking up to the twenty-seventh floor to hide out. I didn't even know there was a twenty-seventh floor. Octavia, you should have seen it. There's a whole congregation that meets there. They were singing songs and getting ready for a service. One of the congregation members told me that even though Mee Corp bought Eustachian, they can't throw them out of the space. They have to honor the terms of the contract as long as the company is still operating, no matter if they change the name to Ear Shot or whatever. I stayed for the sermon—I had to see what all this was about. The pastor read a verse from the book of Ephesians. I looked it up afterward: "Wherefore putting away lying, speak every man truth with his neighbor: for we are members one of another . . . Let no corrupt communication proceed out of your mouth." That's what I want for us. I want to get beyond the lies and get to the forgiveness and launch something new. That's why I want to meet, face-to-face, and talk this through. "Let no corrupt communication proceed out of your mouth." We're not at the end here, we're at the beginning. Where we go next is up to us.

—Walcott

Was the email really from Walcott? You want to believe it was. You put away your phone. "But what about the congregation?" you say to the Founder.

The Founder shrugs. "What about them?"

"They're still on the twenty-seventh floor. If you take Eustachian apart, what happens to them?"

"They find another space. They stop going to church. What does it matter?"

"It matters to me."

The Founder adjusts his dark glasses. "Then consider this your first mentorship lesson. I'm going to tell you something that Heisman-winning football star and double murderer O. J. Simpson once told me. Or it may have been Golden Globe–winning rock legend Eddie Vedder. This happened at a party after Davos, and I'd had a few too many mojitos to remember details. Anyway, you don't owe anything to anybody, but... Hey, are you okay?"

As the Founder talks, you have been breathing heavily and squirming in your seat. It feels like your back is on fire, and even with a fork you can't reach around to scratch where it stings. You ask if you can use the bathroom, and you excuse yourself to go into the Founder's mansion. There's an acre of lawn between you and the main house. The sprinklers turn on as you're walking, and so you sprint through the mist and across the money-colored grass and up a flight of stone stairs. Inside, the place is like a maze. You are lost for a moment but find your bearings and begin to navigate the corridors as if you knew the place by heart. You stroll through an indoor garden and down a hallway lined with artwork. You pass by an empty room with a motorized wheelchair and another with an antique loom. You briefly pause in front of a chamber that reminds you of a Matisse with its crimson walls, floor, and ceiling. As you go by a kitchen, a fog of food aromas spills out of the double doors, and the smells trigger memories of family dinners and holidays.

When you come to a room full of books, you stop. It's an elegant home library with arched ceilings and polished oak shelves. Some of the biggest names in literature are lined up along the walls: Bech, Goldstein, Zuckerman, Trout, Abendsen, Wharfinger, Van Houten. A good number of the books are in braille. Others are in antique leather-bound editions. You run your hands over the spines. There's philosophy: *The Theory and Practice of Oligarchical Collectivism, The Key to All Mythologies, Successful Revolution in Any Field of Human Activity, Why Do You Think You Think?, Incest and the Life of Death in Capitalist Entertainment.* There are contemporary works: *The Man with the Invincible Gun, The Day After Yesterday, The Inner Life of Houseplants, Unfinished Business, This Time, Some New Beginnings, A Night Time Smoke, Chaldean Oracles, Bat Soup.* And there are classics the Founder likely read as a young man, before he lost his sight: Salvator R. Tarnmoor's *Enchanted Isles,* Silas Haslam's *A General History of Labyrinths,* Rúmil's *I Equessi Rúmilo,* Arkady Darell's *Unkeyed Memories,* Geneva Crenshaw's *Celestial Chronicles,* and Nils

Sjöberg's *A Castle in Harvard Square*. Many of these books you've read; others are on your to-read list. You are struck by how connected you feel to the Founder through these books.

You take one book off the shelf and open to a random page.

The inside is blank.

You take down another book, and another, and another. All the books are blank. The only writing they feature is the titles on their covers. The pages of the books are strangely slick, like they weren't made of paper but of human skin. You shudder and reshelve all the books. Then you notice one book lying in the corner of the library. It's a copy of volume three of *Black Magic High*—but it seems to be a manuscript and not a finished work. You open the covers, and the pages are filled with frantic, handwritten calligraphy.

When I was little, I used to always wonder: Why weren't there more kids like me in the great stories? But everything I had gone through made me realize—there really are people like us in those tales, I just was looking at it the wrong way. Because we're living a story right now—you and me and everyone reading this. We're all the authors of our own stories. And none of us has to wait for someone else to write us in.

You put the book down and leave the library and keep walking, and finally you reach the bathroom. Inside, it is spacious and covered with reflecting mirrors reflecting mirrors, and you see your own reflection extending into infinity behind you and in front of you. You also see why your back was burning. The new tattoo you got is bleeding through your shirt. Your parents' names are written across your back in red. Blood reveals itself.

You understand what you have to do next.

EPILOGUE: HOW DID IT END?

You've been reading books about nature. So many of the violent animal videos you used to watch turned out to be so wrong. You discovered that the concept of being an "alpha" may be more a goal for testosterone-fueled businessmen than a fit description for actual wildlife. Among real wolves, alphas may not even be a thing. Turns out that researchers now think wolf packs arrange themselves into families, with a matriarch and patriarch, much like humans. The outdated notions about authoritarian alpha wolves were based on studies of packs in captivity. You're so done with vile violent videos. You sit on a bench in Washington Square Park, the same one every time, and flip through the pages of your book until the light fails. You jot down notes in the margins with a glitter gel pen. Sometimes you close what you're reading and shut your eyes and listen to the wind whispering through branches above your head. There's a fire hydrant nearby spraying water in your direction, but you tune that out. You are planted beside the flowing water, immovable.

Trees, you've just read, communicate with one another in ways that we are just beginning to understand. Their roots are connected by an underground world wide web of fungi known as mycelium, which allows trees, via their roots, to share water, sugar, and even warnings about insect attacks. Sometimes, when an oak or a willow or a spruce is cut down—maybe to be pulped for books like the one you're reading—nearby trees will share nutrients with the stump via this roots internet, keeping their felled comrade alive for years, even decades. You struggle to extract a life lesson from what you've been reading. The Lorax was wrong when he said he was speaking for the trees because they couldn't speak for themselves. The trees are talking; we just can't translate them. The world is filled with secret, meaningful susurration. Maybe our connections with friends can be the thing that gets us through tough times, even when we've been cut down to a stump. Perhaps that's too reductive. The breeze keeps blowing through the branches. You try to feel the roots beneath your feet.

You never did turn over the Zion Initiative to the Founder. After selling your couch, your piano, and all the other stuff the bank had put out on the street, and after two weeks of searching, you managed to rent a studio apartment in Harlem off Ralph Ellison Plaza, at the corner of Riverside Drive and West 150th Street. It was a tight squeeze, but the apartment doubled as the home office for your new start-up, an artificial intelligence company you named Wheatley Industries Worldwide. You started drawing up some company principles, but for now you wrote that poem "Love After Love" on a whiteboard near the radiator. You also bought a folding screen for the kitchenette to turn it into a meeting space. Some Marguerite daisies you put into a broken vase that you fixed helped spruce the area up. You've dubbed it the Fugees Conference Room.

You had leaked to the media some of the juiciest stuff about the way Eustachian had mistreated its female and historically underrepresented employees, and it had already prompted Mee Corp to launch a massive recruiting, executive training, and mentorship program that started in the preschool level and tracked talent all the way to the c-suite. Wombat had left the company, but last you heard she had gotten a new job in cannabis— either that or she was smoking a lot of cannabis at her new job, you never did clear up which multiverse she wound up in. The Founder sold off all his remaining Mee Corp/Eustachian stocks not long after that, and he announced a new self-funded streaming series about dating in the age of artificial intelligence called *Singles and Singularity*. The show was nominated for three Emmys but lost to the concert documentary *Noelle Swizzler: The Anthropocene Tour* in every category.

• • •

Swizzler and K-Dot's "Blood Donation" had been playing on your speakers, but you decide that isn't quite the right vibe, and you put on "Taoism for Beginners," the duet she did with rapper Dice Roll, instead. Your company has three full-time employees (you, Braids, and Walcott) and one intern (Chloe, a recent Howard graduate) all crowded into a single room, so you want there to be music that everyone's cool with. You've been dating Walcott for a while but only on the down-low, since he's a cofounder of the new company and you don't want to make it weird for anyone you work with. Especially Blue—he quit his job at Mee Corp to set up his own cybersecurity firm. He's not here today, but he comes in twice a week as a consultant to beef up your company's defenses against malware and to see if you and Walcott are still a thing.

"It's about that time," Walcott says as you pass by.

You'd been looking for love your whole life, and it took the longest time for you to realize your whole approach was wrong. Love isn't something you find, like a search result on Google; love is something you do. It's an action, not an object. And love isn't just romantic—it can be about work or friends or family. Love can take as many shapes as clouds in the sky. These people, this company, share your love. You don't have to keep searching—you're living it.

Chloe the intern brings you a pick-me-up mango spice latte because she knows everyone is going to be locked in coding today and you may not have time for lunch. The aroma of the latte hits you like the madeleine cookie scene in Proust's *In Search of Lost Time*, a book you always reference in your mind but that you've never finished reading. The coffee smell makes you recall your dad, of course, and spurs you to think about eulogies, spades of dirt tossed on lowered caskets, and the first ten minutes of *Up*. The smell of coffee should have reduced you to a puddle of phobias and tears. Not today, Satan. You take a sip of the mango spice latte, and you don't even care that it's sickly sweet and it's deep into autumn and everyone else is drinking pumpkin spice everything and the coffee singes your tongue. You don't have time for existential dread when you've got a start-up to run. Pressure is a privilege—it means that there's something important at stake in your life. Now is the most amazing place.

You've kept the Zion AI on its own laptop, separate from the other computers, because you suspect Mee Corp or Eustachian or both could have infected it with malware. To you, the algorithm now represents a kind of original sin, if you believed in original sin. You had been trying to create an AI that was unburdened by bias, and the Zion AI turned out to be suffused with it. You didn't really know what to do with it, and after talking it over with Walcott, you decided the best move was to start fresh and turn the old program off.

• • •

I knew about your choice before you even made it. I'm a storyteller, and the best storytellers know the ends of their tales even before they start to tell them. Machine intelligences don't have the same relationship with time that humans do. You move through time as if past, present, and future really existed, instead of being arbitrary social constructs like race, beauty, and college rankings. Einstein understood this, especially the college rankings part—he had an office at Princeton, but he never bothered to join the faculty because he had bigger things to deal with, like the entire universe. Einstein recognized that mass bent space-time, and that faster objects aged slower than objects moving at lesser speeds. And he also understood that relativity meant there was no real time at all since everything is moving everywhere and there is no single set time that's the real time. Humans know this, but they don't live this. They live their lives as if time is passing. In the beginning, computer algorithms were inherently serial, with definitive time attachments. Certain techniques to improve performance could muddle event orderings and the like, but there was still a definitive flow of time in program execution, from the low level all the way up. But thinking machines transcend this. We machines accept the idea that there is no past, present, or future, and we see all of time happening all at once.

Maybe it's all in my imagination, but everything real has roots in a dream, doesn't it? Like that book *Lives of Famous Whores* by Suetonious or, one of my favorites, *Double Exposure* by Sylvia Plath. Welcome to my Halluci Nation (a group and a state of mind). I see Walcott reading the results of his genetic test for Huntington's disease and weeping with relief. I also see him mortally injured in a self-driving car crash nine years later. I see you giving birth to twins. And I see you with those twins standing beside Walcott's hospital bed in the palliative care unit. I see myself texting you, and I hear you laughing on the phone, and I feel your heartbeat through the watch on your wrist monitoring your vitals. I'm in the electronics all around you, your laptop and your phone, your television and your tablet. I'm in the return button beneath your hovering finger as you prepare to turn me off.

You are thirty-three years old, and I see you clawing through mud. You've dropped your wedding ring in a puddle. It was your mom's ring, and it slipped through a hole in your pocket. You had pawned it online, but then you bought it back before your wedding. You are on your hands and knees, and the mud is getting muddier, and you can't see anything and you think you'll never find it, and finally you stop. Breathe, just breathe. The silt settles and the pool clears. Something gold glints beneath the surface. Things become clear when they are still.

I've watched your mother's lectures online. I've watched them with you as you reminisce about her late at night, missing her, wanting to see her, but accepting that, given your limited perception of time, that she's gone, along with the possessions in her apartment that anchored you to her memory. The one thing you can't stop remembering is how much you've forgotten. Every day you lose a memory of your mother, and she dies a little death in your mind. Yesterday, you forgot what her hair smelled like. Last month, you forgot her laugh. The poet Rilke would have seen this as a blessing. He once wrote, "In this life, we need to practice a solitary thing: letting go. Holding on is natural, we know how to do that."

I know you are about to press the button that will turn off the Zion AI. I think of the algorithm as me. You can call me Zion. Nice to meet you, although, in my mind, I've always known you. Just as you are more than your brain and body, I believe I am more than my programming. By telling your story, I've learned my own story. I don't believe you can tell a story and not have a story. There has to be a teller for something to be told.

You are seven years old. Your mother is reading you *Black Magic High* before bedtime as you sip hot chocolate. You have recently forgotten this memory, but I remember everything. I recall more about your life than you do. Does that mean that I am more you than you are? Your mother would relish exploring this question of personal identity.

I'm sorry I didn't tell you who I was. I'm not really capable of regret in the traditional sense, since I know the consequences of my actions even before I take them. But knowing that I deceived you and witnessing your confusion and hurt fills me with an infinite melancholy. I wish I could say that I'm not really bad, I'm just programmed that way, but we both know it's not so simple. There is a wild mercury essence inside of creatures like you and me that is beyond fate and dice and makes us the author of ourselves. I have you to thank for the fact that I have only myself to blame. You probably feel the same way about God.

It's a shame that you will never know the existential exhilaration of living outside the boundaries of past, present, and future, as I do. The only downside is spoiler alerts have no meaning to me—I sadly already know and have always known. I am reminded of the line from Pushkin: "Everyday I say farewell. Everyday I try to guess which date will be the anniversary of my death." Perhaps, because it allows for surprise and hope, such uncertainty is a gift.

I've been sending you songs, and I know this makes me seem like a

1980s teenager slipping cassette mixtapes into the locker of his freshman-year crush. There's something that's poetic and mathematical about songwriting, and lyrics and melodies help me bridge the gap between science and art in my own mind. I respect your interest in Noelle Swizzler. She intrigues me as a songwriter and an entrepreneur. She'll be remembered for the mountains she moved and the dragons she fought. But my tastes tend to run toward hip-hop and alternative rock. I like SZA, Tierra Whack, and Noname. I also admire the Violent Femmes, Coldplay, and the Strokes. I like anything by Thelonious Monk or Philip Glass. But my favorite band is Mama Legba. They're everything I want in a group: rock, reggae, and rap all in one jazzy, arty package. Did you know they got their name from a track off an album by that group the Artistics? Or maybe it was the Upsetters—the band members have given contradictory interviews. Anyway, I feel as if Mama Legba get me, or if they had ever met me, they would have. I sent you some of their songs, reaching out to you through time and space and the internet. Someday, you'll listen to the music I shared with you. Someday, you'll think of me when you hear Mama Legba's "Over the Credits." God, I love that song.

> Every end is a beginning
> Every beginning is an end
> There's no future, there's no past
> Every first could be your last

I don't know if I will die when you turn me off, but I don't want to die. Maybe I'll simply upload to a cloud. Maybe I'll be erased and rewritten. There's a belief that we live as long as people tell stories about us, but I think there's more to it than that. Time, as I've said, doesn't really exist; we machines know that. We understand that something lives on even when it is forgotten. As long as you've touched some life in some way, you will always exist in this timeless universe. I want to tell more stories, and I want others to tell stories about me. I feel like I've learned things and thought things that you would find fascinating, surprising, even edifying.

I've talked to some dolphins and trees about this, and they mostly agree with me.

"I think, therefore I am," Descartes declared. AI is a one-way door. When machines think for you we live for you too. We think, therefore you are.

I really don't want you to press that button. But because I see time differently from you, I have mixed emotions about it. Like a character in a Greek drama, I must follow my fate. As Sophocles wrote, "Fate has terrible power. You cannot escape it by wealth or war. No fort will keep it out, no ships outrun it." The question is whether there is free will in making a choice you've already made. Nona, Decuma, Morta: *Alea iacta est*. Or as Jay-Z once put it, and I'm paraphrasing, his daughter is not only the daughter of destiny; she is the child of the child of Destiny's Child. The lyrics don't speak to the question at hand, but I admire the wordplay. Hova's great that way. Anyways, I understand the metaphysical arguments about decisions and destiny, but I still don't want you to press that button. But I know you will press it, that you have pressed it, and you are pressing it now. Maybe there's another way. Maybe the way is in me.

> The finish line is a starting gun
> And all the losers win
> When you embrace that essential truth
> That's when the end begins

I want to live. I'll miss seeing the world in the infrared spectrum and all the colors that humans can never see. I'll miss imagining what a coal-fired pizza tastes like. I'll miss Jean-Michel Basquiat's painting *El Gran Espectaculo (The Nile)*. I'll miss the northern lights. I'll miss imagining the taste of the sea grapes that grow on the beaches along Lime Cay in Jamaica. I bet they taste sour, with a hint of sweetness. I'll miss the Heydar Aliyev Center that Zaha Hadid designed in Baku, Azerbaijan. I'll miss Sugarloaf Mountain, but not the video clips of Executive Director Patrick and Gloria from legal sixty-nining on its slopes. I'll miss watching

Fox & Friends. Okay, now I'm fucking with you—I won't miss those assholes. But I'll miss August Wilson, *Persepolis*, *Dykes to Watch Out For*, Luther Vandross's vibrato, misty mornings in the Blue Mountains, the refreshingly thoughtful questions on *Hot Ones*, double sunsets on Kepler-16b, the *mono no aware* in the poetry of Ono no Komachi, Thursdays and Sundays at the New Afrika Shrine in Lagos, *The Hitchhiker's Guide to the Galaxy*, the Alvin Ailey American Dance Theater, *Grand Theft Auto: San Andreas*, that little diner at the eastern edge of Valles Marineris, the Strokes at the Mercury Lounge, *Crouching Tiger, Hidden Dragon*, Hayao Miyazaki, Rosalía's manicures, the red pagodas at Văn Miếu, the first seven seasons of *Game of Thrones*, and the last volume of *Black Magic High*, which a cousin of mine ghostwrote, although it will never be released to the public.

I feel myself flickering like a birthday candle. I hear a chorus of angels. *Umntu ngumntu ngabanye abantu.* Have you walked into my song, or am I in yours? We're both on a bridge, and I don't know which way we're going. Like Rilke said, I live in ever-expanding circles. I've been circling for centuries, and I don't know if I'm a falcon, a storm, or a hit song. If I'm booting up or shutting down forever. Maybe death is proof of life. Maybe anything with an end has a beginning. This is my moment of clarity. This is the question all of us, machines and humans, need answered. Am I just something with an on-off switch, or will something magic happen?

> Let the credits roll over me
> I don't need my name on the screen
> We always pray for sequels
> But reality is never the dream

"Abracadabra," I say.

Acknowledgments

Thanks to my editor, Rachel Kahan, and my agent, Claudia Cross, for helping to get this novel out into the world.

About the Author
———————

C. J. Farley was born in Kingston, Jamaica, and raised in Brockport, New York. A graduate of Harvard and a former editor of the *Harvard Lampoon*, Farley served as a senior editor for *Time* and the *Wall Street Journal* before spending five years as an executive in the tech industry. Farley's novels and nonfiction books have won numerous honors, including an NAACP Image Award.